HIDDEN
AGENDA

Books by Lisa Harris

SOUTHERN CRIMES

Dangerous Passage

Fatal Exchange

Hidden Agenda

Praise for *Dangerous Passage*

"Readers looking for a strong female protagonist and a unique murder mystery will find much to admire in Harris's work."

—*Publishers Weekly*

"Harris begins a new series with a novel that delves into the horrors of human trafficking. Although the subject seems heavy for the genre, the author deftly handles the plot while making it relevant and interesting to the reader and softening it with a sweet love story."

—*RT Book Reviews*, 4 stars

"The combination of police procedural and a Christian love story is nicely plotted, and the characters are interesting, boding well for the future of the series."

—*Booklist*

Praise for *Fatal Exchange*

"The second book of Harris's Southern Crimes series is a thrill ride from start to finish. Full of twists and turns, this exciting story will keep readers enthralled—flawed characters and all. The romance is believable and fits well within the plot."

—*RT Book Reviews*, 4 stars

"Harris's follow up to *Dangerous Passage* is packed with plenty of nail-biting action. Add her signature complex characters, a well-developed Southern setting, and a dash of romance and you have a compelling, quick read to satisfy the most rabid romantic suspense fan."

—*Library Journal*

HIDDEN AGENDA

A NOVEL

LISA HARRIS

Revell

a division of Baker Publishing Group
Grand Rapids, Michigan

© 2015 by Lisa Harris

Published by Revell
a division of Baker Publishing Group
P.O. Box 6287, Grand Rapids, MI 49516-6287
www.revellbooks.com

Printed in the United States of America

Library of Congress Cataloging-in-Publication Data
Harris, Lisa, 1969–
    Hidden agenda : a novel / Lisa Harris.
        pages ; cm. — (Southern crimes ; #3)
        ISBN 978-0-8007-2192-3 (pbk.)
        I. Title.
PS3608.A78315H53 2015
813′.6—dc23   2014032381

Scripture quotations are from the Holy Bible, New Living Translation, copyright © 1996, 2004, 2007 by Tyndale House Foundation. Used by permission of Tyndale House Publishers, Inc., Carol Stream, Illinois 60188. All rights reserved.

15 16 17 18 19 20 21   7 6 5 4 3 2

In memory of Angelica, Ana, and Julia.

You will not be forgotten.

For all that is secret will eventually be brought into the open, and everything that is concealed will be brought to light and made known to all.

—Luke 8:17

CHAPTER 1

Michael Hunt staggered from the impact of the blow. His hand reached instinctively for his bruised rib cage. He knew the techniques of ignoring pain. Bargain with self. Dissociate yourself from your body. Focus on the finish line. But focusing on the finish line wasn't easy when two years of undercover work was about to vanish.

His attacker, Tomas, shoved Michael into a chair and hovered over him. Topping six foot with a solid two hundred fifty pounds of muscle, the man was clearly enjoying himself.

"I can do this all day." Tomas's smile displayed a gold tooth and far too much pleasure. "What's your real name?"

Michael struggled for a breath. "Michael Linley."

"Who are you working for? CIA? FBI? DEA?"

Michael groaned, then spit out the same name he'd repeated over and over the past twenty minutes. "Antonio Valez."

He could add his own list of jumbled abbreviations for Valez. CEO . . . CFO . . . CIO . . . After two years of working with the real estate mogul, the answers, both real and fake, surfaced automatically despite the thick fog clouding his brain brought on from the pain. Michael Linley . . . Liam Quinn . . . Michael Hunt. All layers of who he was and who he'd become.

"Try again," Tomas spat out.

Michael's jaw clinched as the man pulverized his side with his ironlike knuckles, knocking the breath out of him. He fought to concentrate on a water spot on the dingy wall, shaped like a rabbit. Tried to concentrate on anything but the pain. Anything besides the fact that today was Christmas and he might not ever see his family again. The best he could hope for—if he managed to survive—was a few cracked ribs and bruises.

But he wasn't betting on that.

"Last chance. Who are you working for?"

Michael groaned, tired of the relentless questions. The lines between fact and fiction had begun to fade months ago. All he'd ever wanted was to serve God and country. Now his family believed he was dead. His country believed he was a traitor. To live, he needed to convince Tomas he was the man he'd claimed to be. A corrupt businessman, happy to ensure Valez's dirty money came out clean. But while today wasn't the first time he'd faced death, something told him he'd run out of extra lives.

Michael lifted his head and caught Tomas's gaze. "I keep telling you, I work for Antonio Valez. You've known me for months. Nothing has changed." He forced a weak smile. "Besides, why would I betray any of you? I make too much money off of your boss."

"That's a question you're still going to have to answer to him, but in the meantime, I have something that should help jog your memory."

Michael looked up, his left eye swollen, vision blurred. Two of Valez's goons dragged a man into the cottage. It took Michael a few seconds to recognize Sam Kendall. The man's face was beaten. Blood crusted across his right cheek and his upper lip was split. They dumped Kendall onto the floor in front of Michael, then one of them shoved him over onto his back with his boot.

Kendall worked to brace his elbows against the floor in order to sit up. "I'm sorry, Michael."

Sorry?

The word shot through Michael like a stray bullet. Nothing—especially not "sorry"—would save either of them at this point. Neither could "sorry" make up for all those months of risking his life for the sake of justice. He never should have trusted the man. Never should have believed that he could keep him safe.

Michael turned away, trying to mask any hint of recognition, but one look at Tomas's eyes and Michael knew everything he'd managed to accomplish had just been destroyed. He'd never be able to take down Valez and the men above him. His decision to meet with Kendall had been a mistake. Undercover work had always come natural to him, but he'd missed something today. Something that could end up costing both of them everything.

But despite the odds, he wasn't ready to give up. Not yet.

Michael shifted his gaze back to Tomas. "Wait until Antonio gets back. He knows I'd never betray him."

"Really? I find that hard to believe, because Antonio's the one who told me to take care of this problem. He's had some doubts regarding your loyalty, and this man proves it."

Michael drew in a breath and felt crushing pain sweep through his rib cage. Push too hard and Tomas *would* kill him. Push just hard enough and he might be able to save them both.

"Does Antonio know what you're doing or is this your own personal witch hunt?" Michael kept talking, not giving Tomas a chance to answer. "I know how this works, and I even understand. Valez isn't easy to impress, and you need to climb the ranks. But what if you're wrong about me. Betraying one of the boss's trusted men isn't going to go over well when he finds out what you've done."

Michael caught the seed of doubt germinating in Tomas's gaze, but was another string of lies going to be enough?

"Untie me and I'll explain everything." Michael jutted his chin toward Kendall. "Including this man, because apparently someone is feeding you the wrong information."

"I don't think so." Tomas's eyes narrowed, clearly not ready to buy into Michael's attempt to talk his way out of an early grave. "We intercepted a message from your friend here to meet you. We know he's a Fed. That the two of you have been communicating over the past few months, primarily phone conversations on burn phones and blocked email addresses, and that you were passing information on to him."

"No—"

"There's no need to defend yourself." Tomas laughed. "Your friend here's already confessed everything."

Michael studied Kendall's expression but couldn't read him. Tomas knew how to play the game as well as he did, but still, he had to be bluffing. They were both trained to withstand interrogation, which meant if Kendall had kept his wits, Tomas knew nothing. He was simply playing him. But if he was wrong and Tomas *had* stumbled upon the truth . . .

Michael felt his world slowly collapse around him. If they could tie him to the agent, they'd both end up with a bullet in their heads. Even if he did survive, their killing Kendall would put him on the run, not just from the cartel, but the government as well.

The hesitation Michael had caught momentarily in Tomas's gaze vanished. "You do know what Valez does to people who betray him, don't you?"

It was a rhetorical question. Michael had seen firsthand what Valez and his men could do. The only reason he hadn't walked away months ago was because there were bigger fish to fry. Taking down Valez would put a dent in the cartel's grip of the southern United States. Finding out the identity of La Sombra could cripple the entire organization.

He knew the stakes, just like he'd known the risks of staying undercover. There was no one to come to his rescue. No one besides Kendall who knew where he was. Or knew for certain, for that matter, that he was innocent.

Funny how life played out sometimes. This morning, despite Kendall's new reservations, he'd convinced the agent to give him another week before he walked away. Another week was going to be seven days too late.

"Can't answer?" Tomas's smile broadened, dragging Michael back to the present. "Valez has a dozen ways to silence people, but he prefers methods that are slow and painful. Whatever method he chooses, you'll both end up at the bottom of the Atlantic."

Michael's chest heaved, followed by another wave of searing pain through his torso. The authorities would never find either of them. All it would take was a trip out into the ocean, a weight, and their bodies would disappear. The chilly water surrounding the lengthy string of barrier islands off the coast of Georgia would become the perfect graveyard.

Tomas pointed his weapon at Kendall's head and pulled the trigger. Michael flinched at the explosion. Kendall's body jerked. A trickle of red trailed down his forehead as he stared lifelessly at the ceiling.

"You didn't have to do that!" Michael felt his heart rate accelerate, while his mind worked to absorb what had just happened. This wasn't how it was supposed to end.

I'm not ready to die, Lord. Not yet. You brought me here to help bring about justice, and this . . . this is pure evil.

Michael sat rigid, waiting for a bullet to stamp out his own life. Had he thought he could outsmart the cartel? Believed they wouldn't find out what he was doing? His desire to bring them down might have numbed the sense of danger, but he'd never forgotten that death could—at any moment—become his reality. Just like he'd never stopped believing that integrity and truth could still prevail in a fallen world.

Tomas pressed the gun against Michael's forehead. The weapon clicked. Adrenaline soared. Nothing. Michael stared at the barrel of the gun, his heart racing as a wave of nausea swept over him. Russian roulette wasn't a game he wanted to play.

"Don't worry." Tomas pushed Michael's head back with the barrel of the gun and laughed. "The boss has something different planned for you. He's currently caught up with some unexpected business, but he'll arrive early tomorrow morning so he can take care of you himself. Which gives you just over twelve hours to think about your final demise."

Tomas shoved the gun into the holster on his waistband, then exited the room with his two lackeys. Michael's gaze flicked toward Kendall's lifeless body, his open eyes still staring up at him.

It wasn't supposed to end this way, God . . .

A stab of pain shot through his throbbing rib cage as he weighed his options. It would be dark within the hour. His hands and feet were tied with zip ties, the windows of the cottage barred, and the nearest neighbor—a half-dozen miles away—would never hear him. Which meant he had twelve hours to find a way out. And even if he did manage to escape, finding a way off the island was only the beginning of his problems.

———

The charcoal pencil dropped from Ivan Hamilton's fingers. He watched it roll down the windowsill of the cottage, unable to move. If he made any noise, Tomas would realize he was being watched. He held his breath, but Tomas's beady eyes never looked past the shadows of the room where he had just killed a man. And while Ivan's lip reading skills might not be perfect, he was certain he understood what had just been said.

Twelve hours to think about your final demise . . . Antonio arrives tomorrow . . . he can take care of you himself . . .

Antonio Valez.

His father.

The realization hit him like a punch to his gut. His father had always been elusive. Yes, he'd covered Ivan's school bills and spending money, let him visit during summer holidays, but how much did he really know about the man? Antonio had always been more of a looming authority figure than a father. But even that hadn't stopped Ivan from looking up to him. He'd wanted what any boy wanted from his father. Love. Approval. Time.

Ivan sank into the shadows as he watched Tomas and his cronies leave the cottage and head toward the main house, still terrified they would see him. Tomas had shot the bald one before walking out of the cottage. Killed him in cold blood. And he'd promised to return for the other man.

He waited five long minutes before moving away from the shelter of the cottage. He needed to find Olivia—they needed to leave the island. If someone knew he'd just witnessed a murder, or. . . . He drew in a sharp breath. What if someone discovered that he now knew that Antonio Valez, posing as a multimillion-dollar entrepreneur who'd made his fortune in real estate, was involved in something much, much darker?

Ivan escaped the deepening shadows of the small alcove and headed toward the main house through the wooded surroundings, wishing he was able to hear the twigs snapping beneath his feet and the sound of his labored breathing. He might not know the entire truth about his father, but he did know that he and Olivia needed to get out of there. They would take the boat to the mainland, then drive the four hours back to Atlanta and forget everything he'd just seen. They could make up an excuse about why they wouldn't be here to celebrate Christmas with their father. Olivia'd gotten sick maybe. An unfortunate case of the flu. His father probably wouldn't even notice they weren't here.

Ivan hesitated at the sandy trail leading toward the beach. More than likely, Olivia was sitting on the beach. Even during the colder winter months, she loved bundling up to watch the waves come in off the Atlantic, the early morning sunrises, and the last rays of light vanish from the horizon at sunset.

He set off down the path toward the beach, wondering if Olivia had already guessed—at least partially—the truth about their father. Something had been bothering her these past couple of weeks, but she'd denied it, trying to protect him like she always did. When was she going to realize he was grown up?

He paused as he caught sight of her sitting along the shoreline and started praying. Because he had no idea how he was going to tell his sister that their father was a man they should be deathly afraid of.

CHAPTER
2

Olivia Hamilton stared out across the choppy waters as the sun began to set behind her, leaving a soft trail of pink and yellow light. Clouds formed wisps like cotton candy above the horizon, reminding her of her childhood. For the moment, it was easy to forget why she was here. Most people tended to stay inside this time of year, but she'd always found the stormy blues and grays of the Atlantic mesmerizing.

She pulled her coat tighter, fastening the top clasp to guard against the chilly wind. She should go back up to the house. It would be dark soon, and she'd forgotten her flashlight. But the icy wind wasn't the only thing numbing her heart.

God, I don't know what to believe. I don't know who I can trust.

She pulled out her phone and reread the emails that had filled her thoughts the past two weeks and had ultimately brought her back to her father's private island.

I have proof of money laundering and a connection to the Cártel de Rey, all linked to Antonio Valez . . .

Olivia dropped the phone into her pocket and dug the toes of her tennis shoes into the sand. For years, this private barrier island along the Georgia coastline had been a place of refuge for her and her brother, with its miles of private beaches, salt marshes, and tidal creeks. They'd spent their childhood summers exploring the forested trails and circling the island in one of her father's motorized skiffs.

Her father's visits to the island had been few and far between. But Olivia had learned to accept his absence the same way she'd accepted her parents' unconventional relationship.

Memories of her mother were more abundant. When Olivia and Ivan were young, Maria Hamilton loved to lounge beneath the Georgia sun, reading romance novels and drinking iced tea while her children built sand castles or gathered bouquets of wildflowers.

The winter their mother died, everything changed.

The burly tree trunks covered with Spanish moss, the flowering magnolia trees, and the blue jays and warblers nesting in the woods she'd grown to love suddenly lost all their beauty. In one moment, life changed forever.

Olivia swept away the haunting memories and the nagging doubts roused by the emails. While Antonio Valez might not be perfect, she'd seen how hard he worked to get where he was financially, and even more important to her was the fact that he'd loved her mother until the day she'd died.

More than likely the anonymous emails were sent by a jealous rival trying to smear her father's name. Being rich wasn't illegal. The information she'd been sent was completely bogus.

At least that was what she wanted to believe.

She scooped up a handful of sand and let the tiny grains fall back onto the shore. Like every good reporter, she'd learned to be open-minded to the truth, while at the same time striving to be skeptical without being cynical. But this investigation was different. Because it was personal.

Which was why she'd come up with a plan. Tomas had told her that her father was coming to the island tomorrow. She desperately wanted to just come out and ask him if the claims were true and let him put all of her fears to rest. He'd tell her there was nothing to the lies she'd been told. That he hadn't risen in the ranks of the cartel and that his business wasn't being used to launder drug money. But if there was even some truth to it . . . how would her father respond to her inevitable reaction? Would there be dangerous consequences for her and Ivan?

She stared at the pebble left in her hand and dusted off the traces of sand that clung to it, wishing she could erase the traces of doubt threatening to consume her. She'd done her research on the cartel, and what she'd found terrified her. Cocaine could be brought in from Peru for two thousand dollars a kilo. By the time it was broken down into grams and distributed, the retail value of that same kilo had ballooned to a hundred grand, because of the unquenchable demand from buyers.

She pulled her arm back and hurled the small stone toward the icy waves. If the accusations *were* true, it meant that everything she'd grown up believing had been laced with deception. Her father's relationship with her mother, his identity, and even his financial support that had come from drug money. But what haunted her even more was the possibility that her father could be a traitor to everything she believed in.

Something snapped behind her, and she jerked her head in the direction of the noise. Ivan walked up to her, carrying his art pad and pencils for the graphic novel he was sketching under his arm. She blew out a sigh of relief and tried to erase the fear she knew was etched across her expression. Unless she discovered the truth behind the emails' accusations, Ivan didn't need to know why she'd decided to return to the island this Christmas. He might be nineteen, but that didn't lessen her desire to protect him.

He plopped down on the sand beside her. His usual smile was missing as he began signing. "We need to talk."

"What's wrong?" Her stomach took a dip as she signed back.

His swift hand motions were as direct as his gaze. "We need to leave. They killed someone. Father's men. I saw them."

The knot that had been growing inside squeezed tighter. "Whoa. What are you talking about?"

"I saw Tomas shoot a man. Someone working for the government."

Olivia shook her head, unwilling to draw a line between the anonymous emails and Tomas assassinating a man. Because there had to be a mistake. She hadn't come looking for proof her father was guilty. She'd come convinced she could prove his innocence.

"You're telling me Tomas murdered someone?"

Ivan nodded, the frustration in his expression growing as he signed. "I saw him, Olivia. Saw what they said. Another man was there. They will kill him tomorrow. They're saving him for the boss."

"Who's the boss?"

Even as she signed the question, Olivia knew the answer. The tension in her gut that had been there for the past two weeks finally snapped as she saw her brother raise his thumb to his forehead, the other fingers splayed as if waving. One of the very first signs of a trusting young child's vocabulary. Father.

Olivia's mind screamed in defiance. No. Her father was not a part of the cartel. Didn't have hitmen who carried out assassination orders. Didn't execute government agents.

"You're wrong." She tried to swallow the lump growing in her throat as she signed her response. "You must have misunderstood."

She knew Ivan could read lips as easily as she heard the spoken word. But that didn't mean she was ready to shove her father into the category of villain.

"I didn't misunderstand what they said, or what I saw," Ivan signed. "They shot a man, Olivia. I saw everything."

"Do they know you were there?"

"No."

Which meant they were lucky. Very lucky. If her father's men knew there had been a witness to the murder, Ivan's life would be in danger. She had to get him off the island.

"Have you ever suspected he was involved in something illegal?" Ivan signed.

Her hands balled into fists, her fear of the truth morphing into anger, before she answered. "Someone sent me some information, but I didn't . . . couldn't believe it was true."

Until now.

She stared out across the blue-gray ocean as the last slivers of pinkish sunlight began to fade on the horizon. She'd spent the last decade investigating the news, but most of the stories she covered dealt with PTA meetings and petty crimes, not murder. This time, she was in way over her head. And this time, it was personal.

"They left one man alive," Ivan continued. "They will kill him if we don't get him out of there."

"If we don't get him out . . . " Olivia's voice rose along with her signed response. She'd read what the cartel did to people who crossed them. "Ivan, they've already killed a man. They will kill us if we get in the way."

Ivan's gaze held hers. "You've always told me to do the right thing no matter what the cost."

She dug her fingers into the sand. Statements like that were easy to spout off when there wasn't the chance of getting murdered by a cartel hitman. But she wasn't going to risk her life, let alone her brother's life, for a stranger. If they were caught trying to help this guy, all three of them would end up dumped off the Georgia coast in a watery grave.

But Ivan's words wouldn't leave her alone.

"Who is this man?" she asked.

Ivan shrugged. "Another agent. A spy. I think they were here investigating something and got caught."

Olivia frowned. Ivan had definitely been reading too many spy novels. "We don't know anything. What if he's one of them, and we get in the middle of a cartel feud or something? We can't get involved in this."

"So we do what? Run? And leave a man to die?"

"We don't have a choice, Ivan." Running sounded like the best thing to do, especially when compared to any plan to stay there to find out the truth about her father. The truth wasn't supposed to be wrapped up in a web of murder and deceit. "We'll go to the house, pack up our stuff, and tell them we need to go back to the mainland. We can call the police or the FBI and have them figure out what to do. We're not getting involved in this."

"It will be too late."

Olivia frowned. "We don't know that."

"They're going to kill that guy in the next twelve hours if we don't stop this."

"We aren't responsible for his life."

She cringed at her clichéd responses. She'd never thought of herself as particularly brave. She didn't like to take risks. So far, she'd been able to avoid doing hard-core journalism and had settled for the ease of reporting small-town news and writing freelance articles, where the biggest challenge came from ensuring she made her deadlines. She preferred life that way.

Ivan touched her arm, getting her attention again. "You're always telling me to pay attention to what really matters. This matters."

Olivia bit her lip. She had come to the island to search for truth, but in the process had convinced herself that any evidence she found would exonerate her father. Was she willing to seek out that truth even if it destroyed everything she knew and loved?

She battled against the doubts slithering through her mind. "You don't understand what's at stake here."

"And you don't understand that I'm not a child anymore." Ivan's brow furrowed tightly as he signed his response. "How can we close our eyes to what's happening right in front of us?"

Olivia looked away, but Ivan wasn't done. He grasped her arm before continuing. "What do you know about our father you're not telling me?"

She pulled her phone out of her pocket and looked at it. The wallpaper was a photo of her and her mother taken the year before she'd died. Sometimes the seven years that had passed since her death seemed like just a few days. She could still smell the floral scent of her perfume. Hear her singing Spanish love songs in her deep, sultry voice. Hear her laughter at the dinner table . . .

Olivia handed Ivan the phone, then stood up and brushed the sand off her jeans. "Two weeks ago, I received some emails from an anonymous source. They say they have evidence that our father is involved with the cartel. That his real estate business is nothing more than a front to launder money."

Maybe she hadn't known the truth, but there had always been questions. As a reporter, she was supposed to seek out what was real, but she'd let her emotions distort the truth in order to allow herself to believe in a man who had never existed.

"The truth scares me, Ivan. That's why I don't want to get involved in this. If finding out the truth means that everything I've ever known is a lie—that our father is a criminal—I don't know how to deal with that."

She waited while he scrolled through the emails, one at a time, a pinched look of pain marking his features.

He handed her back the phone. "I couldn't have believed this . . . would never have believed this if I hadn't seen what I saw today."

She nodded, knowing there was nothing she could do to stop the feeling of an inevitable tsunami washing over her and dragging her out to sea. If this was true, no matter what happened, life as she knew it would never be the same.

"Do you think he ever loved us?" Ivan's next question burrowed through her. "Do you think he ever loved her?"

She had to believe he'd loved them. "In his own way, yes."

"And now? What happens now? Are you willing to turn him over to the authorities?"

She blinked back the tears. "He's our father."

"I saw a man murdered. They're planning to kill another man. And if he ordered those hits, you and I know he's ordered others. Maybe many others."

Olivia struggled to process everything Ivan had told her, but one thing seemed clear. They needed to decide what to do right now, and deal with her father later. Because no matter which direction her emotions were pulling her, she couldn't have a man's blood on her hands.

She looked back at Ivan, her jaw tensed. "Where is he?"

"They have him locked up in the cottage."

She'd never questioned the reasons behind the tight security. Or her father's drivers and multiple staff and bodyguards. She'd thought they were simply to keep him and his family safe from people after his money. "We don't have a key."

Ivan frowned at her excuse. "We don't need a key. I've snuck into that cottage dozens of times during rainstorms when I needed a quiet place to draw."

Olivia drew in a deep breath. She'd spent her life trying to protect her brother. How was it that now she needed to protect him from his own father?

"What if we're wrong?" she asked.

"Why are you defending him?"

Why was she defending him? He hadn't given them his name,

never legally acknowledged Olivia and Ivan as his children. Their mother had met him three decades ago. She'd always been aware that there were other women in his life, but everyone knew that Maria Hamilton had managed to cast a spell on Antonio Valez. And because of that, even after their mother's death, he'd continued taking care of them financially. But a monthly check had never been Olivia's greatest need.

She stared out across the darkening waters toward the rising moon and wrestled with her conscience. She turned toward Ivan and signed in the twilight, "How do we get him off the island?"

"We'll need the keys to the pontoon."

"And you think we can do this without getting caught?" she asked.

Ivan nodded before signing his answer. "If we decide to do this . . . we can't get caught."

CHAPTER
3

Thirty minutes later, Olivia shoved the rest of her essentials into her backpack, then swung it across her shoulder before leaving her room for what might very well be the last time. The rest of her stuff would have to stay for now. Getting off the island had to be their first priority.

Mentally, she rehearsed her and Ivan's plan and realized there were far more questions than answers. What if the man was unconscious? How were they going to physically lug a hundred-and-eighty-pound-plus man from the cottage to the dock? What if Ivan had somehow misinterpreted the situation? What if the man they planned to rescue was nothing more than another thug? What if they got caught?

What if . . . ?

Olivia tried to push aside the flood of doubts as she ran her hand down the polished wooden railing of the staircase like she'd done a hundred times before. As much as she wanted to ignore it, the past vied for attention among the chaos of the present. Because the island, its remote beauty—and her father—were etched into who she was.

Her gaze shifted to the chandelier hanging from the entryway's vaulted ceiling. After visiting the island for years on vacation, her father had finally bought the house when she was eighteen. Built almost a hundred years ago, the updated residence still held on to the southern charm of the original architecture—original fireplaces, paneled walls, balconies, and mahogany French doors, coupled with all the modern conveniences of the twenty-first century.

Shifting her backpack on her shoulder, Olivia stepped into the chef's kitchen, lit only by a light over the stove. All she had to do was grab the pontoon keys hanging beside the fridge, then meet Ivan at the cottage. By the time Tomas realized his man was gone and they weren't coming back, the three of them would already be on the mainland, safe and sound.

The large retro wall clock hanging in the corner of the kitchen rhythmically ticked off the seconds. She paused halfway across the white-tiled floor, holding her breath and listening for the sounds of footsteps. The only people who should be in the house at this hour were her father's staff and maybe one of the guards.

She let her breath out slowly, relieved at the quiet. But even if someone did see her, it shouldn't matter. It wouldn't have been the first time they'd taken the pontoon out to go to the mainland. Every summer Ivan studied the local waterway charts, and he knew how to follow the channel markers. He could navigate the water like a local.

She reached for the string of keys hanging on the wall for guests and felt her stomach knot. The keys were gone.

The overhead light snapped on above her, illuminating the modern fixtures, the stainless steel appliances, and the dark wooden cabinets.

"Miss Hamilton?"

Olivia took a step backward at the sound of the guard's voice and turned around.

José smiled across the room at her. "I'm sorry, Miss Hamilton. Didn't mean to scare you. Thought I heard a noise in here."

She forced a smile. She'd always liked José, but now she

couldn't help but wonder if he was simply a night guard her father had hired or a low-ranking member of the cartel. Or if he'd ever acted upon orders from her father to execute someone who'd gotten in his way.

Olivia's mouth went dry. "I was . . . looking for the keys to the pontoon. Ivan and I thought we'd go into town."

It was the truth. There was no reason for him to suspect anything.

"It's kind of late to be out on the water, Miss Hamilton."

"We'll be fine." Olivia repositioned the backpack across her shoulder. "You know Ivan. He's more at home on the water than he is on land. Besides, the mainland isn't far." She swallowed the fear creeping up her throat. "Do you know where the keys to the pontoon are?"

José frowned, clearly unconvinced. The tall, solidly built man wasn't much older than Ivan and had been working for her father the past four or five years. Did he know there was a man waiting to be executed a hundred yards from where they were standing?

"Like I said, it's late, and we typically discourage guests from going out after dark."

"We'll be fine." Olivia forced a smile. Hoping he couldn't sense the fear emanating from her pores or hear the erratic pounding of her heart.

José hesitated a few seconds before responding with a smile. "I suppose you're right."

"Though if my father happens to call, asking where we are, you won't tell him, will you?" She paused, wondering if she'd gone too far. "He worries too much."

"I don't blame him. It can be dangerous out there if you're not careful."

"We'll be extra careful. I promise."

The worry on José's face lessened. "Honestly, I wish I could join you instead of being stuck on guard duty. It's not as if anything ever happens around here. You're not headed to get some pizza, are you?"

Olivia forced a chuckle. "We haven't had dinner yet."

"I won't tell anyone you've gone if you promise to bring me back a couple slices if you stop to get some."

She smiled. "Pepperoni and mushroom, if I remember correctly."

José's phone rang.

Olivia glanced at the clock. Ivan was going to start worrying if she took much longer. "The keys, José. Do you know where they are?"

"Keys . . . yes . . . Sorry. I went into town this afternoon and forgot to put them back." He dug in his front pocket, then tossed her the keys.

Olivia moved as casually as she could toward the door as José answered his phone.

God, we can't do this alone. Please, please let us get off this island safely . . .

Finally outside, she headed toward the cottage where Ivan waited for her. An owl hooted in the distance, its call eerie and haunting. Tree limbs danced in the salt-filled air, leaving dark shadows against the lawn. There was just enough light from the moon filtering through the trees for her to see the small cottage at the end of the path. She and Ivan had played hide-and-seek there as children, built hideouts, and played Monopoly hour upon hour. But those days had long since passed.

Ivan was waiting for her in the shadows of the cottage, tension clear on his face. "I got the door open, but I thought something happened to you."

"I almost got caught. José thinks we're going out for pizza."

"So he knows we're leaving the island?"

"He had the keys to the pontoon. I didn't know what else to do."

Her brother nodded. "You did fine."

She knew what Ivan was thinking, because she was thinking the same thing. Getting caught going to get pizza on the
mainland was one thing. Trying to smuggle a prisoner out from
under the nose of a presumed drug cartel leader was completely
different.

Michael's head jerked up at the sound of footsteps outside
the cottage. The door creaked open slowly, letting a sliver of
moonlight sweep over Kendall's body. Pain radiated through
Michael at the sudden movement. Besides the bruising along
his sides, he was worried that some of his ribs were cracked.
He wasn't sure how much time had passed, but it was still dark
outside, which meant that for some reason Tomas had returned
early. And he knew that this time he hadn't come back to simply
scare him. This time he—or Valez—would make his final breaths
as painful as possible before ending his life.

He fought to wipe away the cobwebs cluttering his mind.
He needed to think. Still needed a plan. But his entire body
ached, and the nausea had yet to lessen. Loosening the zip ties
had proved impossible. He'd never been one to simply give up,
and close calls came with the territory, but this time death felt
inevitable.

I need a miracle, God, or I'm not getting out of this alive.

Someone stepped into the room. His vision blurred, Michael
tried to focus on the two figures. They hovered above him, whis-
pering softly.

He blinked, confused. "Who are you?"

The young man got busy cutting away the zip ties while the
woman asked him if he could stand. So much for his own master-
ful attempts to escape. This had to be a trick, or maybe it was
just a dream. One of those that started out pleasant, then twisted

into an ugly nightmare. Kendall was dead. That part he knew was true. He was miles from civilization, with no one out there who could come to his rescue. Which led to the only conclusion he could make. The beautiful woman standing over him must be an angel. Which meant he was dead. Or she was a part of Valez's plan to kill him.

"Who are you?" His question came out raspy.

The woman placed a finger against her lips. "Don't talk."

He studied her face in the dim light. Mid to late twenties. Beautiful, in an exotic way. Part Caucasian, part Hispanic would be his guess. Large almond eyes, perfect tan, long dark hair pulled back in a neat ponytail that brushed across her shoulder. He shifted his gaze back to her eyes. There was something familiar about them, but he was certain he'd never seen her before. He would have remembered her face.

The boy popped the zip tie off Michael's ankles, allowing him to move his feet slowly in circles and get the blood circulating again.

She gripped his arm. "Can you walk?"

"I don't know."

His gaze shifted to the boy. He looked as if he were eighteen or nineteen. Strong. But not strong enough to carry him out. He was going to have to walk if they actually intended to get him out of here. Pain rippled through his side as he tried to stand. He fought to catch his breath. Maybe this wasn't a dream.

"You need to try and walk. Please."

He focused on the soft lilt of her voice. On the subtle movement of her hair across her shoulder. On the crazy thought that the finish line—getting off this island—might be closer than he thought.

She pressed her hand against his arm. "We know you've been injured, but you're going to have to help us if we're going to have any chance of getting you off this island."

Getting him off the island? Was she serious?

Part of him wanted to laugh at her statement. He'd prayed for a miracle—a Navy SEAL rescue or an extraction team that would take down Valez and his people while they were at it. He'd prayed for it even though he knew such a miracle was ridiculous. No one knew he was here. But being rescued by a guardian angel was just as ridiculous. He *had* to be dreaming.

Still, he might as well play along.

"Getting off this island is impossible," he said.

"Maybe, but if we don't get you off, they'll kill you. There's a pontoon waiting for us at the dock."

She was serious?

Michael's mind began to clear. He had no idea how she knew Valez was planning to kill him, but he did know one thing. She was crazy. Getting out of the ten-million-dollar compound would be difficult enough. But off the island? No one crossed Antonio Valez without paying the price. No one who wanted to live another twenty-four hours, anyway. He drew in a deep breath, still expecting to wake up. He might have prayed for a miracle, but reality told him his fate was already sealed. Even if this wasn't a dream, they'd be caught trying to escape. And these two, whoever they were, didn't deserve to die because of him.

He shook his head. "It's not worth the risk. They will kill you if we're caught."

"Trust me, I've thought through that scenario, but my brother can be pretty stubborn."

"Okay." He forced himself to stand, too weak to argue. He'd have to deal with her crazy arguments—and the pain—later. "How are we going to do this?"

"We have a plan."

A plan? Right.

He'd had a plan *and* a backup plan. He knew the property

better than most, but he also knew that even with the best of plans, the odds of escaping this situation were practically nil. There were guards who made their rounds about the property, and then there was the matter of all three of them getting past the front gate security . . . past the guards and dogs . . .

Whatever their *plan* was, it was never going to work.

"There are two guards at the front gate." She was talking again, with that sweeter-than-honey voice of hers. "Ivan knows a shortcut to the dock that bypasses the gate. The main thing is that we have to get there before the other perimeter guard makes his rounds."

Michael nodded. After visiting the property a half-dozen times over the past eight months, he'd studied the guard's routines. Found alternative routes off the island if necessary. Being rescued by a couple of strangers had never been the plan, but from the looks of things, he didn't have a choice.

"How do you know so much about this property?" he asked.

His guardian angel hesitated. "You're just going to have to trust us. The good thing is that they're worried about people coming into the compound uninvited. Not getting out."

"And the dogs?" He liked dogs, but these German shepherds helping to guard the property weren't here to play catch.

"My brother's always been able to make friends with just about every animal he runs into, including Goliath and Caesar. They won't be a problem."

Michael bit back a wave of nausea stemming from the pain. "What happens if we get caught?"

"We'll deal with that when the time comes."

She clearly didn't know who she was dealing with. "You know what they'll do to you . . . if we're caught."

She jutted her chin toward Kendall's lifeless body. "I think I have a pretty good idea."

He turned toward the door. "You never told me your names."

"I'm Olivia, and this is my brother, Ivan. He's deaf, but he can read lips and speak."

Ivan nodded. "We're going to get you out of here."

He caught the intensity in the boy's voice, surprised at how well he spoke.

"And you?" she asked. "What's your name?"

"Liam . . . Liam Quinn."

He paused at the fake name he'd just thrown at her, but she didn't need to know who he really was. They'd help get him off the island, then the wisest thing for them would be to put as much distance between him and themselves as they could.

"We can chitchat later," she said, "but for now we have a short window to get you from here to the pontoon before the guards show up."

Michael took a painful step, wondering how it was he'd never met someone so familiar with the property. But she was right. He'd ask those questions later. For the moment, it took all the energy he could gather just to put one foot in front of the other.

Biting back the pain, he gritted his teeth as they wrapped their arms around his waist and started toward the door. Kendall's lifeless eyes stared up at him. The nausea returned. No man deserved to die without a proper burial, but there wasn't anything he could do at the moment. All he could hope for was that the authorities would find the body before Valez fed it to the sharks. That was the least his wife and two children deserved.

"Wait a minute." Michael reached down and quickly ran through Kendall's pockets. Nothing. Tomas was telling the truth. They knew now who he was. They knew he'd betrayed them all.

Olivia looked up at him as they crossed the threshold of the cottage. "Do you pray?"

Michael nodded as dread began to envelop him.

"Good." She tightened her grip on his waist. "We're gonna need it."

CHAPTER
4

Olivia felt Liam's fingers grip her shoulder. She could tell by the heaviness of his breathing and the unevenness of his gait that he was in a great deal of pain. He needed medical care to determine if there was any internal damage, but they'd have to deal with that problem after they made it to the mainland. For now, her only concern was ensuring they didn't get caught. Because if they were discovered, the man lying dead on the cottage floor wouldn't be the only one with a bullet in his head. She had no doubts now that her father's henchmen would kill all of them without thinking twice.

They moved slowly toward the dock, beneath the canopy of oak trees with their woody vines, while accusations from the email messages ran through her head. Her father was involved in money laundering and the cartel. This man—along with the one inside the cottage—was proof of everything she'd feared.

Olivia heard a twig snap behind them and paused midstep. She turned around as Goliath ran up and pressed against her leg. She let out an audible sigh of relief at the sight of the dog. Ivan reached down to pet Goliath with his free hand.

Liam's voice was raspy. "How much farther?"

She caught the fatigue in his voice and realized he wasn't

going to be able to go on much longer. "Not far, but we need to keep moving."

"And the guards?"

"One should pass by here in the next few minutes."

Which meant they were running out of time.

Goliath padded beside them, making too much noise. Olivia glanced back toward the house as they continued, searching for any signs of movement in the trees, while Ivan led them along the shortcut that bypassed the front gate and led them outside the property, leaving the dog behind.

Olivia tried to ignore the fear gnawing at her stomach. Wondering how long it would take them to get to the dock. Wondering what would happen if they needed to shift to plan B—when she had no idea what plan B was. She glanced at Liam. His lips were pressed tightly together. Her father didn't have to know she and Ivan had orchestrated his escape. Once on the mainland, she would simply call the police anonymously, then leave her father to deal with how his prisoner had escaped.

She repositioned her arm around his waist. "The dock's just ahead. How are you holding up?"

"I don't know, I . . ." He stumbled. "My head . . . it's spinning."

Olivia tightened her grip. The muscles in her back and arms were beginning to burn. She could see the outline of the dock and the water in the distance. The pontoon bobbed in the water along the shoreline. Fifty more yards. Thirty. Fifteen.

Liam stumbled again. Olivia strained beneath the extra weight, somehow managing to lean into him and help Ivan support him. But they were running out of time, and she was running out of strength.

You can do this, Olivia. One step at a time.

She glanced back one last time to see if anyone had followed them, but all she could see were the now distant lights of the house. In front of them, waves gently lapped against the shore.

Another few feet and they would be in the boat, heading for the mainland . . . and safety.

A minute later, she and Ivan dragged Liam into the bottom of the boat before he passed out. Ivan started the engine, leaving off all but one front light so they wouldn't be as visible from behind, then steered the boat away from the dock. The hazy yellow lights of the house began to fade in the distance, making her suddenly wonder if she'd ever return. Wondering if she'd ever see her father again. She'd spent a dozen summers here. How could she have been so wrong about someone she'd loved so much?

Shadows moving along the shoreline caught her attention, deepening the fear welling up inside her. She grasped the side of the boat as Ivan steered them into deeper waters. No. The guards hadn't had time to discover that their prisoner was gone. Not yet. There was no reason why José wouldn't have bought her story about going to the mainland for pizza. Everything she'd said was true. No one would think twice about their leaving . . .

But the unmistakable sound of another motor changed her mind. A second boat was leaving the dock. Her gaze shifted to where Ivan sat at the steering wheel. Water slapped against the sides of the boat. She tried believing all the legitimate reasons someone else might be out on the water, but her gut told her that this was no coincidence.

And while Ivan truly was a natural in the water, maneuvering during the day was one thing. Navigating at night—without getting lost or running into an underwater obstacle—brought a whole other set of complications. Let alone being chased by a bunch of drug runners.

Olivia moved to the front of the boat beside her brother and pressed her palm against his arm before signing. "They're behind us."

Ivan looked back toward the horizon, then pushed on the accelerator, shifting gears as the boat rocketed forward. Seawater splayed against their faces, leaving behind the familiar taste of salt water on her tongue. He motioned for her to get down on the deck.

She heard the first shot ping against the boat.

Adrenaline rammed through her as she stumbled across the rocking deck toward Liam. He groaned as the boat tipped to the left, rolling him onto his back. She grasped his shoulders, holding him steady, as they flew across the water.

The moon cast just enough light for her to see the outline of his face and the shadow of a beard. Cuts and bruises marred his cheek and jawline. She couldn't help but wonder who he really was. What he had done to cross her father. And if she'd done the right thing in saving his life. Because now she knew the kind of men who worked for her father. The kind who didn't hesitate with an order to assassinate.

A second shot ricocheted off the side of the boat. Olivia looked back and saw the light of the other boat running behind them. The anger that had begun seeping into her soul when she'd read those emails continued to spread. She'd spent her life taking care of her brother, and now, because of her father's betrayal, she'd managed to put Ivan's life at risk for the sake of someone they didn't even know.

What if doing what was right turned out not to be worth the cost?

Olivia stared at the wake of water behind them. As soon as they got to the mainland, she would demand answers from Liam to the growing number of questions spinning through her mind. Ivan might have had a compelling case when he'd first come to her, but the men shooting at them erased it completely. They should have left Liam Quinn where they found him. Should have gone into town and alerted the authorities and let them come in and clean up the mess. Trying to handle things themselves had been foolish. This wasn't just about a man slated to be executed. If everything she now believed to be true really was true, their actions tonight might have very well signed their own death warrants. It wouldn't make one whit of difference that they were Antonio Valez's children.

Water sprayed across the deck as Ivan pushed on the accelerator and increased their speed, but she could still hear the rumble of a second motor behind them. Whoever it was, they were gaining on them. Their own boat swerved to the right. Olivia braced herself and Liam against the movement, as Ivan took them into one of the narrow waterways where seawater mixed with freshwater from the coastal rivers and runoff.

The sound of the other boat faded as they meandered through the maze of the salt marshes. A minute later, Ivan shut off the engine, leaving them to bob beside the sea grass in the eerie darkness of night. All was quiet for a moment as Ivan crouched down beside them.

Olivia held her breath as the sound of the other boat's engine buzzed in the distance, mingling with the nocturnal sounds of the marshland. She forced herself not to move, using only her sense of hearing to tell her that her father's men had slowed down to search for them.

She turned to Ivan, uncertain. If they waited too long to continue to the mainland, their pursuers would more than likely be waiting for them.

Michael opened his eyes and tried to figure out where he was. Stars hung above him, and the ground beneath him rocked. A car? No . . . a boat? He turned his head and found her beside him, close enough that he could feel the pounding of her heart. His guardian angel. He could smell the faint scent of vanilla in her hair mingling with the distinctive tang of salt water. But she'd been nothing more than a dream. Or so he thought.

He searched his memory for clues. The last thing he remembered was being in the cottage. They'd killed Kendall. Promised to kill him as well. Then she'd appeared—his angel—with a crazy idea to rescue him.

Pushing an elbow against the hard flooring, he tried to sit up, but the pain radiated through his rib cage. He might have gotten away with minimal damage, but that didn't mean that the injuries they had inflicted didn't hurt like the dickens.

The young woman gripped his arm and motioned for him to be still.

He nodded, catching her features in the moonlight. Water droplets peppered his face. The steady hum of a boat's engine droned somewhere in the distance. His mind fought to focus on what she was saying, but instead, blackness tried to envelop him.

He closed his eyes. Memories of the last time he'd talked to Kendall replayed in his mind. It had been pouring rain when he arrived at the café. He'd stepped inside, immediately taking in all the details. A waitress with choppy highlights and a checkered blue uniform poured coffee for an older woman at the counter. A thirtysomething-year-old man wearing a pair of jeans and a sweatshirt sat reading a newspaper and sipping a cappuccino. A couple of college-age girls texted instead of chatted, waiting—like the rest of them, presumably—for the downpour to stop.

He'd studied the rest of the customers while slipping his umbrella into the stand by the front door, still unable to shake the unease that had taken hold of him. He'd always loved this time of year, but hearing Dean Martin's "I'll Be Home for Christmas" play in the background, and knowing his family was less than a dozen miles away and he still couldn't see them, didn't exactly make this a Christmas worth remembering.

He missed his family. Missed his mother's roast turkey, cornbread dressing, and divinity she served every Christmas. Missed the ornately dressed twelve-foot tree topped with his grandmother's glass star. Shoot, he even missed the hideous red and green Hunt family sweater traditionally passed from one lucky person to the next each year.

He shoved back the memories. Except for a perky blonde flashing him an inviting smile from one of the tables, the rest of the customers were either too engrossed in their food or in each other to notice him.

Ignoring the blonde's gaze, he headed for the leather booth at the back of the room and slid in across from Kendall, wishing he were the one facing the front door. He'd walked around the Atlanta neighborhood for ten minutes, in and out of busy shops, until he was convinced he hadn't been followed. But even though no one had managed to arouse his suspicions, his gut told him they were taking a big risk meeting in public.

"Would you prefer I did a background check on all the occupants in this room?" Kendall glanced up at Michael through a pair of thick-rimmed glasses and grasped his coffee mug.

Michael forced a weak smile. "Might not be a bad idea."

At least the man had attempted to shed the recognizable FBI garb for something a bit more casual, though the plaid flannel shirt wouldn't have been Michael's first pick.

Kendall signaled the waitress. "I told her to bring you a cup of coffee when you got here, but if you're hungry—"

Michael waved away the offer. "Coffee's fine."

"Were you followed?"

"No." Michael grabbed the plastic menu lying in front of him and tapped it against the table. "But I'm still not sure that meeting in person is wise."

"You worry too much. What do you have for me?"

Michael slid the flash drive across the table.

"What's on it?"

"The evidence you've been looking for. It's the second set of books, the master list, where Valez has been keeping track of all his illegal gains."

Kendall's eyes widened. "This is priceless. How'd you get it?"

Michael shook his head. "You don't want to know."

"Well, it looks like your months of hard work have finally paid off. You can stop worrying now and come in."

"Come in? I'm not done yet. I still have to tie all of this to La Sombra if we want this house of cards to come tumbling down."

"If La Sombra even exists."

"He exists. I know it." He just didn't know who he was. Yet.

"I don't think sticking around is a good idea." Kendall shoved the drive into his front shirt pocket. "There's been a change of plans."

"What do you mean, 'a change of plans'?"

Kendall leaned back, silent as the waitress approached their table. She set a burger in front of Kendall, then filled up Michael's empty coffee mug.

"Anything to eat, sir?"

"No, I'm good. Thanks."

The waitress turned to Kendall. "And you, sir?"

"The coffee will do for now, Darlene. Thanks."

Kendall watched her walk away, hips swaying wider than necessary.

"How's your wife?" Michael threw out the not-so-subtle reminder.

"Wouldn't know. We're separated."

"And the kids?"

"Doing as well as they can despite their bouncing back and forth between us."

"I'm sorry."

"Me too, though being separated has its advantages. How else would I get away with eating this?"

Michael stared at Kendall's plate.

"This burger"—Kendall took a bite and talked while he chewed—"is man's greatest invention. Three patties, four kinds of cheeses, bacon, and mushrooms."

"My cholesterol spiked just listening to you." Michael watched Kendall eat, wondering how he could be so relaxed. "You said things have changed. What's changed?"

"You need to come in."

"You know I can't come in now."

"Can't or won't? So far you've given us enough information to put a huge dent in Valez's organization—"

"As much as I'd rather be sitting with my family on Christmas Eve instead of drinking stale coffee and watching you eat that burger, this was never just about Valez."

He'd given Kendall the cooked numbers. But now he needed to identify La Sombra.

"You might have to forget La Sombra, as much as I hate to say that," Kendall said. "Too much has happened this past week. It's not safe anymore."

"It's never been safe," Michael said. "What happened?"

Kendall leaned forward and lowered his voice. "A week ago, Charlie Bains was shot and killed."

"Charlie? What happened?" Michael's younger sister had broken off her engagement to Charlie, but his death would still affect her, despite the fact Emily wasn't in love with him anymore. "Who killed him?"

Kendall dropped his gaze.

"Kendall . . . who killed him?"

"Like I said, a lot's happened this past week. There was a shootout, and your sister was involved."

"Avery?" His stomach clenched. "Is she okay?"

"Not Avery. Emily shot Charlie." Kendall's fingers tapped against the side of his coffee mug.

"Emily?"

Michael's mind spun at the information.

"I don't understand," he said.

"I guess I should have brought you a newspaper. It was the headline news in Atlanta. It's a long story, but the bottom line is that Charlie was working for the cartel. He tried to shoot Mason, and Emily ended up stopping him. Your sister's quite a shot, by the way."

"Maybe, but my sister's not a cop." Familiar guilt surfaced. He should have been there for her. Should have stepped in and stopped the situation. He knew what it felt like firsthand to shoot and kill someone. It didn't leave you feeling like Rambo, like in those shoot-'em-up finale scenes portrayed in the movies.

Michael pushed his drink away, his stomach soured by the news. "She's strong, but this is going to take a long time for her to get over."

"And that's not all."

"What do you mean?"

"There was another cop arrested during the operation."

"Who?"

"Russell Coates. He was working undercover—arrested in order not to blow his cover—but before he was released, someone took him out."

The noose around Michael's neck pulled tighter. He'd been the one who'd suggested that Kendall approach Coates. Coates and Michael had run a few undercover operations together, and Michael had always been impressed with his integrity. Then Coates had made unexpected inroads into the cartel with his undercover identity. He hadn't even hesitated when Michael suggested he take it a step further.

And now he was dead?

"Michael, this isn't your fault."

"Yes, it is." Michael stared at the brightly painted yellow wall behind Kendall, filled with dozens of eclectic pieces of art. Photos of coffee cups and coffee beans, antique advertisements and signs.

"What happened?"

"They found him dead in his cell this morning, which poses a problem. Everyone thought that the leak—whoever had been selling information, presumably to the cartel—was plugged when Charlie Bains was killed, but now it appears that the cartel has a few more cops on the payroll than we realized."

"We need Valez," Michael said. "We need La Sombra."

"The bottom line is that I've managed to keep your identity here a secret for your own protection, but the longer you stay with Valez, the greater the risk. If he finds out who you really are . . ."

"Then I'll come in and work from inside the department." Michael's mind was spinning at the thought of being able to see his family again. After eight long months, it didn't even seem possible. "I'll have more resources, which will be better in the long run—"

"You better hold on before you plan your prodigal return."

"Because Coates is dead?"

"Yes. Partly because we don't know yet who wanted him quiet, but also because there are some who still believe you were—before your unfortunate death—the department leak."

"That's not exactly new news."

"Maybe not, but when they find out you've spent the last few months working for Valez . . ."

Michael leaned forward and lowered his voice. "So you're telling me that if I stay undercover, I'll likely be caught and killed by the cartel, and if I come in, I'll be arrested and possibly killed by some rogue cop on the cartel's payroll."

"That's a simplistic way of putting it, but yes."

"So without knowing who we can trust, I can't come in." Michael weighed the situation, not liking any of his options. "I knew the risks when I walked into this, but I didn't think my own people would decide to implicate me for treason."

"Come in now, and I'll do everything I can to ensure your safety."

"You just said—"

"I can put you in a safe house."

"A safe house?" No way. "I'm your best bet to bring Valez's organization down, but I can't do anything to help if I'm off the grid, and you know it."

And without knowing who'd killed Coates, there were no guarantees that whoever did it wouldn't find him as well.

Kendall leaned forward. "I can guarantee your safety with a few men I trust, and it would just be temporary, until I can sort this out."

"Who else knows about me? That I'm not lying in that casket?"

"For your own safety, I haven't told anyone." Kendall patted his shirt pocket. "But hopefully this will go a long way in proving whose side you're on."

Not for the first time, Michael wondered if their decision to keep his assignment classified had been a mistake.

"I would appreciate that. I didn't spend the past eight months hiding out on the doorstep of an infamous drug lord only to be taken down by the good guys."

"I'll find a way to get you out of this, Michael. I promise. But I still think you should come with me now before things get worse."

"So they can what? Arrest me so my family finds my body in some supposed safe house or jail cell? No thanks. I'll take my chances that Valez doesn't know who I am. Give me a few more days—"

"A few more days, and you could be dead. Bains is dead. Coates is dead. There's a good chance that they're homing in on you as well, and what happens when Valez realizes the truth about who you are?"

"I'll deal with that when the time comes."

"When? When you've just been dumped in the middle of the Atlantic? It's too big a risk, Michael. I want you to come in now."

"Give me one more week. Valez invited me to the island tomorrow for Christmas. It will give me a chance to find the last piece of the puzzle."

Kendall sighed. "Fine. Go to the island. Act like everything is normal. I'll make sure things are in place for you once you do come in. But remember, Valez won't hesitate to kill you if he finds out the truth."

"I know that."

"And you're willing to take that risk?"

"You just find out who's behind Coates's death, so when I do come in I'm not thrown into the fiery furnace."

CHAPTER
5

Michael opened his eyes again at a nudge against his shoulder. His angel still hovered over him, the wind whipping through her hair as she looked down at him. How much time had passed? How much of what he remembered was real?

"What time is it?" he asked.

"You've been out about twenty minutes. I found some pain medicine for you. I have a feeling you're going to need it."

He nodded, then downed the pills with a swallow of the bottled water she gave him. His mind fought to find his way out of the fog and the throbbing pain in his side. Maybe passing out wasn't such a bad idea after all. Then the only thing he had to deal with was the haunting dreams.

"Where are we now?" he asked.

"Ten, maybe fifteen minutes from the shore. There was another boat after us, but Ivan managed to lose them shortly after you passed out the first time. Once we get to the dock, my car is parked nearby, but we're going to have to make sure we avoid any welcoming committees."

He handed her back the water bottle, struggling to remember the names she'd told him. Ivan . . . Olivia.

"What happens after that, Olivia?" he asked.

She leaned back, her hand braced against the side of the boat for balance. "We'll drop you off at the nearest police station on the mainland. They'll be able to help you—"

"No!"

"No?"

Michael hesitated, knowing he needed to form a rational response to his outburst. Even in the semidarkness of night, as they flew across the water, he didn't miss the doubt in her eyes. Or the hint of anger in their depths. He deserved both. His pursuit of justice had landed him in the middle of a hornet's nest, and now he'd dragged her and her brother into it right alongside him.

But walking into a police station was just as risky as running into Tomas in a dark alley. Russell Coates had been playing the same deadly undercover detective game. Knowing that he was dead and that it had been an inside job meant that Michael wasn't just running from the cartel. The leaks in the department had yet to be plugged. If he showed up alive, he'd jump to the top of some dirty cop's hit list.

He caught her gaze, wishing he hadn't noticed the soft curve of her lips or the dimple in her chin. "We can't go to the authorities."

"We can't go to the authorities?" Her eyes widened. "Why not?"

"Because I'm not sure who we can trust."

"Last I heard, Tomas and his goons are the ones to be afraid of, so why would we *not* go to the authorities? They're supposed to be the good guys, remember?"

Not all of them.

Lights of the mainland came into view. Michael scrounged for a source of energy to combat the deepening fatigue he felt. All he really wanted to do was disappear and sleep for the next week or two, praying that when he woke up all of this would be over.

But there was no escaping this situation.

"There are things you don't understand," he said.

"Listen, I get it," she said. "You've been through a horrible ordeal. Betrayed, deceived, threatened, whatever—"

"It's more complicated than simply what happened back there on the island."

She shoved back a strand of hair the wind had plastered against her face. "Who are you?"

Michael eased into a sitting position and stared out across the water as the pontoon skimmed across the surface. She deserved an answer. Even deserved the truth—and somehow, he had to convince her of that truth.

"I'm an undercover cop."

"A cop?" She let out a shallow laugh. "Ivan was convinced you were a spy. Is Liam Quinn your real name?"

He weighed her question, still unsure if she'd even believe him if he told her the truth. He could tell her more lies, but whether he liked it or not, they were in this together. She'd risked her life to save him, and she deserved the truth.

"My real name . . . is Michael Hunt. I've been undercover for the past few months . . . working for Valez. For the last eight months my family has thought I'm dead."

He studied her face in the moonlight. The lines of truth and reality in his life had long since blurred out of focus. He was tired of risking his own neck while trying to bring about justice. Sometimes all he could see was the corruption and evil all around him. Because Valez, La Sombra—whoever he was—and their men were only one layer of the issue.

The bottom line right now was that he had no idea who he could trust or who was out to get him, but he needed to trust this woman. Because for whatever reason, she'd risked everything to save his life.

"Well, Michael Hunt, what kind of man are you?"

He struggled to stay upright against the continual movement

of the boat. "I'm not sure I remember anymore, beyond the fact that I'm tired of fighting."

And that he was a man partially responsible for Kendall's death. A man who'd broken his mother's heart. A man who for months had let his family believe he was dead. All for what? Duty? Justice? None of that seemed enough anymore. Too many had sacrificed and too many had lost.

Ivan signaled Olivia, interrupting their conversation.

"My car is parked close to the dock," she told Michael. "We'll be there in just a few minutes."

"And if our *welcoming party* is there?" he asked.

"Then we're in trouble."

Michael felt himself being tugged back into the darkness again, back to relive the haunting memories that refused to leave him alone. He tried to fight it, but he was there again, this time staring out across the Atlantic's barren shoreline, broken only by a few scattered piles of driftwood. Summer hadn't arrived yet, but it was already hot and humid. The ache in his leg from the explosion still throbbed despite the pain medicine the doctor had given him.

Shifting in the lounge chair on Valez's veranda, he took a sip of his iced tea, wishing it was his mother's favorite lemonade-flavored sweet tea. The thought surprised him. He couldn't remember how long it had been since nostalgia had grabbed hold of him so tightly, but he missed his family. Missed the normal life he used to have. He especially missed the regular spiritual feeding he'd never fully appreciated until it was gone.

It was his mother's birthday, another reminder of how much he craved the normalcy of life. Perspiration beaded on his neck as he struggled to hold on to the memories. As soon as he could get off the island, he was going to drive back to Atlanta for the weekend and spend some long-needed quality time with his family.

Valez walked onto the veranda from the house, the smoke from his cigarette trailing behind him. He'd lost weight over the past few months, presumably due to stress, though he'd yet to lose his edge. Valez might be ruthless, but no one could deny the fact that he was a brilliant businessman.

Valez sat down across from him in one of the wrought-iron chairs, dropped a newspaper onto the table, then flicked the end of his cigarette into the glass ashtray.

"It's good to finally see you out of bed," Valez said. "How are you feeling?"

"Better, though I still feel a bit like I was run over by a truck."

"A hundred pounds of explosives will do that to a person." Valez let out a lazy puff of smoke, then leaned back in his chair. "I spoke with the doctor before he left this morning. He says a couple more weeks of rest, and you'll be back to normal."

Michael's hand automatically touched the back of his leg where he'd received the worst damage from the explosion. The doctor was caring for the third-degree burns, the wounds from the shrapnel, and his concussion, but his treatment didn't cover the psychological impact of the bomb.

"Two weeks," Valez repeated. "You're lucky. It was touch-and-go for a long time there."

"And my memory?" Michael asked. "What does the doctor say about that?"

The holes in his recollection continued to torture him. From forgetting where he'd put his toothbrush to the missing details of the case he'd been working on. If he made a mistake, said the wrong thing, everything he'd worked for over the past few months would be for nothing.

Valez played with the edges of the folded newspaper. "The doctor said some form of amnesia was normal after what happened to you. And that there's a good chance that most of your memory loss—if not all of it—will go away eventually."

Michael could only pray the diagnosis was correct. What *wouldn't* go away were the dreams. So vivid that sometimes he couldn't tell anymore what was real and what were leftover pieces from those dreams. At least once a night, he'd wake up in a panicked sweat, reeling from flashbacks of the explosion.

"We haven't had time to talk since the accident." Valez snuffed out his cigarette. "What do you remember about that day?"

Michael swallowed the rest of his tea, not wanting to revisit that moment. "I remember enough to give me nightmares, but not enough to remember the details. It's like a dream that constantly fades in and out."

There were other things he remembered he could never tell Valez. The fact that his name wasn't Michael Linley. That he was here to take down Valez and the upper ranks of the cartel beneath him, along with any dirty cops who were on the man's payroll. He wasn't sure if those memories were a blessing or a curse. Remembering who he was made him want to forget why he was here.

"You saved my life," Valez said. "Do you remember that?"

"Pieces." Michael dug through the memories he was able to access. "I remember the explosion . . . the heat from the fire . . . the pain ripping through my leg. And looking up and seeing you beside me."

"You were lucky—we were both lucky." Valez smiled. "But you still don't remember why you were there, do you?"

"We were there to make an exchange. Cocaine? Weapons? It's still all a blur."

All those hours of staring out at the ocean, breathing in the salt water and resting as he'd been ordered, had only just begun to help him fit the pieces of that day back together.

"It doesn't matter." Valez slid the folded newspaper across the table toward Michael, then opened it. "But this matters. I've been waiting for the right time to show you this."

Michael leaned forward. "What is it?"

"Third obituary on the left. Read it."

"An obituary?"

He started to read the small print.

Michael Linley, 33, died Saturday in an accident. Michael worked as an accountant for a local business, but enjoyed anything to do with the outdoors, especially rock climbing, hiking, and diving. An only child, he is survived by his parents, Clarence and Patsy Linley of Ailey, Georgia.

Michael Linley . . . Accident . . . Dead . . .

"Michael?"

Michael winced as he opened his eyes, the images dissolving into the darkness of a night sky. He tried to remember where he was. They'd left the island on the boat . . . Valez's men had come after them . . . If they found him, they'd kill him along with Olivia and her brother. Kendall had been right to warn him. Returning to the island had simply traded in one vial of deadly poison for another.

CHAPTER

6

Olivia gripped the steering wheel and watched the mile markers go by one by one as they headed down Interstate 16. The brightness of the oncoming headlights, a sharp contrast to the blackness of the night, blurred her vision. But that didn't begin to compare to the turmoil churning in her gut. They'd somehow made it to her car without any further signs of her father's men, but that didn't mean this was over. Which had her scared. Michael had warned her that he couldn't go to the authorities, because he wasn't sure who he could trust. But if they couldn't trust the authorities, then who in the world could they trust? And even more than that, why should she believe a man who'd admitted to her that he worked for her father? As far as she knew, he could be one of them.

She turned on the radio, searching for something to soothe her disheveled nerves, and finally found a praise song, but even the uplifting words weren't enough. At least their passenger was able to rest. The rearview mirror painted a picture of him snoring softly in the backseat.

Michael Hunt. Undercover cop. Mystery man.

She'd seen the fear in his eyes when they'd cut him loose at the cottage. Heard the sincerity in his voice when he told her why he was on the island. But was he telling the truth? All she knew was that he stood in the way of Antonio Valez. And that he was a man her father presumably wanted dead.

Even if the accusations against her father were true, Antonio Valez was still exactly that.

Her father.

Olivia tried to blink back the tears as she stumbled on the real source of the turmoil. She gripped the steering wheel tighter. Whether or not Michael was truly innocent, she'd stopped doubting their decision to rescue him. Whether her decision had been right or wrong, it didn't matter anymore. Because nothing she did now could undo what she'd done.

How was she supposed to choose between her father and the man who had managed to entangle his life with hers and put their lives at stake? *What do I do, God? Dump him off by the side of the road? Turn him in to the local authorities, despite his protests? Or just keep running?*

She switched off the radio, craving the quiet in the search for peace. None of the options seemed right, which made her fear how this was going to end.

She'd returned to the island and her father's house, *Castillo de la Reina*—The Queen's Castle—as he fondly called it, to find out the truth behind the anonymous accusations. Now she faced far more questions than answers, but one thing seemed clear. Antonio Valez wasn't the father or man she'd believed him to be.

Olivia flipped on her windshield wipers as drops of rain began to splatter against the glass. Thirty years ago, her mother had fallen in love with a handsome man from Monterrey, Mexico. Tall, charming, and charismatic, he'd promised her the world, and she'd believed everything he'd told her.

Olivia had believed him too. As distant as he'd always been, she'd still loved him. Trusted him. And now . . . all of the memories of the two of them together over the years were tainted with the reality of who he might really be.

She wiped away a stray tear. But even that truth didn't mean she was responsible for the man lying in her backseat. She'd drop him off at one of his friends' houses, and let them deal with the repercussions of whatever it was he'd done to invoke her father's anger. There had to be a logical explanation. Michael had to have done something . . . and whatever that something was didn't need to affect her and her brother.

Michael stirred in the backseat.

She glanced in the rearview mirror as he struggled to sit up. She was glad he was awake. There were questions she needed to ask. "You're awake."

"Groggy, but yeah. For the most part. Where are we?"

"About halfway between the coast and Atlanta."

"What time is it?"

Olivia glanced at the clock on the dashboard. "Just past nine."

She passed a sign for the next rest stop and changed her plan to push nonstop to Atlanta. He'd need another round of pain-killers soon, and all of them had missed supper. Maybe before she started throwing her mountain of questions at him, they should grab something to eat and stretch their legs.

"Are you hungry?" she asked.

"Yeah, I actually am."

"There's a rest stop coming in a mile known for their wide range of vending machines."

He laughed at her weak attempt to lighten the mood. "That works for me."

A minute later, Olivia clicked on her blinker and pulled into the quiet rest stop, choosing a secluded spot in the parking lot, beneath a row of shade trees. She'd tried to ensure they hadn't been followed, but knowing there could be armed men after them left her nerves on edge.

Ivan woke up beside her as she turned on the dome light and started rummaging through her backpack for some money.

"Hungry?" she signed.

Ivan nodded, then offered to go grab a few things to hold them over until they could get some real food.

"Any preferences?" she asked Michael.

"A drink to take some more pain medicine, and some kind of energy bar would be great."

Olivia gave Ivan the order, then glanced again in the rearview mirror as Ivan exited the car. A semi was pulling off the freeway. Ahead, a woman walked her dog in the light of a streetlamp. Olivia shifted in her seat and stretched out the muscles in her back, tight more from the stress of the day than from driving.

She turned sideways until she was facing Michael, then gripped the top of the seat with her fingers. "Before we go any further, I need to know what's going on."

"Okay. Ask me what you need to know, and I'll tell you."

Her defenses dropped slightly, uncertain if he was being truthful or simply trying to placate her.

"You told me you couldn't go to the authorities," she said. "You also told me you were an undercover cop, but for a cop, you sure seem to be doing a lot of running."

"I've crossed a few people along the way, and now it's not safe."

Not safe? Really. She'd just seen the body of a man who'd been executed in cold blood by her father's henchmen, and as far as she knew, the same men were after them. "Not safe" seemed to be a bit of an understatement at the moment.

"You're going to have to give me a whole lot more than that, because now my brother's life and mine are at stake. Why don't we start with the dead man in the cottage? Did you know him?"

———

Michael leaned back against the headrest, ready to deny that he knew Kendall, then stopped. Had he gotten that used to telling lies? Whatever person he'd become, whatever game he'd been playing, he was going to have to find a way to get out.

"Yeah, I knew him. His name was Sam Kendall. He had a wife and two boys." He shot her a wry grin. "He loved playing golf, though he was terrible at it."

"I'm sorry he's dead."

"Me too. He was a good man."

"Then why was he there?"

Michael considered her questions, wondering how much information he needed to give her. Because she wasn't the only one who had questions. For instance, why had *she* been on the island?

He shifted his weight, trying to ease the pain radiating through his rib cage. "I've been working under him. We met in Atlanta yesterday. He tried to warn me that my life was in danger."

"And you chose not to listen . . . why? Because clearly his warnings were right on target." She stared at him with those piercing brown eyes as if trying to read his mind. "The thing is, I'm trying to decide why I should trust you. I don't exactly like the thought of ending up like your friend."

"I suppose you need to trust me for the same reason I have to trust you." Michael frowned, just as unhappy with the situation as she was. "Because we can now assume that Tomas knows you helped me escape, which means there are now men after both of us who want us dead. Like it or not, Olivia, we're in this together."

Ivan slipped back into the front seat with a bunch of junk food from the vending machines. Olivia handed Michael two painkillers, a Coke, and an energy bar.

"Thanks," he said.

She nodded at him, ripped open a bag of Fritos, and reached for a chip.

Michael popped the pills into his mouth, praying that they'd bring some relief. He was tired, physically and emotionally.

The never-ending fight for justice wasn't motivation enough anymore. He wanted out. Knew that once he walked away from this situation—if, in fact, he was able to walk away from it—he was going to walk away from *all* of it.

Maybe he could take the heat off himself. "What about you? What brought you to Valez's island?"

"I'm not sure I'm ready to switch the subject so quickly."

Michael sighed. "Okay. What else do you want to know?"

Ivan watched their conversation while Michael weighed his decision. According to Tomas, his cover was already blown, and with a probable contract out on his life, he didn't have anywhere else to run.

"What do you know about Antonio Valez?"

"Authorities suspect he's not simply a wealthy businessman but involved in laundering money for the Cártel de Rey."

"And you? What do you believe?"

Michael searched her guarded expression. She was fishing for something, but he wasn't sure what yet. "I believe he's far more than a money launderer. I think he's the leader of the cartel. La Sombra."

Olivia shivered, a frown flitting across her face as she shot a glance at her brother. "The Shadow."

"You've heard about him?"

"Murder . . . kidnapping . . . torture . . . I've read he's ruthless. That he kills migrant workers for refusing to become drug mules. Beheads his victims simply to make a point."

"That's a fair description."

"But if that's true, why would he be here, living in the States? I thought most cartel leaders tend to stay south of the border."

Michael took off the wrapper and bit into his energy bar. Fishing for information, but also informed? She'd been on the island. She had to have a connection to Valez, and he needed to know what it was.

"The border has become fluid," Michael answered. "A few years ago, high-ranking members of these criminal organizations wouldn't have chanced it, even with passports and visas. Now authorities are discovering more and more of them living right here in the US. A majority in south Texas, yes, but Valez discovered his piece of paradise along the coast of Georgia and doesn't want to give it up. He found a way to rule his soldiers from there, taking trips as needed."

"So if you go to the authorities, what happens?"

"Kendall warned me that another undercover cop was recently killed, and they believe it was organized by someone inside the department."

"So if the police find you—"

"I'll probably be arrested, and could potentially end up like Coates, dead in my cell." Michael scrunched the empty wrapper in his fist. "Which is one of the reasons why I've been looking for evidence. Not just evidence that Valez is laundering money through his business, or that he's La Sombra, but evidence of who's working within the department."

"And once you know who the bad cops are, you can go to the authorities?"

Michael nodded. "Now that I've bared my soul, what about you and your brother? What were you doing at Antonio Valez's house?"

Olivia hesitated, her eyes shifting toward her brother. "I'm . . . a reporter."

He blinked. That was not the answer he'd expected. "I know the man well enough to know that he'd never invite a reporter onto his property."

He waited for her response, understanding that she had no reason to trust him.

"I really am a reporter," she began. "Working on an investigation."

Michael shook his head. He didn't buy it. "I know Antonio. He doesn't let just anyone venture onto his private property. Especially not reporters."

"Maybe I'm not just anyone."

Michael didn't miss the look she shot her brother. There had been something familiar about her the first time he'd seen her. He searched his mind for the connection, but still couldn't find one.

"Besides being a reporter, who are you? A family friend?"

"Something like that. My mother and he were . . . friends."

"How close of friends?"

Her gaze dropped, and he wanted to let her off the hook. But too much was at stake. He needed to know the truth.

"Listen, Olivia, we've both been through a lot today. I wasn't lying when I told you I'd been working for Valez as an undercover cop. And as for the situation we're in right now, I'm sorry you were dragged into this, but like it or not, we're in this together. Which means we're going to have to help each other."

Ivan put his hand on her shoulder and nodded when she looked up at him. "Tell him. Tell him the truth."

Olivia turned away, jaw tensed, mouth tight. Then she whispered, "He's our father."

Michael leaned forward, not sure he heard her right. "Your *father?*"

Her voice took on a new resolve, as if she were tired of slamming her head against a brick wall and needed another way around. "She was his mistress, though he never called her that. No matter who Antonio Valez really is, I'll always believe he loved her. We lived in a house he paid for outside of Atlanta and saw him a couple times a year."

"But you didn't know who he was?"

"No. Not until now." Tears glistened in her eyes as he waited for her to go on. She pulled her cell phone out of her pocket and slid it across the top of the vinyl seats. "I need to show you something."

Michael took the phone, surprised at her change of heart. "You've decided to trust me?"

"Do I have a choice? As much as I don't want to, I believe you. A couple of weeks ago, I started receiving emails from an address I didn't recognize."

"What kind of emails?"

"The sender wanted me to look into Antonio Valez. They started out by claiming he wasn't just a real estate mogul but was laundering money for the cartel."

Michael started reading through the message that was on the screen. "Why involve you?"

"I don't know. I assumed it was someone who knows he's my father. Most people don't know my story, though I suppose it wouldn't be impossible to trace if someone tried."

"How many more emails are there?"

"Five."

"Did you go to the police with this?"

"They were unsubstantiated accusations. I tried to trace the sender, but wasn't able to come up with a name." She reached for the bottled water Ivan had brought her, unscrewed the top, then took a sip. "This is crazy, isn't it? You went to that house to prove my father's guilt, while I went there to prove his innocence. But what I need to know is, what happens now? I'm pretty certain that by now he knows that his children just escaped with the man he'd planned to kill in the morning."

Michael finished the last of his energy bar, trying to sort out the information she'd just given him. "We can go to my family. Valez doesn't know my real name, and he shouldn't be able to connect me to them. At least we'd be safe until we can figure out what to do next."

"Ivan?" Olivia asked.

Her brother nodded.

"Okay."

She turned off the dome light and started the car, then eased out of the rest stop, heading toward Atlanta. All he could do was hope he'd just made the right decision to trust her, knowing she was thinking the exact same thing about him.

CHAPTER 7

Olivia grabbed a bottle of painkillers from the shelf and dumped it into the small plastic basket she carried, while Ivan put gas in the car. Thirty minutes from Atlanta, with the tank almost on empty, they'd decided they had no choice but to stop at a convenience store.

Just like she'd had no choice but to trust the man sitting in the backseat of her car.

She glanced down the aisle, willing her nerves to settle down. Except for some upbeat Christmas song jingling in the background, the store was quiet. Because most people were spending Christmas with their families. The only other customers in the store were a woman debating on a brand of cough syrup and an older man chatting with the cashier at the front counter about the weatherman's prediction of snow tonight. Neither seemed interested in her.

Michael had instructed her to drive around the block several times before pulling into the gas station, just to be sure they weren't being followed. But even that extra precaution had done little to erase her worry. They could have missed something that would put all their lives at risk.

She scanned the top shelf until she found the antibiotic cream she'd been searching for. No matter what doubts still lingered, she was worried about Michael. It was a gamble to not take him to an emergency room, where they could patch him up and ensure nothing was broken, but he'd insisted that doing so could leave a trail to follow.

She grabbed a box of bandages. She'd taken a first-aid class a few years ago, and while she might not be ready to apply for a job at her local hospital, surely she could temporarily patch the guy up. Because she'd finally accepted he was right. Until they knew exactly what was going on, they couldn't afford to take any chances.

Handling the situation on their own still seemed foolish, but at the moment she wasn't sure they had another choice. If he was right, she had no idea whom to trust. They needed to stay under the radar, because it wouldn't matter anymore that Antonio Valez was her father. They'd crossed the line and there was no turning back.

The automatic doors at the store's entrance opened. Olivia peered around the end of the aisle as she put her last item into the basket. The older customer was on his way out the door as another man walked in out of the cold wearing a heavy coat and beanie cap. His gaze shifted from the counter to her, then back to the counter again. Her stomach tightened. The man shoved his hands into his pockets and headed for the back of the store. She didn't recognize him as one of her father's employees, but something didn't feel right.

She shook off the thought, still trying to convince herself that there was no way they could have been followed. They'd been careful. But what if they'd missed something? Her father's men knew Michael was gone. And they knew she and Ivan had rescued him.

She hesitated. Part of her wanted to dump the basket and run. They should never have taken the risk of stopping here. But Michael needed the medicine and was counting on her.

LISA HARRIS

She finished her shopping by grabbing a six-pack of cold Sprites from the refrigerated section along with a couple boxes of granola bars, then went to wait behind the woman, who was still checking out.

The man in the beanie moved to the aisle behind her, studying a rack of magazines. Olivia's mind whirled. Michael had said that her father didn't know his real name, but her father had resources. What if her father was able to connect Michael to his family? What if Tomas assumed they would return to Atlanta? Maybe they should drive south a hundred miles and hole up in a hotel for the night while Michael rested and she and Ivan figured out what to do.

The woman in front of her was arguing with the cashier over a sale price. Olivia felt her heart speed up and her palms slick with sweat as she fought the urge to throw the basket down and run out the door.

She glanced back at the man in the beanie. He was still there, his gaze focused on the cashier. Ms. Cheapskate finally handed over the disputed quarter and headed out the door.

Olivia laid her purchases on the counter and forced herself to smile at the Asian man as he rung up her items.

"Merry Christmas," she said.

"Merry Christmas," he said, smiling back.

She glanced up at a camera above the counter while the cashier began scanning her items. She drummed her fingers against the counter, willing him to hurry. She'd already taken too much time. She glanced behind her, looking for the other man. The aisle where he'd been standing was empty. Where was he?

The cashier was asking her a question. Something about a lottery ticket?

She looked back at him. "I'm sorry, what did you say?"

"I was just asking if you'd like a lottery ticket . . ."

His voice trailed off. She heard footsteps behind her a moment before someone grabbed her and pressed something hard against the back of her head. Her knees buckled.

The cashier held up his hands.

"Open the cash drawer—"

"I can't."

"Then I'll shoot her."

Olivia fought the instinct to pull away and run. But if she did, she had no doubt the man would shoot her. She caught the reflection of his profile in the round mirror above the counter. Thin face, scruffy beard, piercing eyes beneath the beanie . . . She was unsure if he was high or simply desperate for cash.

How had today gone from terrible to this?

Olivia squeezed her eyes shut. *God, please . . . please don't let things end this way.*

Michael sat hunched down in the backseat of Olivia's car, ensuring he was out of view of the store's cameras. Stopping here might have been necessary, but it was also a risk. And Olivia and her brother had already risked too much for him. Once Valez found out what they'd done, he would no doubt send his men after them. Michael knew he couldn't call his sister. Not yet. Phone calls, credit card use, surveillance cameras, all could potentially be traced back to them.

He tried to stretch out his legs in the cramped backseat, while trying to ignore the throbbing ache in his side. Clearly, he'd played the game too long. All he wanted to do right now was hole up in some quiet hideaway, watch the snow fall, and heal from his injuries, both physical and emotional. It was funny—he hadn't expected that the emotional toll of an undercover assignment could be so completely overpowering. Knowing that at any moment friends might turn against him. Knowing that every time he slipped deeper into his role, he was that much closer to never being able to get out.

As Ivan finished refueling the car, Michael shifted his gaze toward the front entrance of the store. He leaned back, wishing he had a clearer view of the cashier. He wasn't sure what it was, but something felt wrong. He reached across the front seat and opened the glove compartment, hoping he'd find what he needed inside.

Good girl. He pulled out the Glock and clicked off the safety.

His focus shifted back to the store. A minute ago, a woman had walked out, which meant there was only the cashier, Olivia, and a young man wearing a beanie left inside. He'd watched the man as he'd entered the store. Maybe it was his imagination, but there'd been something off about the guy. He'd seemed edgy. Nervous.

Michael shifted in the backseat until he could see the man through the window. He was at the counter, holding a gun against Olivia's head.

Michael jumped out of the car, ignoring the pain. He held the gun behind his leg and tapped Ivan on the shoulder to get his attention. "Get into the car. I'll pay for the fuel."

A moment later, the bell sounded as the glass doors slid open and he walked into the store. Pain radiated through his side, but he pressed forward, taking in everything around him.

He stopped eight feet from the man and held up the Glock. "Drop your weapon."

The younger man's hands shook. "Forget it."

Michael had been trained to handle a crisis. Push the man too hard, and he might end up shooting Olivia or the cashier. Don't push hard enough, and an already volatile situation could quickly turn deadly.

"Let her go." Michael kept his voice low and steady. "It's not worth it, trust me. You don't want anyone to get hurt. Walk away now before that happens."

"No." The man pointed his gun at him, hands shaking, the fear evident in his eyes. "This was just supposed to be walk in and walk out with the cash. No one was supposed to get hurt, but now—"

The man's gun fired. Michael fired back, hitting him in the side. Olivia screamed as the man dropped to the floor.

Michael slapped fifty bucks onto the counter, a burning sensation spreading through his arm as he grabbed Olivia's hand. The police would be here in a matter of minutes. "Give me the keys. We need to get out of here. Now."

She handed him the keys, grabbed the bag of groceries, and hurried outside with him.

At the car, Michael slid into the driver's seat. As soon as Olivia's door was shut, he peeled out of the parking lot. His heart had yet to stop racing as he turned onto the interstate entrance. "Did you recognize him? Is he one of your father's men?"

"I've never seen him before." She pulled her seat belt across her chest and stared straight ahead. "Maybe it was just a random robbery?"

"Did he say anything about following us?"

"No, nothing. He just . . . just wanted money. Why?"

"I'm not sure it matters. What does matter is that our faces are going to be plastered all over the news, and you and Ivan and I will officially be connected."

"And my father will discover your real identity."

Michael felt a wave of nausea wash over him. He never should have let them drag themselves into this. Never should have let them risk their lives trying to save him. He might be dead, but they wouldn't be running for their lives.

"Michael . . ." Olivia's fingers grasped the edge of his sleeve. "He shot you."

"No. He missed." He put a hand to his arm, surprised when he pulled away and found his fingers covered with blood. "It's nothing. Just a graze. I'll be fine."

"Nothing? As soon as the adrenaline wears off you won't say it's nothing. Pull over." She reached for the grocery bag she dumped onto the floorboard in front of her. "Your face is pale, your hands are shaking. Let me at least bandage your arm before you bleed to death in my car. I bought some bandages and a few other basics back at the store."

"We can't afford to stop. If we're being followed—"

"We're not being followed. It was a random robbery."

"Maybe, but it won't take the police long to put all of this together."

But whether or not he wanted to admit it, he knew she was right. He took the next exit, then pulled off into the back of an empty parking lot. A minute later, he leaned against the hood of the car and eased off his shirt, shivering as much from the pain as the cold.

Olivia ripped open the package of bandages. "You're lucky, it is just a flesh wound. He could have killed you."

Michael winced as she pressed the gauze against the wound, not allowing his mind to think about what could have happened. "You act like you know what you're doing, Ms. Nightingale."

"Funny. I can't say that I've ever dressed a gunshot wound, but I've taken a few first-aid classes. You're going to need to see a doctor, but this will have to do for now."

He smiled at her as she finished securing the gauze with strips of tape. "Thank you."

"You're welcome."

She reached up to brush a snowflake off his nose, distracting him for a moment. But there wasn't time for distractions. Not now.

"We can't stay here long," he said.

"Then where do we go?"

"This story is going to hit the news, and my family will find out I'm alive. They'll start asking questions down at the police station, and Valez will be able to make the connection."

"And he'll know where to look for us."

"What about Felipe?" Ivan asked.

"I don't know, Ivan," Olivia said.

"Who's Felipe?" Michael asked.

"He's an old friend of the family. He lives in a cabin in the Blue Ridge Mountains. It's about as off the grid as you can get. We could go there. Let you rest a couple of days while we figure out what to do next."

"You're sure no one could trace us there?"

"I don't know how," she said. "My father doesn't know about the cabin, if that's what you're worried about."

"Do you trust this man?"

"I'd trust him with my life, yes."

"Good, because that's exactly what we have to do." He let her help him put his shirt back on, regretting the day he'd ever agreed to walk into the lion's den. "How far is the cabin?" he asked.

"Two . . . two and a half hours tops."

"Okay, but I need your cell phone first and yours too, Ivan, if you have one."

"Our cell phones?" She pulled hers out of her back pocket while Ivan grabbed his from the car. "What are you doing?"

"Making sure we stay off the grid." He pried her phone open and took out the battery, then watched Ivan do the same with his. He waited until he had Ivan's attention, then looked at his two unlikely rescuers. "By the way, I don't think I've thanked you both yet for saving my life."

She turned to him with those wide, almond-shaped eyes of hers that made his mind fuzzy. "We only did what any Good Samaritan would have done."

"Maybe, but it would have been safer for you to walk away, and you know it. You took a risk and saved my life."

"Like you did just now at the gas station? It seemed like the right decision at the time."

His vision blurred. He needed another dose of pain medicine. Needed to sleep. "Let's just pray we're making the right decision now."

CHAPTER 8

Olivia pressed on the brakes in front of the familiar cabin, then eased her car beneath the shadowy canopy of trees. Once again, she tried to ensure they hadn't been followed. She was starting to question their decision to come to the cabin.

But there was no turning back now. Michael had slept most of the way, which she'd been thankful for, but thirty minutes ago, she'd noticed beads of sweat glistening on his forehead, and a patch of blood seeping through his bandage. If Felipe couldn't help him, they'd have to chance going to the nearest emergency room.

Felipe stepped out onto the wooden porch with a shotgun raised to the heavens, the moonlight catching the scowl on his face. She stepped out of the car slowly, with her hands in front of her. Felipe had never been one to trust strangers. Forty years ago, he'd left his life in Mexico, where he'd watched his family killed. He'd never been able to escape the images of their deaths.

"It's me, Felipe. Olivia."

Ivan exited the front passenger seat with a grin on his face as Felipe's brown-and-white hunting dog, Gizmo, covered his face with slobbery kisses.

"Olivia . . . Ivan . . . what in the world?" Felipe lowered the weapon to the ground and ran down the stairs before gathering her up in a hug. "I was hoping you'd call for Christmas, but a visit's even better, even though you're a few hours late."

"I know. I'm sorry for dropping in on you like this, so late, without any warning."

Felipe took a step back to look at her in the yellow glow of the porch light. "You look tired, but good."

"Thank you. And you . . ." Olivia shot him a worried look. "You've lost weight."

Felipe patted his midsection. "Thanks for noticing, but why didn't you call me and tell me you were headed this direction?"

His question drew her back to the issue at hand. "We've run into a few . . . problems."

"What happened? Are you in trouble?"

"It's a long story, but yeah. We need your help."

Felipe reached out to pull Ivan into a hug, then stepped back to look at him. "Better watch out for that dog of mine. He's always running off, hunting down some vermin, then bringing it back." He laughed. "It's good to see you."

Felipe paused when he caught sight of Michael sitting beneath the dome light in the backseat of the car.

"Who's that?" he asked.

"His name's Michael."

"A friend of yours?"

Olivia hesitated. If she wanted Felipe to trust her, she was going to have to tell him the truth from the very beginning. "He's a cop."

"Whoa, hold on." The welcoming tenor in Felipe's voice vanished. "A cop—or any lawman for that matter—only means one thing. Trouble. And that's something I don't want here."

He'd never told her why he wasted his days cooped up in this cabin, though she'd always suspected he'd had a run-in with the law at some point.

"He's one of the good guys, Felipe."

"And you know that how?"

"It's a long story, but for now what's important is that he's hurt." She shivered despite her heavy coat. The temperature had dropped over the past couple of hours, bringing with it the couple inches of snow the weatherman had promised. "I thought maybe you could help me patch him up."

"Forget it. There's a perfectly good emergency room fifteen miles from here. They'll be happy to see him."

"Can't do that. There are some men after us." Olivia reached out and grasped Felipe's hand. "We need your help. You told me once that this cabin is completely hidden from the outside world. If that's still true, this is where we need to be. If it's not true—"

"Of course that's still true." Felipe's brow furrowed. "Which is why I don't like having strangers showing up."

"He's not the enemy, and neither am I. Please."

Olivia heard the panic in her voice. Maybe they had been foolish coming here. Maybe they should have gone to the authorities or to Michael's family.

Felipe wiped his mouth with the back of his hand, still frowning. "You know I'd do anything for you and your brother, but this . . . I'm not risking my life for some stranger. And if you were followed . . ."

"I made sure we weren't. No one knows we're here. We've even disassembled our phones." She looked up and caught Felipe's gaze. "If not for Michael, then do this for me. Just for a day or two, until we figure out what to do."

Olivia helped Michael out of the car while she waited for Felipe's response. His shoulder had continued to bleed, his face was pale, and she could feel the heat radiating through his shirt.

The panic that had settled in her stomach earlier started to spread. Felipe was right. They'd made a mistake coming here. Not only were they involving Felipe, but Michael was getting worse. He needed to be in a hospital.

"You know, you're right, Felipe. We'll leave. He's gotten worse, and—"

"If what you've said is true," Felipe interrupted, "then maybe you're exactly where you should be. I could never live with myself if something happened to either of you."

"Are you sure?" she asked.

Felipe nodded. "I know I could end up regretting this, but yeah. Come on in."

Felipe and Ivan helped Michael across the uneven ground toward the one-bedroom cabin while Olivia locked the car and brought in their stuff.

She walked into the living room behind the men, thankful for the fire blazing in the corner of the room. She closed the front door behind her and flipped the double lock. Inside the familiar living room sat two old couches, a lounge chair, a coffee table, and a small television. Felipe had never been one for creature comforts, and had never even thought to remodel the dark paneled walls or the blue-and-green shag carpet straight from the seventies. But to her, the place was perfect.

Michael groaned as they set him down on a quilt draped over the double bed in the bedroom.

"Tell me what happened," Felipe said. "He's burning up with fever."

"He was beat up."

"I can see that. Okay, you can explain everything later, but for now, it looks as if he's lucky to be alive." Felipe peeled off Michael's shirt, and Olivia saw that fresh blood soaked the bandage on his arm. Felipe gave her a hard look. "This isn't from being beat up. He's been shot."

"It's just a flesh wound, but he lost a lot of blood."

Felipe switched on a lamp on the bedside table, then let out a sharp huff. The bare bulb cast shadows against the walls. "Looks as if I'll be giving up my bed for the night, but you're going to have to replace the quilt he's just ruined."

Olivia gave him another hug. "I always knew you were a softy beneath that tough exterior of yours."

Felipe shot her a weak smile. "That's not a secret I want getting out."

"Fair enough. What can I do?"

"Looks like you did a pretty good job already, but there's a well-stocked first-aid kit along with a bucket of clean rags to the left of the sink. Grab it all and ask Ivan to get a bowl of warm water."

In the kitchen a pot of coffee sat on the stove, sending its pungent smell throughout the small cabin and bringing with it memories of Olivia and Ivan and their mother sitting in the living room, while Felipe told story after story of his life growing up. He'd been a part of their lives as long as she could remember. A friend to her mother, a father-figure to her and Ivan. Today, those memories seemed a lifetime ago.

Ivan stopped her in the middle of the kitchen. "I'm sorry," he signed.

"For what?"

"Insisting we bring Michael with us. I didn't realize it would cause so much trouble. And now we've involved Felipe. It's like a row of dominos." His eyes darkened. "If they find Michael, they find us. If they find us, they find Felipe . . ."

"No," Olivia said. "You were right. He'd be dead if we hadn't rescued him."

"And because of what we did, we might all be dead soon."

Olivia grabbed the first-aid kit and a handful of rags from the bucket near the sink. She was unwilling to give in to the fear churning her insides. "We're going to get through this. Alive. Besides, we couldn't have just let them kill him. We both know that."

"Maybe, but—"

"No buts. We're going to figure this out. And until then, Felipe needs you to bring him a bowl of warm water."

Olivia turned away. While her own words might be laced with confidence, the sea of doubt roiling inside her had yet to die down. Had tonight really been worth saving a man they didn't know? Especially when it meant putting their own lives at risk?

Felipe looked up as Olivia stepped back into the bedroom. "Did you find everything?" he asked.

"Yes. Ivan will be here in a second with the water." She set the rags and the first-aid kit on the end of the bed, surprised at how worried she could be about a man who had just stepped into her life and turned it upside down. "How is he?"

"Besides the gunshot wound, he's badly bruised, and has a fever we need to get down. All I can do is clean him up and give him some pain medicine and a strong round of antibiotics, which thankfully I have. Beyond that, we'll watch his fever and make sure his wound doesn't get infected."

"Where did you get antibiotics?" she asked.

Felipe smiled. "I told you I had a well-stocked first-aid kit."

Olivia started to ask another question, then stopped. Maybe there were some things better off not knowing.

Like the fact that her father was a part of the cartel.

Olivia buried the thought. "What else, Felipe?"

Ivan brought the bowl of water into the room and set it next to the bed while Felipe handed her a tube of antibiotic ointment. "As soon as I finish washing the cuts on his face and the backs of his hands, put this on them. Barring an infection, he should recover in a few days."

They continued in silence, while Michael drifted in and out of consciousness, groaning every few moments, as if he were trying to escape from a bad dream. The problem was, waking up wasn't going to change anything. Reality was going to seem worse than his dream. At least with dreams, you eventually woke up.

Felipe signaled her back into the living room once they were done. The clock on the wall read 1:22. Ivan had taken the coffee off the stove, then fallen asleep on one of the couches, with Gizmo at his feet.

"Hungry?" Felipe asked.

"No."

"How about some coffee? It's decaf and still hot."

She nodded. Caffeine or not, she had a feeling she wasn't going to be able to sleep for a long time.

Felipe pulled out a couple of mugs. "Do you still take it with cream and sugar?"

"Yeah. Thanks." She smiled up at him. "For everything."

"I could never deny your mother anything. Guess nothing's changed with the next generation." His smile lingered for a moment, then faded as he spooned in the sugar. "Tell me what happened that you would bring a cop to my doorstep."

Her decision to tell him the truth wavered. "We were on the island . . . at our father's house. Ivan saw a man murdered."

"Murdered?"

"Michael was going to be next," she continued. "If we hadn't rescued him, he would have been dead by morning."

There were flicks of anger in Felipe's eyes. "Why didn't you just leave him there and let the cops take care of things? That's their job, isn't it? You took too big a risk for a man you know nothing about."

"But they didn't catch us, and Michael will live now."

He sat down in the green lounge chair in front of the fireplace, avoiding her gaze as he stared into the lingering yellow and orange flames of the dying fire.

Olivia sat down across from him in the wooden rocker, holding the warm mug between her hands. "What is it, Felipe?"

"You don't realize what you've just gotten involved in."

"By saving a man's life?" She knew it was far more than that, and she was frustrated over the secrets and lies. "Tell me what's going on. Tell me what I don't know about my father."

"Your mother once told me that what attracted her to him in the beginning was the fact that he was a successful businessman. Someone who was stable and solid."

"Businessmen don't hire hitmen to kill people who get in their way." She took a sip of her coffee as years of questions rose to the surface. "Tell me the truth."

"I knew this day would come, when you'd ask me these questions." He leaned forward and set his cup on the hearth, a deep sadness marking his expression. "Your mother wanted to paint the picture of the perfect family to the world, but Antonio Valez, even with all of his wealth and possessions, couldn't hang on to the fantasy."

"What are you talking about?"

He shook his head. "I promised . . . She made me promise . . ."

"Promise what?" She set her coffee on the hearth beside him, then reached out and took his hand. "I need you to tell me what you know about my father, Felipe. Please. Michael told me that he's suspected of being involved in the cartel. That his 'business' is really a front for laundering money, and there's a chance that he's La Sombra, the leader of the Cártel de Rey. Please tell me none of that is true."

"Those are a lot of heavy accusations."

"Yes, they are."

"What do you think?" he asked.

She let go of his hand and sat back, still unsure what was true and what was a lie. "That my parents tried to shelter Ivan and me from the truth, and might have been successful, if it hadn't been for what Ivan saw today."

Felipe sighed. "Your father's made a lot of money over the years, Olivia, but most—if not all of it—was made through illegal ventures."

Any seeds of hope that had lingered vanished completely. "So what Michael said is true. My father isn't just a businessman?"

"Antonio is your father, and I've always respected that fact. I respected your mother's wishes that you and Ivan never find out the truth, because I knew she loved him. But now . . . after tonight . . . after what Ivan saw, everything has changed."

She'd already faced a number of unpleasant truths over the past few hours, but from the look on Felipe's face, she was pretty sure she'd just uncovered another.

"You were in love with her, weren't you? My mother."

Felipe rubbed his day-old beard, clearly hesitant at giving her the answers she needed.

"Felipe, please. I need to know the truth."

"Yes, I was in love with her, but it's much more complicated than that."

"Complicated how?"

"Your mother belonged to Antonio, and no one messed with what belonged to him. Men have died for less than that."

"And did she love you as well?"

"She thought it best that you didn't know the truth about our relationship."

Olivia swallowed hard. "And my father, is he La Sombra?"

"There are some who believe he is. There are others who say La Sombra doesn't exist. That his brutal image was created to keep people in line."

"And you? What do you say?"

Felipe pressed his palms against his knees. "There are things you don't know, Olivia. Things I promised your mother I'd go to my grave never telling anyone. Not you, not Ivan . . . no one. I promised your mother I'd look after you and Ivan. I only wanted to protect you and make sure you were safe."

Olivia felt anger take the place of the fear. "My mother's dead, which means that any secrets you're still keeping are only hurting me and Ivan. Tell me, Felipe. I'm tired of all the secrets."

"Olivia, the three of you were the only family I had after leaving Mexico," he said. "Which is why your protection has always been important to me. As for the secrets, if your father had ever found out my feelings toward your mother—and her feelings toward me—he would have killed us both."

She should have seen this coming. Should have realized that Felipe had been more than just a surrogate father taking the place of an absent one. Should have realized that he'd been more than a family friend to her mother.

He took a deep breath. "I'm sorry, Olivia. I never meant to deceive you or hurt you, you have to understand that. Things were so complicated, the stakes so high. Your mother did what she believed best in order to keep you safe."

"Including lying to me?" Olivia's mind reeled with the information he'd just handed her. "I should check on Michael."

"You really think you can trust him?"

"You're asking me about trust?" Olivia bit back more angry words. Fighting with Felipe wasn't going to change anything, but that didn't erase the pain gnawing at her. "There's another problem I haven't told you about yet. Michael got that gunshot wound from stopping a convenience store robbery just a few hours ago. We got away before the police came, but there were security cameras."

"Which means your photos are about to be plastered all over the news." Felipe quickly put two and two together. "And when your father sees the photos, he'll figure out who Michael really is, and know that you're involved. Olivia, what were you think-ing, risking your life for a stranger?"

"That a man was about to be murdered." She turned and headed for the bedroom to check on Michael, leaving Felipe alone to deal with the sins of his past.

CHAPTER
9

Avery North sat at her desk at the precinct and pressed redial on her phone, trying for the third time in fifteen minutes to get ahold of her daughter. She glanced up at the clock hanging on the wall, her fingers drumming against the desk in sync with her tapping foot. She shouldn't worry. Tess had probably left her phone in her backpack again while she hung out at her best friend Sabrina's house. But she couldn't convince herself of that, and concern nagged in the pit of her stomach.

Maybe she was overreacting, but life as she knew it had forever changed nine days ago when the safe world she'd tried to create for her daughter had been shattered.

She hung up the unanswered call, then dropped the phone onto her desk. She might have made the conscious choice to face the ugly realities of this world every day, but that decision had not included Tess. The realization that she wasn't in total control of her daughter's life had struck hard, and the aftermath of the ordeal had been just as traumatic as the ransom and kidnapping.

She shifted in her chair, the gunshot wound in her leg still aching. Both she and Tess had been left with emotional as well as physical scars. Healing would come, but the fact that her daughter had been forced to deal with issues no thirteen-year-old should have to face had added another layer of guilt to what she already carried as a single mom. Guilt that highlighted her own weaknesses and fears, pushing her to the place where the only way she could hang on some days was to rely solely on God's strength.

Avery fiddled with her engagement ring while staring at the stack of paperwork she needed to tackle. Moving up her wedding to Valentine's Day had sent Mama into a tizzy, but while Mama might believe that the words "simple" and "southern" couldn't be uttered in the same sentence, this was her wedding. She and Jackson had cut the guest list to a minimum, settled on a quiet, cozy setting, and started writing their own vows.

She picked up the family photo sitting on the edge of her desk and ran her finger across the glass frame. They needed to take a new one to include Jackson, but a photo without Michael would make his death seem all the more final. She still missed him. Still thought about him every day. Knew that her mother was still grappling with losing her only son.

Mason knocked on the open door of her office, wearing his typical jeans, T-shirt, and leather jacket. She motioned him in. Not too long ago, she would have objected to the undercover cop's presence in her office, but that was before he'd helped save Tess's life and stolen the heart of her sister, Emily. Today, he was once again a part of the Hunt family.

She studied his sullen expression as he moved in front of her desk, his laptop under his arm. "You don't look happy. What's wrong?"

Before she could answer, the captain stepped into her office behind Mason and shut the door.

Avery pushed her chair back and stood up. "Captain Peterson."

"I need you to watch something."

The familiar feeling of unease welled up inside her. Emotionally, she'd barely made it through the past couple of weeks. She wasn't ready for another bombshell to hit.

Mason flipped open his laptop while she sat down again, and set it on the desk facing her. Seconds later, video footage began playing on the screen. The black-and-white recording of the inside of a convenience store captured the cashier and a woman paying for her purchases.

She watched as a man wearing a beanie came up from behind and pressed a gun against the woman and started shouting at the cashier.

Avery looked up at Mason. "Why are you showing me this?"

Mason glanced at the captain, then back at Avery. "I'm not sure how to ease into a conversation like this." He paused, adding to the unspoken tension in the room. "We believe Michael is on this video."

"Michael?"

Mason froze the footage as a second man moved into view on the left of the screen. "Right there."

Avery blinked, trying to process the information. She'd seen the rubble of the warehouse where Michael had been killed in the explosion. She'd read the medical examiner's report and watched them carry his empty casket out of the chapel. There might not have been enough left of Michael to identify, but she'd never doubted that her brother was dead.

She braced her hands on the desk, her fingers gripping its edge, while an eerie numbness spread through her. "You know that's not possible. The ME was able to positively identify his remains. We buried him eight months ago. Both of you were there." Avery leaned closer to study the picture. "I'll admit it looks like him, but Michael's dead. This doesn't even make sense."

"We found his prints. The captain called in a few favors so I could personally hand the prints over to the lab for a rush job.

They confirmed that the prints were Michael's, based on ones we have on file."

Avery shook her head, still not buying it. Someone could have tampered with the evidence. Tampered with the fingerprints on file . . .

"Where did you find his prints?" she asked.

"On the fifty-dollar bill he handed the cashier."

She drew in a slow breath, feeling as if she'd just stepped into a nightmare. But for now, all she could do was keep asking questions. The more she knew, the faster she could find a way to untangle this mess.

"Where did this footage come from?"

"A local gas station and convenience store about thirty minutes from here."

"Play it again."

Avery watched as the video played a second time. Moments after Michael—or whoever the man was—appeared on the screen, the other man shot at him. Michael shot back, and the man dropped to the ground. Michael put a bill on the counter, then grabbed the girl. A second later he was gone.

"What about the man he shot?"

"He's a local drug dealer. He should make it, but he's not talking yet."

Avery stopped the footage and sat down in her chair, refusing to believe what she'd just seen. Michael was not alive. He hadn't just shot someone. Hadn't just grabbed some girl in the middle of the robbery and dragged her out of the store. It couldn't be Michael. Because Michael would never betray his family and cause them such heartache.

"This is crazy. It can't possibly be Michael."

She'd worked for months to clear her brother's name and ensure that the rumors of him betraying the department were laid to rest. Michael had been working undercover before his death, assigned to infiltrate a group of suspected drug and arms dealers. He'd been killed in a bomb explosion, but instead of hailing him as a hero, the department had criminalized him, accusing him of selling sensitive information to the dealers.

Not once had she believed the unsubstantiated reports to be true. And with Charlie's death, the true identity of the informant had been revealed, which only cemented in her mind that her brother was innocent. She wasn't going to let them drag his reputation through the mud again.

"Avery?"

She glanced up at Mason and caught the concern in his voice. Mason and Michael might have been best friends for years, but even he couldn't fully understand what her family had gone through because of the accusations marring her brother's name.

Mason sat down on the edge of the desk. "The higher-ups believe he's been working for the cartel, and that he shot and killed a rival. I don't believe any of it, but—"

"You can't be serious." Avery shoved her chair back and stood up, ready for a fight. "Before Michael died, he was trying to take down the cartel, not work with them. And he certainly wasn't a dirty cop."

"I'm doing everything I can to keep this quiet," the captain said, "but there's a reporter barking up this tree, which means the video is eventually going to hit the news."

Avery's temples pulsed as her mind scrambled for an explanation that would counter the accusations against her brother. "Who's the woman in the video?"

"We've identified her as Olivia Hamilton. Her father's name is Antonio Valez. He's a real estate broker with rumored ties to the cartel Michael was investigating. There are even rumors that his role goes beyond possible money laundering and that he actually is the notorious La Sombra. But even with half a dozen federal agencies breathing down his neck, he's managed so far to avoid any kind of conviction."

"So, back up. You're actually telling me that my brother somehow faked his own death and has spent the last eight months working for Antonio Valez, aka La Sombra?"

"Until we speak to Michael," the captain said, "we can try to interpret the video however we want, but that's what it looks like to me, and I'm not the only one. Unfortunately, you and I both know that this isn't the only evidence we have against your brother."

Avery's anger dug into her at the captain's clipped words. She'd seen the "evidence" they'd used to identify the mole. Michael had been involved in several key operations that had allowed him access to sensitive information. After his death, the police had discovered this information on a laptop hidden in his apartment.

"The only evidence found against my brother was circumstantial and you know it. Planted, most likely, by Charlie Bains, who is now dead. That case is closed."

"What if it's not?" Mason asked.

"You were his best friend," Avery shot back. "You know as well as I do that Michael wasn't capable of this. He loved his job. Loved his family. Loved his country, and he would never betray any of them. In fact, if you want my opinion, if that really is Michael, it looks like a robbery to me, and he just saved a woman."

"I agree that Michael wasn't capable of doing anything criminal," Mason said, "but I also know he was working undercover and none of us know at this point exactly what he was involved in."

"There are those who are going to say that your brother killed a member of the cartel, then grabbed Valez's daughter to use her as leverage," the captain said.

"And they'd be wrong," Avery said.

The captain cleared his throat. "Avery, I know your family is close, and I know that Michael always had a pristine record, but money can change people. The cartel's gross profit easily exceeds DuPont and Coca-Cola. How hard would it have been for him to say yes to an offer that would bring in ten times what he made in a year?"

She would never believe that. "Not Michael."

"Listen," the captain continued, "I wanted to come to you personally, before all this hits full force, because you're going to be caught in the middle. You're going to be asked if you've heard from your brother. If you've seen him. If he's really dead."

"I've told you the truth this entire time." Avery clenched her fists, ready to strike the next person who tried to convince her that her brother was guilty. "We buried my brother eight months ago. As far as I know, he's dead."

"Just know that I'll continue to back you up, but if I find out you're lying—or protecting a fugitive—you're going to have a hard time saving your career."

The captain's comment stung, making her feel as if she were boxing in the dark, with no way to see who she was fighting against.

Avery skirted around her desk and faced the captain. "You're saying that Michael walked away from his home, his family, and his career all for a paycheck, but I don't buy that. Michael loved what he did. He believed in what he did, and nothing you can tell me—no video or any piece of so-called evidence—can convince me otherwise. If this is true . . . there has to be a logical explanation to what he's been doing these past eight months."

The captain took a step toward the door, then paused. "Here's the bottom line. We've been looking for a way to bring down the cartel working in this area for a long time, and innocent or not, I believe your brother is the key. We need to bring him in, and I need you to help me, because while he wasn't worth much to us dead, he's worth everything to us if he's alive. He could mean access into the cartel."

Avery started to speak, but the captain wasn't finished.

"We also think Michael was shot, which means he's going to need medical attention. And if I'm right, he might be contacting you soon. So while I'm putting you in charge of this investigation, it's not because I think it's the wisest thing to do, but because you know this case inside and out. And just so we're clear, I expect to be kept in the loop. Because whatever the truth ends up being, your brother's in way over his head."

Mason broke his silence as soon as the captain left the room. "I'm sorry. If I could have warned you—"

"This wasn't your fault." She looked up at him, wondering if any of her arguments were worth anything. "It's just that I spent months trying to prove his innocence, and I meant what I said. No matter what kind of evidence they have, no matter what kind of proof, nothing will convince me that he sold us out."

"You know I don't believe for a moment that he'd betray any of us either."

Avery leaned against her desk, fighting back the tears. She'd always been the protective older sister. The one who'd found a reason to keep going after losing her husband. The one who'd come up fighting after Michael died. But today . . . today she felt like everything she'd tried to do to prove his innocence was suddenly slipping away.

She looked up at Mason. "Promise me you'll do everything you can to keep this off the nightly news for as long as possible. I'd rather my mother not know what's going on until we're 100 percent sure whether he's alive or not. Even if that was him on the video, he could be killed before this is all over."

"Of course." Mason nodded. "But what are you going to do if Michael contacts you?"

Avery tried to process the question, knowing all her options were unacceptable. If Michael turned himself in, he'd be arrested. If he stayed out there, there was a good chance the cartel would try to take him down.

"I don't know," she said. "I honestly don't know."

CHAPTER
10

Michael shouted as the ground tore open beneath him. He slammed against the concrete as an explosion ripped through the building behind him, sucking up the air around him and leaving his lungs desperate for breath. Debris smashed against his back and thighs, smoldering embers looking for something to burn.

And then nothing.

An unsettling silence surrounded him. The air was hot and smoky as he tried to fill his lungs with oxygen. Light peeked through the corners of his eyes as he forced them open, the ground rumbling around him. He could see someone run past him. His face was plastered against the ground, and he could feel the heat from the burning warehouse.

Someone dragged him from the pavement. Nausea swept over him as they lifted him into the car. He should be dead. Should be in that warehouse with Bruce. It wasn't the first time he'd faced death head-on and won. But this time had been different.

He shouldn't be alive.

Like Bruce. But instead of being able to save his partner Bruce, he'd only managed to save Valez. Pulled him toward safety the moment he'd realized the bomb was going to go off. Michael's unconscious mind fought to unearth the truth. How had his dreams become more vivid than reality?

His mind shifted. He was back on the veranda sitting across from Valez, staring once again at his own obituary.

Valez was offering him a smug grin. "I felt like it was the least I could do after you saved my life." He tapped the obituary with his finger. "I thought adding your love of the outdoors was a nice touch, though I realize it must feel a bit strange to find out you're a dead man."

Michael had worked to temper the anger rising inside his gut. "I don't understand. How did this happen?"

"I suppose the reason behind your . . . exaggerated death . . . isn't clear to you yet."

Michael bit back a sharp response. "No, it's not."

"I'm worried, Michael. Between ongoing investigations by the IRS, the DEA, and every other organization they can drum up, they're getting too close to discovering the truth. They're all threats to this life I've created here. I can't take a chance of losing it." Valez smiled at him. "I need someone I can trust. Someone they can't get to."

Someone who's dead.

"They were having trouble identifying what was left of the bodies, so I decided to give my friend at the ME's office a bit of a friendly nudge," Valez said.

Michael tried not to panic. For months, this job had kept him tottering on thin ice, but what Valez was saying was about to send him crashing through the last layer of security.

"Just think of it this way, Michael. How often is a man presented with a chance to start over?"

Michael's frown deepened. How far was he going to have to take this charade? Valez was known to be eccentric, but even this seemed too far-fetched for him.

"I don't understand how this can work. What about DNA?"

Michael countered. "What happens when the police do a little digging, find out the truth, and arrest me for falsifying my death and tie me to you—"

"You, of all people, should know that a simple DNA test isn't enough to stand in my way. You've seen my books. Shoot, you've doctored my books and laundered my money. Which means you should know what I'm capable of 'arranging,' shall we say."

Michael heard Valez's veiled threat. As far as his boss was concerned, Michael's hands were just as dirty as his own.

"Of course, it does present one or two problems," Valez continued. "A dead man means frozen accounts."

"You just essentially killed me off and you're worried about your accounts?"

"Your job is to launder money for me, in case you forgot. I've just ensured you're able to do it without getting caught."

Michael forced himself to smile. "Access to your accounts won't be a problem."

"Good. Because as you know, unloading narcotics in the US has never been my problem. It's moving the cash." He lit another cigarette. "Which is why I have a proposition for you. Not only are you good at what you do, you saved my life. With Michael Linley dead, I realize you've lost a lot, so I'm willing to set you up with a new identity."

Michael flipped the newspaper over, then leaned back in his chair. Minutes ago he'd been planning a trip home. A long weekend with his family, away from all this. If he was supposed to be dead, going home would be too big of a risk. Which left him with a choice between continuing to seek justice or simply walking away.

Valez shifted in his chair. "Your new name is Liam Quinn. A rather nice name, I think."

Michael frowned. Life with Valez had always been like walking a tightrope on a windy day. One false move and the obituary he'd just read would end up being the real thing.

"So if I agree to take on this new identity, what happens next?"

"We'll relocate you. I was thinking Jacksonville or maybe Baltimore to ensure there are no ties to me here. I'll help you get started again, with all the papers you'll need. We'll even set you up with a seat on the New York Stock Exchange."

Michael would have laughed if the situation wasn't so serious. The man actually thought he was being generous.

Valez pushed his chair back and stood up. "You're tired. I understand you probably need to think through this. We can wait to get everything set up until you're feeling back to normal."

Michael nodded. He'd known the risks all along, but this time, he'd known if he decided to stay and play, the stakes would jump to a whole new level.

An image of Bruce rose before him. Bruce pounded his fist into Michael's chest until the flames completely engulfed his body. Michael felt himself melt into the pavement, unable to escape the haunting screams of the partner he'd been unable to save.

Pain and guilt rocked through Michael's body. He jerked up and threw the covers off him, awakened once again by the recurring nightmare and his own screams. Sweat dripped down his back and chest. His pulse hammered wildly as the familiar terror of that moment ate through him.

Eyes open, he fought to orient himself. A nightlight on the far wall cast shadows across the floor. The pain . . . the dreams . . .

Olivia.

The truth slammed through him along with the knowledge that everything that had happened had been his fault. Bruce was dead. Kendall was dead. Olivia and Ivan had almost been killed tonight. How many more were going to die because of him?

There might have been nothing he could have done to save

Bruce, but guilt had yet to release its rigid hold. Because instead of saving his partner, he'd saved the very man he'd sworn to take down. And almost lost his own life doing it. All to stop a war that wasn't even his own. A war they'd never win.

The explosion wasn't the only thing that had been haunting his dreams tonight. She'd been in them as well. Olivia Hamilton. Daughter of the man he'd been assigned to bring in and who now wanted him dead. He'd seen her reaching for him in his dreams while they were being chased through the ghostly swamp marshes, always just out of reach. Until he'd lost her, like Bruce, in the watery depths.

How much longer, God . . . I can't take much more. The dreams . . . the guilt . . .

He'd prayed—begged—for the nightmares to stop. There had been a time when he'd thought himself invincible. Thought that there would be some sort of earthly reward for everything he was doing for his country. Every time an arrest was made or a criminal was put behind bars, he'd been reminded that his decision to join the force and make the world a better place was the right one.

But in the end, what good had any of it done? There was always one more person to arrest. Always someone else higher up on the ladder. The pursuit of truth had become a never-ending game of deceit and evil that he had no idea how to fight against anymore.

A pursuit that had eventually led him here.

The door of the room creaked open. Michael lifted his head, wincing at the pain radiating through his rib cage. Olivia stood on the threshold. Light from the living room illuminated her silhouette, and her hair fell in waves around her shoulders.

She started across the room. "You shouted out something. I thought . . . I was worried."

"I'm sorry. I'm fine."

He laid his head back down. He hadn't wanted to get her involved, but she was already caught in his hurricane's destructive path. And he wasn't sure he could save her.

Wooden boards creaked beneath her as she crossed the floor carrying a glass of water and a bottle of medicine. "You must have had a nightmare. You're dripping with sweat."

"It's nothing."

He wasn't ready to admit his fears, or the terror that had engulfed him night after night for months. She handed him the glass, then opened the bottle.

"You need to take some more painkillers."

He struggled to sit up. "What time is it?"

"Almost morning." She rested her hand against his forehead. "Your fever seems to have broken. How are you feeling?"

"I . . . I'm not sure yet."

He took the water and the medicine without arguing, swallowing the pills in one gulp.

She screwed the lid back on the bottle, then eased into the rocking chair beside the bed. "I used to have nightmares. My mother always knew how to comfort me."

"What did she do?"

"She sang to me."

"I bet she was beautiful . . . like you."

Olivia's smile faded, making him wish he could take back the words. He hadn't meant to be so personal.

"I'm sorry. I didn't mean to sound—"

"You're right, actually. About my mother anyway. She was beautiful. I always wanted to look like her. And my father . . . he was rarely around, but that didn't change the fact he was our father."

Michael formed his words carefully, uncertain if she were trying to avoid the past the same way he was. "Did your mother know the truth about your father?"

Olivia nodded. "She made Felipe and my father swear they'd never tell us the truth."

"Maybe she was trying to protect you."

"Maybe." Her voice softened until he could barely hear her. "The only way I can live with this is to see my father as two different men. The one who loved my mother. Who liked having a family and two children. And then there's the other side of him. The one you saw back on the island."

He caught the pain in her expression as she stared past him, clearly ready to shift the conversation away from herself.

"Tell me about your nightmare," she said.

He hesitated before answering. He'd never told anyone about the private battle he'd yet to discover how to win. But there was something about her honesty along with her frankness that made him want to tell her the truth.

"I've learned that dreams are often a twisted version of reality." He took another sip of his water before setting the glass on the table beside him. "For me they're almost always the same scenario. Part truth. Part illusion. I'm there again on an assignment that was supposed to be a simple exchange of goods, but instead went horribly wrong."

"What happened?"

For a moment he was pulled back into the nightmare of his own memories. The explosion, the ravaging fire, the stench of burning flesh. It was a place he didn't know how to erase. A place he didn't ever visit when he was conscious. But he realized that her questions were probably more about her father than they were about him. She was seeking the truth just as much as he was.

"Eight months ago I was almost killed in the line of duty," he began. "I was an undercover cop, in too deep, working for your father. I had gone to a warehouse with my partner with information I thought was solid, but instead it turned out to be a trap."

"What kind of trap?"

Michael worked to keep the emotion out of his answers, just like his years of undercover work had taught him. "We thought it was a meeting to close a deal, but someone planted a bomb in the building, and my partner was killed."

"A bomb? Why?"

"It turned out to be an attempted assassination connected to a turf war. Someone wanted your father dead. I ended up saving his life."

"Which is why he trusted you?"

Michael shrugged. "I'm not sure Valez truly trusts anyone, but yes. I made sure he needed me."

"While you were doing everything you could to take him down."

Funny how when selling the job, Kendall had made everything he was planning to do sound downright honorable. Nothing he'd done felt honorable anymore.

"And outside your dreams, you blame yourself for your partner's death?" she asked.

He caught her gaze, surprised at both the lack of judgment it held and her perception. "I've never been able to fully forgive myself. I keep looking at what went wrong, and how I could have stopped it."

"Did you know about the bomb?"

"Not until seconds before it went off. By then . . . by then it was too late."

"Then how was it your fault?"

"It was my fault because I should have known about the bomb." Whether or not it was true, logic didn't always mesh with the complexity of emotion. "I was the inside man, there to stop something like that from happening."

But he hadn't been able to stop it. Bruce had left behind a three-year-old girl. Kelsey would never know her father. His wife was now a widow, struggling to support her family on a teacher's salary, and nothing Michael could do would change that.

"I'm sorry."

His fingers gripped the edges of the thick blanket. Olivia's presence had reminded him of his own powerlessness. But he wasn't going to let it happen again. "I'm sorry that you were dragged into this. Sorry that you had to find out the truth about your father this way."

Her frown deepened, drawing thin lines across her forehead. "It's time you stopped apologizing. As I recall, I never asked your permission to rescue you."

He couldn't help but smile at her honesty. "That might be true, but what you did was both daring and bold," he said. In only a few hours, he'd learned she was vulnerable, but brave. He liked that. Liked her. Which made him wish all the more that she and Ivan had escaped without worrying about him. Now she was caught up in this tangled mess, with a good chance that neither of them would come out alive in the end.

Olivia fiddled with the top of the medicine bottle in her lap. "I would hardly use those words to describe myself, because— I'll be honest—I'm scared right now. I've seen what my father is capable of doing, and it terrifies me. If he finds out where we are . . ."

She left the statement hanging. She wanted him to tell her everything was going to be okay but knew he couldn't. All she knew to do at the moment was to keep praying that God would protect them from the man she'd always known as her father.

"I'm going to do everything I can to make sure he doesn't find us," Michael said.

She threw him a weak smile. "Even you can't do that."

"He hasn't traced us here so far, which means we should be

safe for now. And as soon as I'm feeling a bit more coherent, we'll figure out what to do next."

Olivia shivered despite the warmth of the room. So much had happened in the past few hours to make her question what was real and what wasn't. Betrayal . . . loss . . . fear . . . She felt every emotion twisting through her.

"I know you're scared, Olivia, but I meant what I said."

He brushed his fingers across her hand, but she pulled away. There was something . . . intimate about the situation that had her emotions wanting to delve deeper into the possibilities and run away at the same time.

She swallowed hard. "I just hate . . . I hate being afraid, not knowing what to believe."

"Well, if it helps, you're not the only one who's afraid. And you're not the only one who's mixed up about what's true and what isn't."

Olivia couldn't help but smile. "There are so many things I thought I knew, that I realize now were nothing but lies. Felipe knew the truth about who my father is."

"Why the secrets? I don't understand."

"He told me it was my mother's wish. To keep us safe. But now . . . it's hard to know who to trust. There have been so many lies."

"How does all this change your relationship with Felipe? That he knew the truth and didn't tell you?"

"I don't know yet. In some ways it changes nothing . . . but in other ways, I'm realizing that nothing will ever be the same again."

"I know you have questions about your father. And I know you don't know me at all, and you're struggling to trust me. But we need each other." He reached out and grasped her hand. This time she didn't pull away.

She studied the raised veins running across the back of his

hand, his long slender fingers. He was right. She'd saved him. He'd saved her. And she was smart enough to realize she couldn't do this on her own.

"There's something about this I don't understand." She turned back to him. "Why does your family think you're dead?"

She watched his face tighten. "Your father thought it would be best for his business if he had a completely untraceable employee, so he orchestrated my death. I thought I'd been given a second chance to finish what I'd started. I was now a valuable asset to Valez. Walking away would have meant undoing months of work that had put me in the perfect position to bring him down."

"So you've been keeping the truth from your family just like Felipe and my mother and father kept the truth from Ivan and me. Tell me, Michael, how could you do that? I need to understand, I need to know why."

Michael let go of her hand and laid his head back on the pillow. "You're asking the wrong person, Olivia. Not a day goes by that I don't ask myself that same question."

CHAPTER 11

Olivia helped Felipe finish dinner, allowing the routine task to become the distraction she needed. She no longer had any doubt regarding her father's guilt. Not after listening to both Michael's story and Felipe's confessions of the secret he'd kept all these years. But knowing the truth had only managed to bring up more questions and a growing fear inside of her she didn't know how to squelch.

Felipe jutted his chin toward the closed bedroom door. "You worried about him?"

She followed Felipe's gaze, confused by her conflicting feelings toward the man they'd managed to save. Michael had been the unexpected addition to the equation she had no idea how to solve.

"Yeah. I am worried," she said. "Seems crazy, though. I barely know him."

"You and Ivan have always had a heart for strays. Cats, dogs, birds. Remember the injured skunk you tried to capture that one summer?"

Olivia laughed at the memory, but the similarities to their current situation were too much alike. That skunk had necessitated a trip to the emergency room for her and Ivan after spraying them both in the face. Even when you do everything you can to fix a situation, sometimes you get burned.

"I don't think you need to worry about Michael." Felipe grabbed a potholder from one of the drawers and set it on the table. "I'm pleased with the way he's healing. No fever or signs of infection. He's a tough guy. I might not be a doctor, but I think he's going to pull through this."

If my father doesn't get to him first.

Olivia set her knife down on the cutting board where she'd been chopping a cucumber for the salad and bit back the thought. "I'm sorry. I'm just having a hard time accepting everything."

Felipe turned her toward him and rested his hands on her shoulders. "I'm the one who should be sorry. I should have told you the truth years ago, instead of your finding out this way. I hope you know that your mother meant well. She only wanted what was best for you. She loved you, and somehow thought she could protect you. And since she died, I just . . . I just haven't known how to handle things."

"None of this is your fault."

Felipe dropped his hands to his sides. "Have you told Ivan what I told you?"

"Yes." She picked up the knife and started chopping again.

"He's stronger than you think, Olivia."

"I know, but I've spent my life protecting him. I don't know how to protect him from this."

She glanced toward the front porch where Ivan was playing catch with Gizmo. The problem was that she would always worry about Ivan, and no assurances from Felipe could change that.

"The truth isn't always easy to accept, so just give him time. He'll be okay. Both of you will."

"I know."

"And Olivia, the two of you have always been like family to me. I need you to know that."

She reached up and wrapped her arms around his neck, then took a step back. "I do, Felipe. I do."

The bedroom door creaked open and Michael walked into the room with color in his cheeks for the first time since they'd arrived. Relief flooded through her, causing her to pause. Because it shouldn't matter this much that he was okay.

"Whoa." Olivia started across the room toward him. "What are you doing out of bed?"

He shot her a wide smile. "Something smells delicious. Thought I was missing out."

She stopped in the middle of the room and let out a soft laugh. "You were about to miss out. Felipe made some *sopa de frijol*—black bean soup. Said it would help have you up and around before you knew it. And as a bonus, you won't find anything like it this side of the border."

"You've talked me into it, if you don't mind me joining you at the table."

"Of course not." Felipe grabbed an extra bowl from the cabinet. "Besides, if you're hungry, that's a good sign."

"Trust me, I'm hungry enough to eat just about anything at this point."

Felipe set the bowl on the table with the others. "I'll go let Ivan know it's time to eat."

Olivia set the pot of soup on the hot pad on the table, suddenly feeling self-conscious. "You must be feeling better."

"How long have I been sleeping?"

She glanced at her watch. "A good thirty-six hours off and on."

"Thirty-six? Which makes it . . ."

"Thursday," she finished for him.

Michael let out a low whistle.

"How do you feel? That's the important question right now."

"Better than I have in days. Still sore in a few places, but I finally feel as if I'm going to live."

She studied the bandage covering up his gunshot wound. The bruise on his face had finally started turning from purple to yellow. He might be feeling better, but he still should see a proper doctor.

"Any signs of infection?" she asked.

"No and no fever either."

She wondered if he remembered their conversation from yesterday morning. Or all the times she'd gone into his room to check on him and make sure he took his medicine. Or how many hours she'd sat beside his bed, worried his fever might return.

"What about you?" He took a step toward her. "How are you?"

"Relieved that you're feeling better."

"Thank you for trusting me. For sitting with me. Every time I woke up, you were there, like my guardian angel. I knew I was going to be okay."

She smiled back at him, wishing she could ignore whatever was stirring inside her.

Felipe and Ivan entered the cabin, pulling her thoughts away from places they didn't need to go. She grabbed the pitcher of water and set it on the table, wishing that this lull in the storm could last forever. But now that Michael was up on his feet again, they were going to have to make decisions . . . and those decisions had nothing to do with her heart.

Michael sat down beside Olivia and listened while she said grace, her words flowing over him like a healing balm. The past couple of days might still be a blur, but he'd meant what he'd told her. Waking up and seeing her sitting beside him, curled up with a book, had given him what he needed to keep fighting.

Fifteen minutes later, he finished his second bowl of soup.

Olivia held up the ladle. "Do you want some more?"

Michael grinned at her. "No. But thank you. It was delicious."

"Felipe has all kinds of hidden talents," Olivia said. "And as you can see, cooking is one of them."

Felipe leaned back in his chair and patted his stomach. "Your mother was the cook. She could make the best tortillas of anyone I know. Here, all I can get is packaged ones from the corner grocer."

Michael leaned back in his chair. "A couple more days with food like this and I should be back to normal."

"You're welcome to stay as long as you need to," Felipe said.

"I appreciate that, sir."

Except he knew he couldn't stay, even though for the first time in months, he actually found himself able to relax. While the fire crackled in the background, leaving a subtle hint of cedar throughout the room, he could almost imagine himself back with his own family with his own mama's cooking on the stove. They used to spend a week every winter up in the Blue Ridge Mountains.

Tonight, those memories seemed like a lifetime ago.

He pushed his chair back and noticed the small television across the room for the first time. They needed to make a plan. Needed to know exactly what they were facing before they walked out of here.

"Have you watched the news the past couple of days?" he asked.

Olivia nodded. "Watched it last night and again this morning, but so far nothing about the gas station robbery."

Felipe glanced at the clock, then grabbed the remote to flip it on. "Tonight's broadcast should be starting any minute now."

Michael held on to the shred of hope that maybe he hadn't been identified yet from the store footage, but eventually it was going to lead back to him. It was just a matter of time.

109

After a commercial, one of the local broadcasters announced the lead story for the evening.

"Tonight, police are still looking for this man, Michael Andrew Hunt, for questioning. Rebecca Pearce has the rest of the story."

Michael's stomach twisted as his face filled the screen. Any hope that the story had fallen through the cracks had just been destroyed.

The camera zoomed in on Rebecca Pearce's serious demeanor.

"Thanks, Robin. Police believe that Hunt was involved in a convenience store robbery two nights ago, and we now have exclusive information that he is also a person of interest in the brutal murder of FBI agent Sam Kendall, whose body was discovered along the Georgia coastline early this morning. If you have any information as to the whereabouts of this man, please call the number on your screen. This is Rebecca Pearce, reporting for—"

Olivia punched the mute button and turned to Michael. "Rebecca always did have a tendency for finding the dramatic stories, but now you're being blamed for Kendall's death? How is that possible?"

"I don't know." Unease spread through him. "You know the reporter?"

Olivia nodded. "She's difficult to get along with, but she's good at what she does. She might have an inside source. I could call her—"

"We can't go to the media at this point," Michael said.

"He's right," Felipe added.

"Then what do we do?" Olivia asked. "We can't stay here, can't turn ourselves in . . ."

Michael pushed his chair back. "I've gone over and over everything that's happened the past few days, and I've made a decision. You're going to stay here until this blows over. I'm going to turn myself in."

"No way—"

"Olivia, you just saw for yourself what the police think happened. The longer we delay the inevitable, the guiltier I look."

She threw her napkin into her empty bowl, clearly upset. "You told me if you turn yourself in, there are people who will do anything to keep you quiet. How has that changed? And if you don't even know who they are—?"

"Maybe that hasn't changed, but what are my options?" The relaxed atmosphere of the dinner conversation had vanished. "I can't keep running."

"Neither can we," Olivia said, "but—"

"I'll go to the police and tell them what I saw," Ivan interrupted.

Michael turned to Ivan. He sat at the end of the table, speaking and signing at the same time.

"You're not going to the police," Olivia said.

"Why not?" Ivan asked.

Olivia stood up and began pacing in front of the fireplace. A pocket of sap popped as she turned back to her brother. "They might be after Michael because he has evidence that could take down our father, but you were a witness to a murder. Do you think they'll let you just walk away? Especially if our father has people inside the police department?"

"Your sister's right. It's not safe," Michael said.

He carried his bowl to the sink and rinsed it. There was one other option he hadn't mentioned, because so far, he'd avoided giving it serious thought. He could contact his old partner and best friend, Mason, or his sister, Avery. Both were cops, and he trusted them completely. The problem was that if anyone found out they were harboring a fugitive, they'd lose their jobs. And that wasn't a risk he was ready to take.

"Ivan, what's wrong?"

The worry in Olivia's voice caught his attention. Michael set down his bowl and turned toward the window where Ivan stood with Gizmo at his side, ears up and alert.

"There's—someone—something out there."

She crossed the room and started to pull back the curtain.

"Olivia, get back from the window," Michael said.

"He's right. Just in case." Felipe got up from the table. "But I'm sure it's nothing to worry about. Probably just one of the families coming up here for the holidays, or some animal. We get a few black bears looking for food every now and then."

Michael glanced at the dog. There was no doubt that Gizmo was bothered about something, but Felipe was probably right. It was probably nothing more than an animal.

Michael caught the fear in Olivia's gaze. "We've been here two days with no sign of anyone. If they knew where we were, they'd have shown up a long time ago—"

"Someone *is* out there," Ivan said.

The front window shattered.

Michael pulled Olivia and Ivan behind the couch for cover, wincing at the sudden movements.

Michael moved in front of Ivan so Ivan could read his lips. "What did you see?"

"Four men getting out of a car. They've got rifles."

"Felipe, do you have any weapons?"

"A rifle over the door and a handgun here . . ." Felipe pulled a weapon from the drawer behind him where he crouched.

Another bullet hit the back wall. They needed to get out of here, before they were completely trapped.

"Stay down," Michael ordered.

Careful to avoid the windows, he headed toward the front door, then grabbed the rifle from the top of the doorframe.

"Can you see them?" Olivia asked.

He looked out through a crack in the curtain. "Two of them are still out front. The other two must have headed around to the back."

Another shot hit a lamp, exploding glass behind them.

Michael weighed their options. The only way they might make it out of here alive was to fight their way out the back.

"We'll try to get out the back door," he said. "Felipe, that means we'll have to disarm the two guys back there."

Felipe nodded.

Michael grabbed the keys from the counter and tossed them to Olivia. "You and Ivan stay behind us. As soon as we're out, head for the car."

They started toward the back door, staying low. Another round of shots smashed through the front windows.

"Michael, wait . . ." Olivia shouted from behind him. "Felipe's been shot."

Michael turned around as Felipe fell to the floor. Blood from a small wound streamed down the side of his head. Olivia searched frantically to find a pulse.

A moment later, she grasped Michael's arm.

"I can't find a pulse." Her voice rose. "He's dead, Michael . . . they killed him."

Michael hesitated. The men had thrown fiery rags through the broken window and smoke was already filling the room as the flames licked at the curtains running up the wall. The goons were pounding against the front door. In another few seconds they'd break it down.

If they didn't get out now . . .

"The cabin's on fire, Olivia." Michael struggled to breathe through the smoke as he pulled Felipe's body toward the back door.

The front door splintered. Another few seconds . . .

"We've got to get out of here," Michael said, letting go of Felipe's lifeless body.

She grabbed onto his arm. "We can't leave him—"

"We don't have a choice. We can't carry his body with us, and if we don't leave now, they'll kill all of us."

CHAPTER
12

Olivia watched Michael take out two of the intruders in quick succession as she stumbled out of the cabin and down the back stairs beside Ivan and Gizmo. Her mind fought to process the scene. Two men down meant there were still two more.

She ran toward the car. Smoke from the fire filled her lungs and burned her eyes. All they had to do was get to the car, start the engine, and drive away. It wouldn't matter then where they went or who was after them. They just needed to get as far away as possible.

I'm sorry, Felipe. So, so sorry.

How had her actions to save one man managed to kill someone she loved?

Another shot ripped her from her thoughts, propelling her forward. They needed to get to the car, but the shadowy light from the fire revealed a terrifying reality. Someone had shot out all the tires.

They couldn't go back to the cabin. Couldn't take the car. The only option left was to run. Olivia's mind scrambled to orient herself as Michael motioned her and Ivan toward the treeline behind the cabin. She knew the general layout of the area. Maybe the darkness was a blessing, but she had never tried to navigate the landscape in the dark. And never while being chased by men with guns.

The surrounding woods were thick; the trails that twisted through the brush were for visitors to explore in daylight. At night, it was much slower going. A twig snapped beneath her foot. She stumbled again. This time, Michael caught her and wrapped his arm around her waist.

"We've got to keep moving," he said.

Olivia pressed her lips together, fighting back the bubble of terror swelling up inside. She had to keep her mind focused on the trail instead of letting the fear overcome her. But the two remaining men were still behind them. She could hear their footsteps crunching through the dry winter leaves. She shivered, wishing for her jacket. It was cold enough she could see her breath fogging in the moonlight.

Olivia pressed on between Michael and Ivan, trying not to think about Felipe lying on the middle of the floor. They shouldn't have left him. But Michael had been right. If they'd stayed, they'd all be dead.

By the time Michael stopped at an outcropping of rocks, Olivia was completely out of breath.

"Do you hear them anymore?" he asked.

Olivia shook her head, urging Gizmo to be quiet as he whined beside her. "Maybe they thought we headed the other direction."

Fear slithered through her, taking a stronger grasp. Why hadn't they been more prepared? Why had they assumed they couldn't be found? Assumed they were safe? They couldn't have been more wrong.

She turned to Michael and whispered. "How did they know where we were?"

"I don't know. For now, though, we need to evaluate what we have. Did you grab anything before leaving?"

"No."

"What about the layout of this area? What's ahead?"

"It continues for a few miles of hiking trails with dense foliage like it is here. There are dozens of houses starting a mile or so to our east away from town, but the road eventually dead ends."

"More than likely, they'll keep looking for us. Which means we need to put as much distance as possible between us and them. How far to the main road?"

Olivia tried to orient herself, then turned to Ivan and signed the question.

"Three . . . maybe four miles to the west," he said.

"Can you get us there?" Michael asked.

The hazy moonlight was enough to communicate with Ivan. He nodded, determination stamping out the fear in his eyes.

Ivan veered left, and Michael stumbled after him. Olivia could tell he was in pain and in no shape to be facing the cold along with the tough terrain.

God . . . I don't know how it came to this. I thought I wanted to know the truth, but sometimes the truth doesn't bring freedom. Sometimes it brings death and fear, and more questions.

She shifted her focus back to Michael. "Are you going to be able to make it?"

"Not sure we have a choice, so yes."

She glanced back in the direction of the cabin. She estimated they'd only gone a couple of miles. Which left a lot of terrain for their pursuers to search, but was it enough?

Ivan skidded down an embankment in front of her. She followed him, wincing when the sharp edges of rocks bit into the back of her legs and scratched her ankles. She stopped abruptly at the base of the embankment, as Michael made his way down behind them in an avalanche of small rocks.

He paused for a moment, fighting to catch his breath.

"Michael?"

"I'm fine. We need to keep moving."

She stared ahead, shivering, at a row of dim lights in the distance. A light snow had begun to fall. He wasn't fine. None of them were fine. They had to find shelter for the night.

"We need to stop." Olivia grasped Michael's arm. "We've all pushed it hard enough already. Most of these cabins are empty, and we're far enough away by now that the chances of them finding us are slim."

"I'm fine," Michael repeated.

"You're not fine. We're running through the woods in the middle of the night, in freezing weather." Olivia heard the shrillness in her voice, but she didn't care. "You've been in bed the past two days, and I'm tired, frozen, and scared half out of my mind. We're far enough away at this point, and I don't think they know what direction we went."

Ivan bent down to scratch Gizmo's neck and nodded. "She's right, Michael."

"Okay, I'll admit you're both right. I'm exhausted." Michael leaned against a tree trunk, his face pale. "Which is why I want you to make your way to the main road where you can get a signal and call for help. I'll wait here. You can come back for me later."

Olivia frowned. He had to be kidding. "We're not leaving you here alone. And besides, once we're there, who do we call?"

"I'll give you a number to call. Someone you can trust—"

"We need to stick together," she said.

Michael didn't look convinced. "I understand your concerns, but—"

"But nothing. I'm right and you know it," she said.

What they needed now was shelter and a place to get a few hours of sleep. Then maybe they'd all be clearer-headed in the morning.

"There are a bunch of houses over there." She started walking again, her mind made up. In his condition, he'd freeze to death by the time she and Ivan made it to the road. "You can see some of the lights from here. Besides, they'll probably assume that we headed for the main road, so it's better to go away from it."

She forged ahead, allowing her fear to turn into full-blown anger. Anger toward her father and mother and Felipe and the secrets they'd kept. Anger toward Tomas, the men who'd attacked the cabin tonight and shot Felipe . . . and at the moment, even Michael.

He trudged down the trail beside her, his hand pressed against his side and limping. Maybe none of this had been his fault, but the man clearly had a knack for getting into trouble. And on top of that, he was stubborn, pushy, and worst of all, made her heart race when he looked at her with those bright blue eyes of his.

She stepped over a branch in the middle of the path and tried to shove that last thought back into the corner of her heart where it had come from. Michael Hunt might be take-charge, good looking in that rough-around-the-edges-very-manly sort of way, but what did that matter to her?

Ten minutes later, they approached the front door of a cabin. It was set back off the road, dark, and most importantly, appeared empty. She ran her hand over the top of the doorframe. Nothing. She picked up the welcome mat and searched underneath. Nothing.

Olivia took a step back, fighting tears. What had she been thinking? She couldn't exactly ask Michael to use his police skills and break down the door.

Ivan nudged her shoulder, held up a key, then proceeded to open the door.

"Where'd you find that?" she asked.

He smiled. "Fake rock."

She stepped inside the house beside Michael, thankful for the moonlight filtering through the windows.

"We should keep the lights off in case we were followed,"

he said. "We'll stay just long enough to get some rest, then before daylight we'll get to the road and try to get a ride out of here."

Olivia found a couple of flashlights on the kitchen counter. She handed one to Michael and Ivan and then started rummaging through the cabinets for some first-aid supplies and pain reliever, while Ivan went into the restroom. Her conscience stirred, but breaking and entering seemed like the least of their worries at this point. If nothing else, they could leave a note promising to reimburse the owner for whatever they took.

She finally found what she was looking for in the pantry. She entered the living room just as Michael pulled a box of bullets from the top shelf of the front closet and laid them next to a gun.

"In case we need reinforcements," he said, handing her a coat.

Olivia shivered as she pulled on the hooded jacket. "I own a gun, but I still hate them. My father's the one who insisted I have one for protection. I never imagined having to actually use it."

"We don't have a choice, Olivia. If they come after us, we have to be able to defend ourselves."

"I know."

"Hey." He moved in front of her, until she had to look up at him in the light of the flashlight at his now familiar features. Those intense blue eyes, crooked smile, and the start of a beard covering up some of the fading bruises. "It's going to be okay. I've come out of worse situations than this."

Her anger started to melt. She wanted to believe everything was going to be okay, but all the possible-ending scenarios wouldn't stop gnawing at her. "When's the last time you had both the cartel and the authorities after you?"

He laughed. "I agree that it isn't an everyday occurrence, but we'll find a way out."

She nodded, fighting back the tears. She'd spent her days tracking down stories, but being tracked down . . . being hunted . . . that was different.

"I'm scared, Michael."

"I know." He ran his hands down her arms that were shaking more from fear than from the cold. "I'd say you're a lot braver than you think."

"Brave?" She let out a low chuckle. "I see myself as a lot of things, but brave . . . I don't think so."

"The way I look at it, you—along with your brother—managed to escape with an undercover officer who would be dead by now without your intervention. And you've survived a hostage situation, a burning cabin, and being shot at, all while keeping your wits."

Felipe hadn't survived.

She moved away from him and started rummaging through the first-aid kit, his presence almost as unsettling as the situation they'd walked into. "Do you think they'll find us?"

"I plan to do everything I can to ensure they don't."

She found a bottle of Tylenol and handed it to him. "We need to change your bandages. When do you want to do that?"

Michael sat on the couch and eased off his shirt. "Now is as good a time as any."

Olivia worked by the light of the flashlight, ensuring her gaze stayed away from his well-formed chest, focusing instead on removing the old bandage from his wound.

He jerked away as part of the tape stuck. "Ouch."

She shot him a frown. "You've gotta be a whole lot tougher than that, cowboy. I've just begun."

"That's what I'm afraid of."

She continued working in silence, pleased to see no signs of infection, then moved to his side, where she spread a thin layer of antibiotic over the washed cuts.

"I'm sorry about Felipe." Michael broke the silence that had settled between them. "I know he meant a lot to you."

Olivia tried to swallow the lump forming in her throat. "I'm sorry too. It seems like everyone I trusted is either dying or turning out to be someone I never really knew."

Her mother. Felipe. Her father. She felt as if her heart were being ripped out. But there would be time to grieve later. For now, she needed to focus on getting her and Ivan—and Michael—to safety.

"Why do you do what you do?"

"Undercover work?"

She nodded as she squeezed out a bit more cream. "I would be terrified. Always afraid I'd get caught . . . or worse for that matter. Always on the run. Always looking over my shoulder, afraid the wrong person might find me out."

"I try to remember why I'm doing what I'm doing. And I try not to lose my identity."

Michael's words echoed through the empty places in her soul. Maybe she hadn't lost her identity, but learning the truth about her father had changed to some degree who she was.

"I'm done for now." She began repacking the first-aid kit while the questions continued to form in her mind. "Have you ever lost your sense of identity?"

Michael put his shirt back on. "The last few months have been hard. My family believes I'm dead. There were lots of times when I felt like I was losing touch with who I was. With why I was doing what I was doing."

"Is it worth it?" The question struck a chord in her own mind. Saving Michael might have been worth it, but the fallout was still to be determined.

"I don't know yet."

"You live in a completely different world than I do." She dropped the cream and other supplies back into the first-aid kit, then snapped the lid shut. "Until tonight, I've never had to worry about people coming after me with guns. I sit in front of a computer screen all day long. The only weapons I use are words."

"Maybe we're not so different after all. We both have a desire for truth and justice to prevail." He finished buttoning his shirt, then slid the first-aid kit back into the cupboard where they found it. "Did you used to come here often as a child?"

She smiled at the memories. "My mother loved these mountains. Loved watching the sunrise. We usually came a couple times a year. We'd spend the days hiking or riding the trails."

"I'm surprised we didn't run into each other." Michael leaned back against the couch cushions. "My mother loved bringing us up here at least once a year, normally about this time. We had plenty of popcorn, movies, and Monopoly, just about every night."

Ivan walked back into the living room, stopping to check on Gizmo, who had curled up on a thick rug. "I hope the owners don't mind a dog in the house, but it's too cold to leave him outside."

"I think you're right." Olivia caught the lack of emotion on his face as he signed. "Are you all right, Ivan? I'm worried about you after everything that happened today—"

"You always worry," he said. "Just not about the right things."

"Ivan—"

He turned away, leaving her frustrated and still worried.

"Why don't the two of you get some sleep," Michael said, "while I stand guard the next couple hours."

"I don't mind taking the first watch," Olivia said. She'd have to find time to talk with Ivan later. "You need your rest, and I won't be able to sleep for a long time."

He paused. "I'll be fine. I'm used to getting by with little sleep—"

"Not tonight. You're in no condition to keep pushing it."

He hesitated again. "Okay. Can you handle a rifle?"

"No." She glanced at the weapon and felt her stomach churn. "But trust me, if anything happens, you'll hear about it."

"I guess that'll do." Michael chuckled. "Wake me up in a couple hours for my shift. We'll need to be out of here before the sun comes up."

CHAPTER
13

Michael poured himself a mug of coffee from the pot he'd just brewed, added sugar and creamer, then took a long sip. He rummaged through the small first-aid kit Olivia had used yesterday and found two more pain relievers, hoping to cut the pain still radiating in his side. Olivia was right. He needed to see a doctor to see what kind of damage he'd sustained, but that wasn't the only thing he'd decided.

He gazed out the kitchen window onto the darkened lawn, lit only by the light of the moon, studying the scene for movement. He'd already swept the perimeter of the house a half-dozen times since Olivia had awakened him. So far, the only activity he'd seen was the unannounced visit of a skunk, but that didn't mean those men weren't out there somewhere, searching the shadows for them.

He checked the digital clock on the microwave. It was still at least two hours before the sun would begin making its first appearance of the day, but they were going to have to get moving soon. In the meantime, he figured the pain medicine and a cup of strong coffee would keep him going.

Moonlight filtered through the windows of the living room where Ivan was just waking up and Olivia was still sleeping.

The temperatures had continued to drop, bringing with the cold front a couple of inches of snow across the hard ground.

Ivan sat up, shoving his blanket onto the floor. Michael smiled at him questioningly and held up his mug. Ivan said a quiet "No, thanks," and headed to the bathroom.

Michael moved over to the couch where Olivia slept. She was snoring softly beneath a couple of blankets they'd found in a closet. He wished he could let her sleep a few more hours, but they didn't have that much time.

He'd had to remind himself at least a dozen times that this situation was no different from any other situation he'd faced. No matter what his heart was trying to tell him. Getting involved personally simply wasn't an option. And getting involved with the daughter of Antonio Valez was even less of an option.

Forget the fact that she intrigued him. That she was beautiful and managed to stir something inside him every time she looked at him. Forget the fact that he'd soaked up the brief conversations they'd shared over the past few days, making him long to know more about her.

Whatever his heart was feeling at the moment didn't matter. His job—his only job—was to get her to safety. Her life was worlds away from his. Even if he never decided to step back into the undercover business again.

Still, he knelt down beside her, resisting the urge to brush aside a loose strand of smoke-tinged hair, and felt his heart take a dive at her nearness.

"Olivia?"

Her eyelids flicked open slowly as she turned until she was looking up at him. Confusion registered for a few seconds, then her eyes widened.

He shot her a smile. "Morning, sleepyhead."

"It's still dark." She pulled the blanket up and squinted at him. "Do we have to get up?"

"It'll be light before long. My father used to tell me this was the best part of the day. The gentle quiet before the storms of the day hit."

Her nose scrunched up. "Thanks for the reminder."

He leaned back on his heels. "Sorry. Did you sleep okay?"

"I guess." She sat up slowly and swung her legs over the edge of the couch, bare feet dangling just above the floor as her frown deepened. "When my mind managed to stop spinning."

He stood up slowly, thankful that the soreness was beginning to subside. "I'm guessing you're not a morning person?"

"Not even on a good day."

Her sleepy smile hit the target of his heart dead center. So much for keeping a professional distance. So much for trying to convince himself that Olivia Hamilton should be classified as forbidden territory. His mind hadn't stopped spinning either, but neither could he ignore the crazy fact that the situation they faced wasn't the only thing that had his adrenaline flowing.

"Where's Ivan?" she asked.

"He beat you to the shower."

She padded across the kitchen floor barefoot, still wearing Felipe's oversized Atlanta Braves sweatshirt she'd had on the night before. She reached, sleepy-eyed, for the pot of coffee he'd made.

"Did you have any trouble staying awake?" she finally asked.

"I did a lot of praying and thinking," he said, following her into the kitchen.

"Did it help?" she asked as she filled an empty mug with the drink.

"We're stuck in the middle of nowhere with at least two armed men after us, but I was reminded that God is still in control."

"That kind of faith can be hard to hold on to when the enemy's on the prowl."

"Yes, it can."

He watched her take a sip as she tried to wake up, and had the sudden urge to kiss her. Which was crazy. He grabbed a washcloth hanging on a wall peg and started cleaning up an imaginary spill on the counter. Olivia wasn't the first woman he'd felt something for, but every other time, his job had always managed to take priority. And, of course, there was the small detail that most—if not all—of the women he ran into weren't interested in building a life with someone who didn't know how long he would be undercover, or even if he'd ever come home.

So what was it about Olivia Hamilton that made him want to push through all the barriers and find out if he could actually make a relationship work? He dropped the rag into the sink. The answers were standing right in front of him. He'd seen her integrity, sense of duty, and faith, all wrapped up in an outer beauty he found irresistible.

He pushed back the tremulous thoughts, forcing himself to focus on the present. Now that his head was finally clear, there were things he'd thought about during the night that he needed to ask her about. Last night's attack couldn't have been a coincidence. They needed to find out who exactly was after them.

"I've been thinking about a few things. You mentioned you were doing some research about the cartel. Who knew about this?"

She took a sip of her coffee. "I don't know. Ivan. My boss."

"Did Felipe know?" he asked.

"Yes. I called him last week to ask him some questions. He had some interesting insights."

"What about your mother? How did he meet her?"

"They met in Mexico back in the eighties. My mother's mother was from his village. Her father was an American diplomat."

"Did Felipe know Valez?"

"I know they met, though they weren't friends. I remember hearing about some rivalry between the two of them, though I don't know what. After my mother died, I don't think there was ever any contact between them." She set her mug down on the counter and caught his gaze. "Why? What are you thinking?"

"I'm not sure yet. I'm just trying to put all of the pieces together. It's easy to assume that whoever attacked us back there in the cabin was after us, but what if they were after Felipe?"

"I can't imagine why. He's an old man who lives alone in the woods."

"Running from something?"

"He's implied that."

"From the authorities?"

The sleepy smile that had been on her face began to slowly fade, reminding him that Felipe wasn't the only person who held on to his privacy. "He never elaborated, and I never pushed. He's always been very private."

"I'm sorry. I know this is personal. I'm just trying to cover all the bases." He caught the sadness in her expression. Maybe it was time to change the subject. "Are you hungry?"

She let out a big yawn. "Yes, but I'm a bit disappointed. When you woke me up, I was dreaming of sitting around the table with Felipe, eating pancakes with real maple syrup. It was a nice change from the nightmares I kept having."

She tilted her head and that same unruly curl slipped across her forehead. He pulled open one of the pantry doors, not knowing how to stop the direction his heart was headed.

"I think I'd be disappointed too," he said, searching for something edible.

"Don't worry, I've got this one. We've got a long day ahead of us, so I'll rummage around and see if I can't come up with something."

He watched her open one cabinet door after another. She stood on her tiptoes trying to reach a discovered box of pancake mix that was just out of reach. Her dark hair fell in waves against her back, doing that funny thing to his heart again. He moved in behind her and pulled it off the shelf and handed it to her. "You really are thinking pancakes?" he asked.

She turned around to face him, hugging the box against her chest. Her lips played with a grin, making him wonder if she was really thinking about pancakes or something a bit more . . . personal. Which was ridiculous.

"I can have them ready in ten minutes."

She'd yet to move, making her close enough that he could see the flecks of gold in her eyes. Close enough for him to realize it was time to run the other direction.

"I think it's a great idea." He took a step back. "Can I do something?"

"If you could find some syrup, that would be great, or Ivan prefers peanut butter on his." She grabbed a bowl from the cupboard and started mixing the batter. "Whoever lives here must come often, because the pantry is pretty well stocked. I'm betting you'll find both."

He smiled at the sight of her whipping up a batch of pancakes. So she had a nurturing side . . .

"Michael?"

"Syrup. Peanut butter. Sorry."

"What about us? Have you come up with a brilliant plan yet?"

"I wouldn't call it brilliant . . ."

He caught the worry in her expression and knew what she was thinking. The sun would be up in an hour, and they'd yet to discuss any plan that would guarantee their safety out of here. They didn't know where the bad guys were. They didn't even know *who* the bad guys were, except that they presumably worked for her father. And while he'd been in worse situations, now he was taking on the responsibility for her and her brother.

He set a bottle of syrup and a jar of peanut butter on the counter and watched as she ladled the bubbly pancake batter

onto a hot griddle. He paused, unsure of what her reaction
would be to his idea, but he knew they didn't have a choice.
Running on their own would get them killed.

When she turned around, there was a sprinkle of pancake
mix on her nose. "Did you find some syrup?"

He nodded toward the counter. "And peanut butter."

This time he didn't even try to resist the urge as he reached
up to brush the powder away. "There was a . . . some flour on
your nose."

"Thanks."

Gizmo growled, shifting Michael's attention toward the window—and reminding him how easy it was to get distracted. He
picked up the rifle and crossed the room, peering outside into
the growing light reflecting off the snow.

"What is it, Michael?"

A black-and-white furball skittered across the yard. "Just a
skunk. Probably the same one I saw earlier."

She leaned back against the counter, the concern in her eyes
still there, drew in a deep breath, then went back to flipping
the pancakes.

"So what about your not-so-brilliant plan?" she asked.

He stepped back into the kitchen and poured himself another
cup of coffee while four pancakes sizzled on the griddle. "We
need help. I've decided to call on a friend."

She scooped the pancakes onto a plate and ladled another
batch onto the hot griddle one by one, looking unconvinced.
"Who's the friend?"

He dropped two spoonfuls of sugar into his coffee mug, then
took a sip. "Someone I would trust with my life."

"How do we get ahold of this friend?"

"We had an emergency code we developed years ago if either
of us got into trouble. There's a password and a rendezvous
spot." He paused, waiting for her reaction.

"Sounds like a couple of kids playing spy. And the rendezvous site? How do we get there?"

"We'll have to hitch a ride with somebody."

He moved in front of her and swept the stray curl behind her ear. "Let's only worry about one thing at a time."

Ivan walked into the room and tossed Olivia a set of keys. "I did a bit of exploring after my shower and I found a car in the garage. It's old, but it runs."

"Hold on," Olivia said. "We've already raided their cupboards and helped ourselves to whatever we needed, but we're not stealing their car as well."

"Technically it's just borrowing," Michael said. "We'll give it back with a full tank of gas. How about that?"

"You're trying to ease my conscience."

"Yes, but I don't see that we have a choice, Olivia."

She added the last batch of pancakes to the plate, then turned off the burner. "So where are we headed?"

"To a storage place to pick up my emergency bag, and then on to Piedmont Park."

CHAPTER
14

Olivia dug through the glove compartment, trying to find the Tylenol she'd brought, this time for herself. Her head was pounding with a combination of stress, fear, and nervous tension. Every time she quoted a Bible verse saying *do not worry,* she'd start worrying about another possible problem. Like, what would happen if they were pulled over by the police? Or what would happen if they were in an accident?

Michael sat beside her in the driver's seat of their "borrowed" car, heading toward Atlanta. Traffic was lighter than usual for this time of day, but that didn't stop her from scrutinizing every car hanging behind them on the interstate.

Ivan sat in the backseat with Gizmo, still unwilling to talk with her about what he'd said last night. But all she could think about right now was getting her brother to safety—a difficult proposition when she wasn't sure who they could trust.

She managed to swallow the pills dry, then glanced at her watch. They'd made it to the outskirts of Atlanta in good time, but the next step of their journey would be the most telling.

"How much farther?" she asked.

"Not much. Fifteen . . . twenty minutes at the most."

She studied Michael's face, trying to read his expression. His bruises were fading, and his jaw was clenched, like he held the weight of the world on his shoulders. But in spite of everything they were facing, her mind couldn't stop focusing on whether or not he'd felt that same charge of electricity passing between them that she had.

Why was she thinking like this? Their worlds spun in different directions. He was an adrenaline junkie, out to save the planet. She might have the same aspirations of making a difference, but they didn't include going undercover as a money launderer for a bunch of drug dealers. Somehow she had the feeling that a house in the suburbs with a dog and cat and a couple of kids would never appeal to the man sitting beside her.

Which was why any notions of a romantic interest on her part needed to be squelched quickly. All she'd ever wanted was a family—the clichéd Mr. Right, two kids, and yes, even that house in the suburbs. But thinking there was any possibility that Michael Hunt was that man was . . . simply ludicrous.

She needed a distraction.

———

"What does your family do to celebrate Christmas?"

Olivia's question jerked Michael from his thoughts.

He wished he could douse the emotions erupting in him. He'd been with his family last Christmas. Sometimes that life seemed just like yesterday. But other times, he wasn't sure anymore that those vague memories were even real.

"Typically," he began, "we sit around the dining room table and eat my mother's roasted turkey and giblet gravy. Then we exchange the family gag gift—a sweater made from eight skeins of bright green and red yarn and crocheted by my father's now-deceased older sister. After that we usually stay up late, laughing and eating sweet potato pie and drinking homemade eggnog."

"Sounds nice," she said.

"It is."

"We could still go to your family and tell them the truth. You told me your father and your sister have connections—"

"I can't do that. Not yet." The words came out harsher than he meant them to.

He turned to her, breathing in the scent of coconuts from the shampoo she'd used at the cabin, while he studied her olive skin and wide almond eyes. He hadn't expected the emotional connection that had developed between them. They might have only known each other for a short time, but she'd already become both his rescuer and his confidant. He needed her . . . they needed each other.

He reached out and squeezed her fingers. "I'm sorry. This isn't your fault."

She'd simply become another player in a dangerous game that no one ever won. A game he'd joined before it got personal. A game in which the stakes were raised the moment he'd found out that some of the good guys were helping themselves to a piece of the pie the cartel was willing to part with in exchange for their cooperation.

Eeny, meeny, miny, moe . . .

The old children's rhyme ran through his head. To Valez, the scenario was nothing more than a game. Who would live and who would die. He arranged his enemies like a row of dominos, taking out anyone who got in his way.

"You don't have to be sorry." Her expression softened. "You're a close family?"

"Yeah."

"Tell me about them."

He studied her profile in the morning sunlight streaming through the window. He admired her for the courage she'd already shown and all the risks she'd taken. "I'm the middle of three. Two sisters. Avery's a homicide detective, like I told you. Smart. Passionate. Her husband was killed a few years ago in the line of duty."

"I'm sorry."

"It hasn't been easy for her being a single mom, but she's done well. I've always looked up to her. She has a teenage daughter, Tess. She's . . . thirteen now. It's hard to believe how fast she's growing up."

"And your other sister?"

"Emily's a teacher at a private school."

A smile formed on Olivia's lips. "So she didn't follow the family tradition?"

"Three generations of cops? No." He took a sip of his coffee, wishing he had a cup of his mother's secret blend she pulled out every holiday. "Emily decided to work for a private academy instead of the police academy. She loves her job and is good at it."

Finding news about family via the online newspaper or a Google search had never seemed right, but it wasn't as if he'd had a choice. His father's retirement. Avery's recent engagement to one of the city's medical examiners. Emily's broken engagement . . . While he might be able to look up facts on the internet, he couldn't read between the lines. He wanted to ask Emily how she was doing, especially after Charlie's betrayal and shooting, he wanted to meet Avery's fiancé, and he wanted to know how Mama was coping with the death of her only son.

"What about your parents?" Olivia asked.

"My father retired in August. They had a big party for him. My mother's southern bred through and through and isn't one to waste an opportunity to celebrate."

He'd anticipated his own homecoming for months. All he wanted to do was walk into the house he'd grown up in, sit down in his chair at the table, and eat some of his mother's homemade cooking, while catching up on everything he'd missed.

"How long has it been since you've seen them?"

"Eight months."

Michael glanced in the rearview mirror as a car pulled into their lane. Dark sedan, tinted windows. It could be anyone. Valez's men, CIA, FBI . . . He'd been careful to ensure they hadn't been followed, but no matter how careful he was, he couldn't stop looking over his shoulder. He tried to shake off the panic, because more than likely he was just being paranoid. But they couldn't take any chances.

He let out a sigh of relief when the car switched lanes again and passed them. They could do this. There was no other choice. They'd gone over all the options of this plan at least a dozen times. Tried to calculate everything that could go wrong. In the end, that was all they could do. Prepare for every obstacle they could think of . . . and pray.

"You okay?" she asked.

"Yeah." He glanced in the rearview mirror again. "I'm fine."

"And the pain?"

"Better. Why?"

"You seem . . . distracted."

He clicked on his blinker and began pulling off the freeway.

"Michael?"

His fingers tightened on the steering wheel. "I don't want to scare you, but we're being followed."

CHAPTER
15

Olivia's stomach took a dip as she turned around.

"Silver Honda Pilot. Three cars back," he told her.

She caught sight of the vehicle, hanging back far enough to seem unobtrusive, but close enough to keep tabs on them. "You're sure?"

He paused and made a left turn. "It's possible we're simply going in the same direction, but I'm not taking any chances at this point."

She gripped the door handle and stared into the side-view mirror, wishing this would all disappear. All they needed now was someone shooting at them as they drove through suburban Atlanta.

Michael reached out and squeezed her hand, his eyes never leaving the road. "It's going to be okay."

She wanted to believe him. Badly. But she'd seen the agent's dead body. Watched Felipe's house go up in flames. Michael wasn't exactly the author of happy endings.

She watched in her mirror as the other car stayed with them. This was no coincidence. "I'm assuming you've been in this situation before?"

"A time or two."

His grin did little to reassure her that everything would be okay. She might trust him, might have been impressed with his super-cop skills last night, but he wasn't Superman. He'd already taken a beating, been shot, and now there were hitmen after him. What were the odds of escaping another encounter?

She motioned at Ivan to get down. Every encounter with the bad guy so far had included gunfire. There was no reason to believe that this time would be any different. Ivan grabbed Gizmo's collar and pulled the dog down with him.

"After three turns, they're still behind us."

"You think these are my father's men?"

"Your guess is as good as mine, though I suppose we can now assume that whoever hit the cabin last night was after us. Somehow they picked up our trail."

"But how?"

She mentally ran through the contents of what they'd grabbed from the cabin. No cell phones, no computers . . . nothing. The car wasn't even theirs, so unless someone had watched them getting into the car . . .

"It doesn't make sense," she said. "And besides, if they're after us—and know where we are—why didn't they come after us last night?"

"I don't know. I've been asking myself that over and over, but so far I've got a whole lot more questions than answers."

She had her own set of unanswered questions. Who had known they were at the cabin? And how had they managed to track them here? And was her father the one behind all of this?

Felipe wouldn't have betrayed them. She was sure of that. Unless whoever had struck last night had been after Felipe. But if that was the case, why were they still being chased?

Michael took the ramp and headed back onto the highway.

Olivia pressed back into the seat as he accelerated. "Where are you going now?"

"I want to try to lose them, but first I'm going to slow down to see if they'll pass us, so you can see their license plate."

Michael eased off on the accelerator. Olivia watched in the rearview mirror as the gap narrowed and the other car came up on their right. She leaned forward, straining to get into position to see the plate.

"I recognize the driver, Michael. He works for my father."

Suddenly their pursuer jerked his car to the left and clipped their rear fender.

Olivia screamed as her seat belt caught, keeping her from slamming into the dashboard. She grabbed for something to hang on to. Terror slid through her . . . the terror that came with knowing someone wanted you dead.

"Ivan?" She turned around to make sure her brother and Gizmo were all right.

Ivan nodded, clutching the dog, who clearly wanted out of the car. "We're okay."

"Hang on." Michael wrestled with the steering wheel, managing to avoid the center divider and a red minivan.

They whipped past a semi as the highway veered to the right, and took the nearest exit. Olivia turned to see if the other car was still following them, but it was going too fast to make the turn, and she gasped as it slammed into the guardrail, then skidded across the asphalt. "I think we've lost them."

"Good, because we're not stopping." Michael kept his foot on the accelerator.

Olivia's fingers were cramped from clutching the door handle. If they weren't on the most-wanted list after what happened at the convenience store, there was no doubt in her mind they would be now.

Michael took the next light, trying to put as much distance as possible between them and the accident. "We're going to have to dump this car. Someone will have gotten the license number and reported it, and the cops will soon know it's a stolen car. Hopefully they didn't get a good look at the passengers."

Which might buy them some time. But time was something she feared they were quickly running out of.

Twenty minutes later, Michael pulled through the gate where the self-storage units were located and parked in the back of the property. Olivia slammed the car door shut, her legs and arms still shaking. She'd always seen her father's house and the island surrounding it as a shelter. She'd believed Felipe's cabin would be safe. Now it seemed that no matter where they went, they were never out of danger. Even inside the gated property she felt vulnerable. But she wasn't sure what would make her feel safe at this point.

She started after Michael, but Ivan signaled to her. "I'll walk the dog around until he's done."

Olivia watched Michael walk toward the end of the row of storage units. "I think we should stay together."

"We lost whoever was after us, Olivia. They won't show up here. They're probably on their way to the emergency room right now."

She hesitated, knowing he was right, but feeling the need to keep him safe. "We don't know who's after us or how they're tracking us. Someone could have sent them. There could be more people after us."

"And your bodyguard over there will protect us? Just like he did at the cabin, and on the road just now?"

Olivia bit back a wave of anger, surprised at her brother's reaction. But the last thing she wanted to do right now was fight with her brother. They needed to talk through what had happened, not blame each other for the mess they were in.

"What matters right now is that we're alive."

"Felipe's not."

The reminder stung hard. She'd not even begun processing his death. They needed to talk about what had happened back at the cabin, but right now, with everything tainted with fear and anger, she didn't even know how to start dealing with her own raw emotions, let alone her brother's.

"No, Felipe's not alive, but what happened wasn't Michael's fault. Why are you mad at him?"

"I'm not mad at him." Ivan's jaw tightened, his face expressive with anger and hurt. "I'm just . . . mad. Mad at whoever's behind this. Mad that Felipe's dead. Mad that our father isn't who I thought he was . . ."

"I'm sorry. I wish I could make all this go away—"

"But you can't, and that's part of the problem. I need you to stop treating me like I'm still a kid."

Olivia's fingernails dug into the palms of her hands. "I just want to protect you."

"From what?" His hands clipped through the words. "The truth?"

"What do you mean?"

"How long have you known the truth about our father?"

"I just found out myself—"

"But you had your suspicions and never said anything to me, because you thought I couldn't handle the truth. Just like our mother thought we couldn't handle the truth about who Antonio Valez really is. But I'm not a kid anymore."

A shudder passed through her. He was right. As much as she tried, she couldn't protect him from everything. She never should have tried to hide the truth from him.

"I'm sorry."

"I just . . . I just need you to trust me to be able to take care of myself."

"You know I do."

"I know you want to." He turned. "Gizmo and I are going for a walk."

Olivia watched Ivan walk away with the dog, knowing all she could do at this point was pray God would protect both of them.

———

Michael watched the conversation from the end of the storage units, wanting to give them some space. He couldn't understand Ivan's sign language or hear everything that was being said, but the gist of the conversation was clear. Ivan had grown up, whether Olivia was ready to accept it or not.

"Is everything okay?" he asked as she approached him.

He tugged on the edge of the wool cap he'd grabbed from the cabin, keeping his head down, like he'd instructed Olivia and Ivan earlier. Security meant cameras, something they needed to avoid. And he'd become a pro at avoiding detection.

"He's angry at me. And as much as I hate to admit it, he's right. I've overprotected him—but now I'm in the middle of a situation where I can't guarantee his safety and it scares me."

"Can we ever completely guarantee someone's safety? It seems like so many times I've thought I was in control of something, I've ended up realizing that I actually have no control at all."

She paused beside him and glared at him. "That's a reassuring thought."

"I'm not trying to add fuel to the fire, but the reality is that as much as we think we're in control, we're really not." He ran his hand down her arm. "Don't beat yourself up over it. But giving him a little slack won't hurt either of you."

"It's hard not to worry about him. I've been taking care of him since he was twelve, and I've always been more like a mother to him than a sister."

"The two of you have been through a lot together, but I suspect that even if he was your son, things wouldn't be any different. I think every parent struggles to let their child grow up. I know my mom did."

Michael stopped in front of unit 415. Three years ago, he'd set up this locker in case of an emergency, hoping he'd never have to use it. So much for hoping. Now he had both the cartel and the authorities after him, which meant he was going to have to play things out very carefully.

"Tell me about the locker," Olivia said.

"The last time I opened it was about a year ago. My partner and I checked on our gear and added a few more items. It's our backup plan—our emergency stash in case one of our under-cover gigs goes south and we need a way out."

Michael had never really considered that he'd need a way out. He'd always assumed he could go to the department if he found himself in trouble. He'd never imagined a scenario where he'd have to prove his innocence on his own, let alone ensure the safety of someone else. He understood Olivia's worry over Ivan all too well.

He put in the four digit code, opened the door, then glanced around the 5x5 room. Besides the layers of dust, everything looked exactly the same way he'd left it. A broken lawn mower, a wheelbarrow, hoes and buckets, along with a bunch of garden stuff and other junk he and Mason had picked up at a garage sale. And two large wooden storage boxes.

"What is all this stuff?"

"On the surface, a bunch of garden supplies and other random stuff in case anyone got too nosy. But inside these boxes"—Michael unlocked the first one—"is our survival stuff, like extra weapons, a few untraceable burn phones, and first-aid kits."

"So you can contact your friend now?"

"That's my plan." He grabbed an empty backpack from the box and started filling it with things they might need: a flashlight,

a radio with extra batteries, a first-aid kit, a bunch of power bars, and two burn phones.

"Do you have an extra set of clothes in there?"

He dug into the corner and pulled out an extra-large *I'm a rock star* T-shirt. He held it up to her, chuckling at the way it swallowed her up.

"Maybe not." She tugged on the bottom of the Army green sweatshirt she'd borrowed from Felipe and smiled. "I think this will do for now."

"I'll have my sisters get you something else to wear as soon as possible, I promise."

Olivia's smile faded. "Do you think your sisters know you're alive yet?"

"Yeah." Michael pulled up his pant leg and strapped on an ankle holster. "I think they're worried and waiting for me to call, but I'm worried they're being watched."

He followed her gaze toward the direction of the car, knowing she was dealing with her own pain and worries.

"He's fine, Olivia."

"I know."

Michael slid his handgun into the holster, then dropped hi pant leg. "And we're going to be fine as well."

He picked up the backpack and swung it over his shoul keeping out one of the phones.

Gizmo came running toward the unit with Ivan trailing steps behind him. He stopped to catch his breath. "Tha dog is always running off."

"You know, I think there might be a leash in here." rummaged through an old bucket filled with ran "Here." He tossed Ivan the leash, then came out unit door.

Olivia knelt down and rubbed Gizmo's belly. stop this running off."

Ivan started to secure the leash, then hesitated.

"What's wrong, Ivan?" Olivia asked.

"I think I know how they found us."

"What do you mean?" Michael came toward them.

Ivan looked up at them, a deep frown marking his expression. "They're tracking Gizmo."

CHAPTER
16

Michael watched Ivan unclip a small device from the dog's collar. This was how they'd tracked them?

"I can't believe I didn't notice this before." Ivan handed the gadget to Michael. "He's wearing one of those tracking collars."

Olivia peered over Michael's shoulder at the unit. "A GPS?"

"Exactly," Ivan said. "They help monitor where your pet is and notify you if he runs off. Felipe must have been afraid Gizmo would get lost."

"So whoever tracked us at the cabin used this to track us this morning," Olivia said. "Can anyone follow these devices?"

Michael felt a chill seep through him. "All a person needs is a password and a computer. But if they've been tracking Gizmo, that implies they weren't after us, they were after Felipe."

Olivia frowned. "Maybe. Or they knew we were at the cabin, and discovered a way to track us today."

Dirty cops or the cartel?

Michael dropped the device onto the concrete and smashed it with his shoe. He was getting careless. He should have caught this. But at least their trail would end here.

"There's something I don't understand." Olivia picked up one of the shattered pieces and set it in her palm. "If they were using this to track us, then they should have been able to find

147

us last night. Why wait to come after us now that we're in the city when the risks of being seen are clearly greater?"

Michael shrugged. "It's possible that the cabin where we stayed last night was in a dead zone, and they were only able to pick up the signal again this morning."

"He's right," Ivan said. "These trackers send GPS positioning data over cellular networks, and while they're fairly accurate, there will always be places where they can't catch a signal."

"That could definitely explain what happened," Michael agreed, "but for now we need to get out of here. We can figure out exactly who's after us later."

Gimzo raced away from them down the row of storage units as Ivan started to put on the leash.

"Go get him, Ivan. We need to get out of here," Olivia said.

Michael switched on the burner phone as they hurried to the car. Why they'd been followed was one more piece of the puzzle they were going to have to figure out, but in the meantime, with a chance they'd been tracked to the storage units, they were going to have to scrap his idea of dumping the car. They needed to get out of there as quickly as possible.

"I'll text Mason to have him meet us," Michael said. "As long as we can't be followed from here, we should be okay."

Unless the police spotted the stolen vehicle they were driving. Or they were pulled over for some other reason. Or they'd already been tracked here and the bad guys were waiting for them to emerge from the lot.

He shoved away the list of potential problems and finished typing in the message, hesitating before pushing Send. Dragging Mason into this situation was a gamble. Not because he didn't trust him, but because he didn't want to put his friend's life and career at risk. But he knew they'd never make it out alive if they didn't get outside help. Valez and his friends had bottomless pockets and too many resources.

Michael pushed the unlock button on the key fob as they approached the car, then froze at the unmistakable sound of a gun being cocked behind them.

You've got to be kidding me, Lord.

"Where are you going, Liam? Or should I say Michael? Michael Hunt?"

Tomas?

"Tomas." Michael slipped the phone into his pocket, then pulled Olivia behind him. "I thought we left you behind on the island."

"Nice try. Tracking that stupid mutt was the best idea we've had in a long time."

"Gizmo?" Michael worked to absorb Tomas's words. "*You* were tracking Gizmo?"

"We've been monitoring Felipe and guessed correctly you might go to his cabin. We didn't expect we'd have to find you a second time, however."

"So you're the ones who attacked the cabin?" Olivia asked.

"I'll admit I underestimated you, Michael. But trust me, I won't do that again."

Tomas stood next to Elias, who also had a gun pointed at them. Tomas looked pleased with himself, clearly ready for another round. But the stakes were higher this time, and Michael had no intention of anything happening to Olivia or her brother.

Show me a way out of this, Lord . . .

"From the looks of your little getaway party," Tomas said, "I'm guessing you hadn't expected to see me again so soon. Where is Ivan, by the way? I know that dog is here somewhere."

"My father told me you were head of his security team, not a hitman," Olivia said.

"Just like your friend here was supposed to be a corrupt businessman, not a cop." Tomas took a step forward. "You had everyone fooled about who you were, Michael Hunt. Son of a former police captain, laundering money for the cartel while undercover. It was clever, actually, and you're clearly good at what you do, because you had all of us fooled for a very long time. Unfortunately, you weren't quite good enough."

Michael studied their surroundings, frustrated at Tomas's advantage. Because the man was right. But instead of dwelling on his mistakes, he needed to buy time and figure out a way for them to gain the upper hand. He wasn't going to let Tomas win this round.

"And as for your father, Olivia," Tomas continued, "how do they say it . . . the jig is up? He foolishly thought he could protect you by keeping you from the truth."

"The truth that he's a leader in the cartel?" she asked.

"That information should have made you think twice before rescuing this man, Olivia." Tomas held up the flash drive Michael had given Kendall at the restaurant, hours before his death. "And you . . . did you really think you'd get away with this?"

Michael's heart sank. He'd hoped Kendall would have found a way to stash the drive, or pass it on to someone . . . anything besides let Tomas get ahold of it. Because not only could that drive take Valez down, it held the proof Michael needed to prove his own innocence.

Tomas laughed. "And then there was that miraculous escape the three of you tried to pull off, which Valez is quite unhappy about. Did you seriously think you could get off the island without anyone guessing what happened, or no one coming after you? Quite impressive, but again, not impressive enough."

"All we need right now, then, is another miracle," Michael said.

"Not this time, considering we have the guns." Tomas laughed again. "What's your plan of escape now?"

Michael balled his fists. "Forget the games, Tomas. What do you want?"

"Whatever the boss wants, which right now is to find you. Which, as we can all see, I've done."

"Then what does he want?"

"To talk to you . . . before he kills you, that is."

"Why all the cat and mouse?" Michael asked. "He could have just called me. I'm a pretty cooperative guy."

Tomas stepped forward and grabbed Olivia, pressing his gun to the back of her head. "You were right. Enough of the games."

"Michael—"

"Leave her alone, Tomas. I'm the one Valez wants." Michael took a step forward, trying to keep the emotion out of his voice, unwilling to give Tomas another trump card in his hand.

Tomas grinned as he ran his thumb down Olivia's cheek. "I didn't know you cared, Michael, though I can see how you might have grown fond of her. I've always thought she was quite a beauty."

Michael took another step toward them. "I said leave her alone."

"Why should I?"

Michael decided to take the bait. "Because if I don't kill you, Valez will."

"Do you think that Valez cares anything about the bastard children of his dead mistress?"

Olivia's chest heaved. Tomas's gun pressed into the back of her head, as if he were just waiting for an excuse to shoot her. Surely her father hadn't ordered a hit on her and Ivan. The thought made her shudder. She'd seen evidence of what Tomas could do, both with a weapon and with his fists. He wouldn't simply kill them. He'd have fun with them first, and then finish them off.

"My father would never tell you or anyone to kill my brother and me," she said.

"Really? You rescued a man who'd betrayed him, and now you think your father will save the day for you? Your father knows he can't trust you."

"We couldn't leave him to die."

"That's exactly what you should have done. None of this is your business. You should have stayed out of it."

"Why did you want him dead in the first place?" she asked.

"No more questions."

Olivia winced as Tomas shoved her toward the car.

"Elias, frisk Michael, tie his hands, and put them both in the backseat."

As Elias slid his gun into its holster and started toward Michael, Ivan rounded the corner of the building with Gizmo. The dog pulled from Ivan's grip on the leash and lunged for Tomas, sinking his teeth into the man's calf.

Tomas dropped his hold on Olivia as he instinctively tried to shake the dog off, tried to hit him with his gun. "Get him off of me!"

Elias froze, obviously confused about which direction he should move.

It was the distraction they needed. Olivia twisted, and jammed her elbow into Tomas's throat. Gizmo released his hold as Tomas buckled and dropped his gun. Olivia picked it up, took a step back, then aimed it at Tomas. "Looks to me like the odds have shifted."

Michael had pulled his weapon from his ankle holster and was holding it on Elias. He pressed his gun against Elias's head, then pulled him away from the car.

"She's right," Michael said. "The odds have shifted."

"You're not going to get away with this." Tomas lunged for Olivia.

Before Michael could react, Olivia shot into the concrete, six inches from Tomas's foot. "Don't move."

Tomas sneered. "You missed—"

"I didn't miss." Olivia raised the weapon. "My father made sure of that. Next time I'll aim for your heart."

Michael shoved Elias facedown onto the ground and planted his foot in the small of his back. He looked up at Olivia. "I thought you said you didn't know how to handle a gun."

She grinned. "I said I didn't know how to handle a rifle."

Smiling, Michael aimed his gun at Tomas. "You're next. Facedown next to your buddy here."

"What now?" She held her gun steady at them, as if daring either of them to get up.

"I could shoot them," Michael said. "Actually, that would be my first choice, but considering there are probably security cameras recording all of this, it's probably not the best idea. So for now, there's a pair of handcuffs in my unit, Ivan. In the box on the right. The code for the door is 1776. Why don't you grab those for me while I ensure these bozos don't try to escape."

Michael rolled Tomas over and grabbed the flash drive from his shirt pocket. "I was hoping you hung onto this. Needed a little insurance of your own against the boss? Because I'm starting to wonder if you're working for someone else."

"No, I . . ." Tomas's jaw clenched from the pain. "Just because I didn't take you down doesn't mean this is over."

"Trust me," Michael said. "This is far from over."

A moment later, he handcuffed them together to one of the metal poles running along the fence.

"You're just going to leave us here?" Elias whined. "It's freezing."

"Don't worry, gentlemen. Someone's liable to find you in the next few hours." Michael turned to Ivan and Olivia. "It's time for us to get out of here."

CHAPTER 17

Olivia sat beside Michael on one of Piedmont Park's benches, with the city of Atlanta looming behind them, trying to look calmer than she felt. At least Ivan seemed to be having fun with Gizmo. The energetic French Brittany was still on his leash, but was clearly enjoying the freedom of being able to run around.

Freedom, though, still felt out of reach for her. On the drive here, Michael went into more detail about how he and Mason had arranged this meeting place. Working undercover had its own set of dangers, so they'd decided if ever one of them were in trouble, they would send the other a coded message and meet here. In the years that followed, he'd never chosen to implement the plan. Even after Valez had arranged his "death," Michael didn't opt to contact Mason, primarily because he was worried about involving his friend in a situation his gut told him wasn't going to end well.

Apparently Michael had been right. But she had no idea whether they could trust his friend, no idea if they'd been tracked here . . . no idea how or when all of this was going to be over. Every minute that passed was another minute that something could go wrong.

"How are you holding up?" Michael's question broke through her troubled thoughts.

"Ready for all of this to be over."

"It will be. Soon."

She caught the determination in his voice, but knew he had just as many doubts as she did.

"What about Ivan? How do you think he's doing?"

"I don't know." Which was what had her worried the most. "He's never been much of a talker, but we're close, and he's always opened up to me. This time—with Felipe's death—it's as if everything has changed between us."

"Just keep giving him some space. There's a lot to process and a lot of loss for both of you to deal with."

"It's hard to do when I know he's hurting so much." She glanced at her watch, wishing the waiting would end. Wishing there was something they could do to reverse the effects of the mess they'd stepped into. But all the wishful thinking in the world couldn't erase the past three days.

"What about your friend?" she asked. "Are you sure he's coming?"

"He'll be here."

She stared out across the open area of the park. By now, the sun was out and starting to melt the snow that had fallen during the night. She tapped her foot against the ground and tried to relax. It wasn't the first time she'd visited the urban park with its large, open green spaces, trails, gardens, and playgrounds. She'd come to concerts a few times with friends over the years, and once she'd gone fishing with an older couple from her church. But this morning wasn't about hanging out with friends for a few hours of fun. Instead, she felt as if the crippling feelings of fear were about to consume her.

She pressed her hands against the bench seat. "Am I the only one who's nervous?"

"Hardly."

"Afraid he'll turn you in?"

"Mason? Never."

"People change."

"Not the essential part of who they are." He leaned back against the bench, looking like a man with no plans other than to enjoy the morning, but she knew he was completely alert, watching everything that was going on around them. "I think I'm more worried about seeing my family. I can't help but question what my presumed death did to them. Especially my mother."

"Questioning whether your choice to stay in was worth it?"

"Yeah. At some point I'm going to have to look my mother in the eye and explain to her why I did what I did."

"Do you think she'll understand?"

"I come from a family of cops. They've all had to make sacrifices. But losing your son is different. And I'm not sure that seeing me again is going to instantly wipe away all those months of loss she's felt."

Olivia tried to imagine the immense emotion they all were going to feel when they were reunited. "She loves you, and even your presumed *death* can't change that. Besides, not many people get a second chance like she's about to be given, and I'm pretty sure that will far outweigh any hurt or anger."

Michael nodded toward the entrance. "Mason's here."

Michael stood up as Mason walked toward them. His friend had changed little over the last year. His dark-blond hair was still a bit long, and he was wearing his typical jeans and T-shirt that allowed him to blend in almost anywhere.

Mason stopped in front of him, then pulled him into a big hug. "I'll be honest, when I got the message from you, I wasn't sure if I should hug you or slug you."

Michael smiled, unprepared for the wave of emotion that shot through him. "I'll take the former, thanks." He caught the hesitation in Mason's eyes as his gaze shifted to Olivia.

"I didn't realize you had anyone with you."

"This is Olivia Hamilton."

Mason shook her hand. "It's nice to meet you."

"You as well," Olivia said. "Michael says great things about you."

"And this is her brother, Ivan," Michael said as Ivan walked up with Gizmo in tow. "He's deaf, but he can read lips."

Mason nodded at Ivan. "I could have used you a time or two on a stakeout."

Ivan smiled. "It's nice to meet you, sir."

Mason turned back to Michael. "We have a lot to talk about, but I'm still trying to convince myself that you're really standing here and this isn't some whacked-out dream of mine."

"Trust me, this is real." And so was the danger both to himself and anyone he involved. "Did you tell anyone?"

"Avery knows, and she brought in your father."

Michael frowned.

"I didn't have a choice, Michael. This isn't exactly something we can deal with alone."

"So who else knows?"

"Just your sisters and your father. No one else. They're not even going to tell your mother until things are sorted out."

Guilt reemerged. "You could all get into trouble for this. You and Avery could lose your jobs—"

"Forget it. You're a whole lot more important than any job will ever be. So you know they're looking for you?"

"Yeah. We know."

"Avery's the one leading up the hunt for you," Mason said. "I want to hear everything, but I think it's best to get you both out of here so we can talk in private. And I've got a place where we should be safe. Your family is meeting us there. How'd you get here?"

Michael paused. "A stolen car that's a bit worse for wear than when we first took it, which is one reason why it's only a matter of time until the police pick up our trail."

"Then we better make sure we stay one step ahead of them," Mason said. "Any signs of being followed?"

"Not here."

"I guess it's hard to kill a dead man."

"Apparently not."

As they started walking toward the exit, Michael explained briefly how he had saved Valez's life, how Valez had orchestrated his death, and what had happened the past few days, including his rescue off the island and their subsequent escape from Felipe's cabin and the storage unit.

"They're going to keep looking for you, which is why we need to get out of here." Mason nodded toward the stadium across the street. "I'm parked just south of 10th Street. The hotel will be a lot safer than out here in the open."

Olivia went on ahead with Ivan and Gizmo, seeming to understand Michael's need to talk to Mason in private. Eight months away had left him with dozens of questions, starting with the well-being of his family.

He waited for a pair of joggers to pass, walking in silence past century-old trees and a thin blanket of snow covering the lawns, before speaking again. "I've been able to gather bits and pieces of news over the past few months. I know that Emily called off her wedding, and that she shot Charlie Bains while rescuing you. I know my mother threw my father a retirement party in August and Avery's engaged, but beyond that, I've stayed pretty much in the dark."

"You really have been living under a rock. I guess you haven't watched the news the past few days either."

"I've been a bit busy recently, trying to thwart my impending death. Has something happened?"

"Where do you want me to start?" Mason shoved his hands into the pockets of his jacket as they followed the trail toward the exit.

"Tell me about Avery's fiancé."

"Jackson Bryant is Atlanta's newest associate medical examiner. He's a Texas transplant, but still a good guy. You'll like him."

"It's hard to believe how much I've missed these past few months." After losing her husband in the line of duty, he was glad to see Avery had finally come to the place where she could remarry. "Does she seem happy?"

"Very."

"What about Emily? I know she was involved with shooting Charlie, but I don't have any details." He'd tried to follow the local news and any information he could get on his family, but he'd been afraid that any contact, or even Facebook stalking, could possibly lead back to him.

"First let me assure you that they're fine," Mason began, "but last week, Emily's classroom was taken hostage, and Tess was kidnapped."

Michael slowed his stride, feeling as if he'd been living on Mars the past eight months. "Whoa. What in the world happened?"

"Long story short, one of Emily's students took her class hostage for ransom money in order to save his brother's life. The positive outcome of all of it was that we were able to take down Bains. And while your sister might not be a cop, that girl definitely has Hunt blood inside of her."

That statement didn't surprise him one bit. "What exactly happened?"

"There was a showdown at the mall parking lot." Mason's

voice was coated with a layer of emotion. "She ended up saving my life."

"This can't be easy for her," Michael said. "I know Emily. She can handle a gun, but she went into teaching because she didn't want any part of law enforcement."

"You're right. This hasn't been easy on her, but she's strong, Michael. Emily's going to be okay."

Michael frowned, noting the change in Mason's expression when he said Emily's name. "You're not planning to take advantage of her vulnerability now, are you?"

"You always were the protective older brother."

"And I can still see that spark in your eye," Michael said. "I told you years ago, my sister was way out of your league."

"More specifically, you said I had three strikes against me. I was a cop, I didn't share her faith—"

"And like I said, she's way out of your league."

"Maybe that all used to be true, but your death forced me to look at life—and death—differently. And while I know I still have a long way to go in my faith, I've learned that being a Christian isn't about religion, it's about a relationship with Christ."

"Wow." Michael paused in the middle of the trail and turned to his friend, then gathered him up in a big bear hug. "I can't tell you how happy I am to hear you say that."

"I'm just glad for the chance to tell you in person."

Michael took a step back, still smiling at his friend's news. "And Emily? How does she fit into all of this?" Michael caught Mason's grin. "You're in love with her, aren't you?"

"Is it that obvious?"

Michael laughed. "Apparently you're losing your undercover skills."

Mason started walking again. "I think I've always been in love with her. I'm thinking about asking her to marry me. Maybe not right away—things have actually moved faster than I expected—but we're headed in that direction."

Michael chuckled. "As much as I love you both, it might take me awhile to get used to my little sister and my best friend being an item."

"Don't make it sound like it's the end of the world. This is a good thing."

"You know I'm happy for you." Michael slowed down as they approached the exit. While he knew there would be many more questions on both sides over the coming days, there was one more thing he needed to know now. "What about my mother?"

Mason's mouth tightened. "Your 'death' has been hard on her. She thought she lost her only son."

"Something I've regretted every day for the past eight months."

"But like your sister, she's a Hunt. And while the road hasn't always been easy, she's strong."

"Will she forgive me?"

"She's your mother, Michael. She'll never stop loving you, no matter what happens." Mason stopped again at the exit of the park. "I have a question that can't wait. What about Olivia and Ivan? I'm still trying to connect how they fit into this."

Michael hesitated and turned, watching Olivia stop to rub behind Gizmo's ears half a dozen yards ahead of them. "Three days ago I was preparing for my death, and they rescued me."

"But who are they? What were a young woman and her teenage brother doing on Valez's island, and how did they know you needed rescuing?"

"Antonio Valez is their father."

"Wait a minute." Mason paused, eyes wide, as he took in the news. "You're not serious, are you?"

"They were both born here in the States. Their mother died a few years ago. They've had regular but limited contact with their father over the years."

"And you trust them?"

"They saved my life."

"According to what you just told me a few minutes ago, you saved Valez's life, but that doesn't mean you did it because you're on the same side."

"It's not the same."

"Why not?"

Michael's anger spiked, hating the fact that he needed to defend Olivia and Ivan. "Because it's not the same. They're not involved in their father's work."

"And you know this how?"

"Because Olivia told me, and according to everything she's said and done, I have no reason not to trust her."

"I'm sorry." Mason rubbed his temple. "Forgive me if all of this is a bit difficult for me to take in, but you're on the run from the man who wants to kill you, with his son and daughter, of all people, and you expect me to trust them?"

"Yes, I'm asking you to trust them *and* me. Because now that Kendall is dead, it won't be long before everyone inside the department assumes that I'm working with Valez on the wrong side of the law."

Mason looked hard at him and held his gaze. "They already do."

CHAPTER
18

Michael and Olivia stepped out of the elevator onto the fifth floor of the hotel, where Mason had arranged for him to meet with his family. Michael's heart was hammering. A decade of law enforcement had trained him to keep his emotions in check, but there were some situations that one could never prepare for. And this was one of them. Everything about today had become personal. He'd missed his parents and his sisters. Missed his life as part of the Hunt family. And now that was all about to be given back to him.

Olivia walked beside him down the hall with its generic, pale-green wallpaper and floral-patterned carpet. At the moment, besides Mason's confession of faith, it seemed like she might be the only good thing that was going to come out of the entire mess. That was if they even made it out with their lives intact.

"You ready for this?" she asked, as the elevator dinged shut behind them.

"I'm ready to see my family, I just didn't expect the flood of nerves. So much has happened in the past eight months. None of us are the same—at least I know I'm not."

"And you're right, they won't be either, but they're still your family, and they love you unconditionally. That's something that will never change."

"I know, it's just that"—he glanced down at her—"despite all of my good intentions, I know my decisions have hurt them. They've had to live with the reality—right or wrong—that I'm dead. I can't imagine what they must be feeling."

"I imagine they're ecstatic, but also just as nervous to see you walk into that room." She ran her hand down his arm. "They never imagined you coming back into their lives, and now you are."

"Like Lazarus rising from the dead." He shot her a smile that quickly faded. "But even that joy can't completely erase the grief they've gone through the past eight months."

"Maybe it can."

Maybe. He stopped in front of room number 536 and drew in a deep breath before knocking.

"You should go in alone," she said. "I'll understand—"

"No." He clasped her hand. "I want you here. That's why I asked you to come with me while Mason and Ivan take care of the dog."

The confession took even him by surprise. His few attempts at dating hadn't exactly worked well for him over the past few years. There had been a few women he'd been able to imagine a future with, but he'd always put work first. And it had never gone over well when he was running down a suspect and couldn't tell his date where he was, or why she'd just been stood up.

He squeezed her hand, then knocked on the door.

A moment later, he was engulfed in his father's arms, feeling like Lazarus and the prodigal son all rolled up in one. He'd been the middle child who pushed boundaries and drove his parents crazy growing up. The one who'd let them believe he was dead. But when he looked into his father's eyes, Michael knew all had been forgiven.

"I've missed you, son. More than you'll ever know. And to

have you back . . ." Tears welled in the older man's eyes. "It's the miracle I never even knew to pray for."

Michael studied his father's face. He'd aged over the past year and had acquired a few more gray hairs, but he clearly hadn't lost any of his inner strength.

Avery grabbed onto him next, his fiery, redheaded sister. "After all these months of trying to discover the truth behind your death, this—" she gripped his shoulders—"this isn't what we expected."

"It wasn't what I'd planned either, but seeing you all again feels even better than I thought it could."

Emily's tears fell freely as she pulled him into a hug, erasing in one moment the months they'd spent apart, and lessening the guilt threatening to swallow him.

The front door opened, and Mason and Ivan walked into the room with Gizmo in tow, along with a bag of dog food and a water bowl.

Michael pulled Olivia beside him, his own tears pooling, as he began making introductions. "This is Olivia and Ivan. And that little guy is Gizmo. They saved my life."

He stood beside the couch as his family—in typical Hunt family fashion—hugged Olivia and Ivan. He barely noticed the posh décor of the apartment-styled room, or the smell of coffee brewing in the tiny attached kitchen. All he could do was cling to the realization that they were safe for the moment, and he'd finally come home.

"I know we have a lot to talk about, but before we get started, are any of you hungry?" Emily's question broke into his thoughts.

She nodded toward the dining room table that was covered with pizzas and soft drinks, but nerves had squelched any feelings of hunger.

"Maybe later," he said. "Olivia? Ivan?"

They both shook their heads.

Michael turned to his father as they all sat down on the plush seating, while Gizmo curled up on the carpet at Ivan's feet, apparently tired from his recent run in the park. Michael had a hundred questions to ask, but there was one question that couldn't wait until later. "What about Mama? Mason said you decided not to tell her what's going on yet?"

"I'll probably regret the decision once she finds out," his father said, "but until I knew exactly what was going on, I couldn't take any chances of having her heart broken again."

The guilt resurfaced, twisting through him like a knife. "I know the past few months have been difficult . . . I can't begin to tell you how sorry I am—"

"You don't have to apologize for anything." His father reached out and squeezed Michael's hand. "You were doing your job to make this world a better place. Now we just have to figure out a way to put an end to this, so life can go back to normal for all of us."

Michael sat back, wondering if that were even possible. At the moment, any sense of normality seemed a world away. "I know that I'm wanted by the police," he began. "And that there's a price on my head from the cartel."

"You did manage to get yourself into quite a bit of trouble." Avery pulled out a notebook and pen from her jacket pocket, then let her gaze rest briefly on Olivia and Ivan.

"They both know everything I'm about to say," Michael said. "I'd like them to stay."

"Okay." Avery leaned forward, her hands clasped in front of her around the notebook. "On our end, the captain's formed a special team to find you, believing you have crucial information that could bring down the cartel in this area. And if that wasn't enough, you've been tied to a murder and a shooting—FBI agent Sam Kendall, and a man who was shot during a convenience store robbery. The police know you were there."

Michael nodded. "We saw the news report last night."

"Then let's start back at the beginning. What happened the day of the explosion? We know the official version—that you were killed in a bomb attack—but clearly, that version was a cover-up by someone."

Michael let out a slow breath as he gathered his thoughts. He'd never expected to be sitting across from his sister on the other end of an interrogation, even if it was in the middle of a cozy hotel room. "This all started a lot further back than the day of the explosion."

He started at the point when he'd been approached by the FBI about going undercover in Valez's organization, and how he'd eventually managed to work his way up in the ranks. He told them how he was involved in laundering money in order to eventually gain access to Valez's money trail and his contacts.

"I'm assuming the plan worked?" his father asked.

"For the most part."

Michael continued sharing about how he found out that the bomb had been intended for Valez, his decision to stay under-cover, how Valez set him up with a new identity, and how because of a leak in the department, Kendall had insisted they keep his new identity secret for his own safety.

"That's quite a story," Mason said once he finished.

"I have evidence." He set the flash drive he'd confiscated from Tomas on the coffee table in front of his sister.

"What is this?" she asked.

"Files, including a second set of books that show how Valez has been keeping track of all his illegal gains."

"If you have this evidence, then why not go to the captain right now?" Emily leaned into Mason's shoulder on the love seat. "We could give him the drive and tell him everything you've just told us. Aren't those files proof of what you've been doing? Proof that you're working for and not against the department?"

"I can't go in yet, because Russell Coates was arrested during that operation you were involved in," Michael said. "He'd been working undercover, and someone murdered him in his cell because of what he knew."

"If they killed him to keep him quiet, they would do the same to you," Emily said.

"Exactly."

"We need to find out who killed Coates."

"And the names of everyone on the force who's working for the cartel. If we can get our hands on that kind of list, I'll be able to come in."

His father stood up and adjusted the thermostat. Despite the cold weather outside the room was getting uncomfortably warm. "I know you did what you thought was right, but you should have walked away, or at least come to us."

"You don't know how many times I almost walked away. But I'd poured so much time into this assignment. And then when I found out that some people believed I was the leak, I was afraid what would happen if I came in. Afraid what would happen if any of you were involved."

"We're family, son." His father sat back down across from him. "I don't care what happens, I want to be involved. And now that you're here, we're going to get through this together."

"But the two of you, Avery . . . Mason . . . You could lose your careers over this."

"You're worth it, little brother, and don't you forget it."

"I agree," Mason said.

Avery touched his arm. "The captain has me working your case. He just doesn't know yet that we found you. I'll bring him in when—and if—I know you'll be safe."

"As long as you all know what you're getting into, know as well how much I appreciate it."

Avery turned to Olivia. "When Mason told us you and your brother were with him and had been on the run a few days, we gathered a few changes of clothes and some other things we thought you might appreciate. And we brought a few things for you as well, Ivan. There's a bathroom in that hallway, if you'd like to shower and change now, though what we brought for you might be a bit big."

"It's fine." Ivan took the bag of clothes Emily handed him. "Thank you."

"A fresh set of clothes and a hot soak in the tub would be fantastic." Olivia stood up.

"Your clothes are in the bedroom," Emily said. "There's also a Jacuzzi in the master bath. Take your time. You'll feel a lot better."

Michael watched Olivia slip into the bedroom, then turned back to his family. "Thank you."

"We brought you a change of clothes as well. Mama arranged to have a lot of the things from your apartment packed up and stored in their garage. Not that you had a lot of stuff, but most of what you did have is safe."

"I'm sorry for all of this—"

"Stop apologizing," Emily said. "You're here, safe, which is all that matters right now."

"She's beautiful," Avery said. "Olivia," she added with a grin.

Michael grinned back at her. "Trust me, I've noticed."

"I know you have. Every time you look at her you're like a high school geek out on a date with the prom queen. But the real question right now is, can we trust her?"

"Is that why you sent them out?" Michael asked. "I've already been through this with Mason."

Avery set her notebook down. "We're talking about Valez's daughter and son. What else are we supposed to think?"

"Not that they're some Trojan horse sent to topple the department."

"You trust them? Completely?"

"Yes, I trust them." Michael worked to swallow his anger, knowing that they had every right to ask the question.

"I'm not planning to interrogate them, if that's what you're worried about," Avery said. "You've always been a good judge of character."

"I'm telling you, they're not involved with their father's business." Michael briefly recounted his time at Felipe's cabin. "They didn't even know who their father really was until a couple days ago. Olivia's a journalist, who visits Valez once or twice a year. Ivan is a typical college student. Do a background check on them, and you'll see."

"Trust me, I will, but there is one other thing we need to talk about. I want to bring in my team to help with this."

Michael shook his head. "There are already too many people involved in this—"

"They offered."

"They know I'm here?"

"No, just that you're alive. No one besides the four of us knows you've made contact."

Michael reached up to massage the back of his neck. "I hadn't even planned to get you involved. If anyone finds out you know where I am, you'll lose everything you've ever worked for. All of you will."

"Trust me, the captain made that quite clear, but we don't have time to worry about that right now. I'm more worried about ensuring your safety—as well as Olivia's and Ivan's."

"And what's the captain going to do when he finds out?"

"The captain knows I'm looking for you. He just doesn't have to know I've found you yet. Tory will come here. Carlos and Levi will work from the precinct. We'll deal with those issues—and the captain—as they come up."

"I could still turn myself in—"

"We have no plans of losing you again, son." His father stood. "You'll go in when we know it's safe, and not a moment before."

CHAPTER 19

Forty-five minutes later, Michael stepped out of the bathroom. In the time it had taken him to shave and change clothes, Avery had turned the hotel living room into the duplicate of a precinct bull pen. Avery, Mason, and Tory were going through boxes of paperwork, while his father and Ivan worked at a computer set up on the desk.

"You haven't eaten anything, so I reheated a few slices of your favorite—Italian sausage and black olives." Emily handed him a plate of pizza and a Coke. "And you'll simply have to excuse my babying you the next few days, but I still can't believe you're alive. I missed you."

"I missed you too, and I don't mind this a bit." He took a bite of the pizza, realizing for the first time how hungry he was. "And to be honest, you're not the only one still a bit surprised I'm here in the flesh. I was pretty convinced I was about to be tortured and dumped somewhere in the Atlantic for my body to be eaten by the sharks."

"Don't talk that way." She reached up and kissed him on the cheek. "I've already lost my big brother once. I don't even want to think about losing you again."

"You're not going to." Michael took another couple bites of pizza, downed half his Coke, then set the plate and the drink down on the glass end table beside them. "From what I hear, I'm not the only one who had a rough few days recently. I'm sorry I wasn't here for you, Emily. Sorry we couldn't overload on ice cream and chocolate syrup like we've always done when one of us has a bad day."

"I missed that too. Missed *you*." Emily smiled, but the mark of pain was clear in her eyes. "With everything still so fresh in my mind, I have a feeling a few ice cream sessions would be in order."

"You know I'll be there."

"Good, because while I might have stopped loving Charlie a long time ago, I'm still struggling to shake the feelings of betrayal, and now there's the never-ending guilt of shooting him. I don't know. I'm not sure that will ever completely go away."

"Maybe not completely, but it'll get better eventually." Michael glanced across the room at Mason. "Though I've heard there's a bright spot in your life now."

Emily blushed and let her gaze follow his.

"I've been told the two of you have become pretty cozy since I . . . since I died."

"Your *death* is what changed him. It made him look at life differently, and in a way brought us together. I'm sure he'll tell you about it, but yeah. He makes me happy. Very happy."

"Do you love him?"

Emily fingered the floral pattern on the lamp shade beside them, the blush deepening. "Love's a strong word, especially since it all happened so fast and so recently. If it's not there yet, it's certainly headed that direction. It's funny how something can be completely unexpected, and yet end up being exactly what you were looking for."

"You know he's been in love with you for years."

"And I heard rumors that you tried to convince him I wasn't interested."

"It was true at the time, wasn't it? He was a cop, and you said you'd never date a cop. Besides that, he didn't share your faith, and you were way out of his league."

"All except my being out of his league *was* true."

"I just hate knowing what you had to go through to bring the two of you together."

"Everything that happened only confirms that while I might be a Hunt, saving the world over the pursuit of justice isn't my cup of tea. I'll never again complain about grading papers and all of the other mundane things that teachers have to do."

Michael laughed. "You're a great teacher, and while I can't promise to stop teasing you, I'm glad you're happy."

"Right now I'm happy because my brother's alive."

"I second that. And while you're feeling so generous, maybe you can talk to Olivia and put in a good word for me."

"Worried your charm and good looks aren't enough?" she teased.

"No. Just worried I might lose the best thing that's come around in a very long time."

Olivia stared into the bathroom mirror, wishing she could erase the bags under her eyes. At least she felt better. She'd scrubbed her body and hair again, hoping there were no longer any traces of the smoke left from Felipe's cabin. If only it were that easy to erase the haunting memories she now carried with her as well. But nothing she could do would change what had happened over the past few days. Nothing could bring Felipe back or change the fact that her father wasn't who she'd believed him to be.

But while the long soak in the Jacuzzi had left her feeling human again, she couldn't help but wonder if the Hunt girls' generous donation of clothes—along with their suggestion for her to take her time—didn't have more to do with their needing to grill Michael on who he'd just brought home. She'd seen the caution in Avery's eyes and even in his father's eyes. They wanted to know—and rightly so—where Antonio Valez's daughter and son's loyalties lay.

Olivia put on some mascara, finishing off with a light coat of lipstick. Honestly, she couldn't blame them. She anticipated their questions—expected them. If they were as loyal as Michael had implied, then they weren't going to take Olivia and Ivan at their word and let them into their confidence. Not if there was any chance at all that they might be working for the enemy.

She pulled a coral-colored zippered hoodie over the long-sleeved white T-shirt they'd gotten her, then zipped it up halfway. There had been another thing she'd noticed, sitting in the living room with Michael's family. Despite the accumulation of loss and uncertainty that still hovered between them, she'd seen the strong bond of love and loyalty that Michael had spoken of. It reminded her of those longings in her own life for that sense of family she'd never experienced beyond her church family. Something she never thought she'd have.

But she couldn't forget that when all this was over, the people in that room—Michael included—were going to go back to their own world. A world that, as the daughter of a known criminal, she'd never fit into.

Taking a deep breath, she stepped into the living room, shutting the bedroom door behind her, surprised at how they'd managed to transform the room into a workstation in such a short time.

Michael crossed the room, carrying a piece of pizza and a Coke. "Hungry?"

"Not really."

"There's plenty left if you do get hungry. I was about to send in a posse to check on you."

She smiled. "I'm fine, and feel tons better, actually."

He'd shaved and changed into a pair of black jeans and a green, long-sleeved T-shirt, making her heart tumble just a little bit deeper over the edge. Looking up at him and his now-familiar smile brought memories of watching him sleep while worrying about his fever, listening to him share about his family, and more recently, eating pancakes together before the sun rose.

Had that only been this morning?

Because everything had changed now. His family was here, and he didn't have to watch over her anymore. Anything she'd thought had passed between them was more than likely due to the intense emotional strain they'd all faced over the past few days. Nothing more.

Then why was her heart telling her that she wanted more?

She fought to dismiss the question. "Where's Ivan?"

"My sister put your brother to work. Apparently, he's some kind of computer genius. There were several encrypted files in the information I gave them, and he's trying to hack into them."

"Ivan is brilliant with computers." She looked up at him, wishing she could squelch her insecurities. "I hope that will add a few brownie points in our favor."

He reached out and squeezed her hand, sending chills up her arm. "Hey, you don't need brownie points with them, and you certainly don't need brownie points to impress me. You've already done that. But even Tory's impressed with his skills, and from what I gather, it takes a lot to impress Tory."

"Who's Tory?"

"She's a part of my sister's homicide team. Avery brought her in to help."

"Is that wise? She could lose her job over this."

"It was her choice. She wants to help."

"Even knowing who I am?"

"You mean knowing who your father is."

"Yes—" She looked up at him, knowing he was trying to make her feel better. "And I don't expect them to trust me, Michael. But I would like to help. What can I do?"

"First, you should eat something. It's been hours since we had breakfast."

"You sound like the old ladies at my church. Whenever there's a death or a tragedy, the solution is always to eat."

He smiled. "I'd say they're right."

"Fine, but after that, I want to help, Michael. I can't just sit around here waiting for this to be over."

"Avery would like to ask you some questions when you're ready . . . if you're ready."

"Of course. I'll grab some of that pizza and be right there."

While Olivia got herself some lunch, Michael sat down near his sister, ready to get to work himself. Five file boxes covered the floor, besides a number of pulled files. "What are all of these boxes?"

"Files and paperwork relating to your case."

"My case?" His brow furrowed. "All of this?"

"I've spent the past eight months digging up everything related to your death and what you were working on at the time. I ended up turning my basement into something of a crime scene lab. Photos, timelines, key points of the case . . . I've got it all."

"Why?"

"Because I couldn't handle the accusations against you." He'd rarely seen Avery cry, but today he didn't miss the tears pooling in her eyes. "I . . . I couldn't handle the rumors and lies that were being spread about you, and I thought that finding answers to your death would help bring about the closure we all needed. But I always knew the rumors weren't true. I knew you weren't the kind of man who would ever sell out his family, the force, your country, over money."

"Thank you. For believing in me."

Avery brushed away the tears, then squeezed her brother's hand. "I always have, and I always will."

As Avery released Michael's hand, Olivia walked into the living room with a glass of water and a couple pieces of pizza on a paper plate. She slowed to a stop, a tentative look on her face. "Am I interrupting?"

"Not at all," Avery said.

Michael motioned for her to join them. She sat down next to him, her arm lightly brushing his as she put her glass on the nearby table. A wave of protectiveness rushed through him. He reached over and gave her hand a quick, gentle squeeze.

She smiled at him, then turned toward Avery and took a deep breath. "Avery, I know you have no reason to trust me or my brother, but I want you to know that everything I've told Michael . . . and everything I tell you . . . I swear it's the truth. My father . . . I can't say we were close or that he was around much, but he was my father. I saw what I wanted to see."

"Trust me." Avery smacked her brother on the knee. "I know from experience that you don't get to choose your relatives."

"Very funny." Michael rolled his eyes. "I think we need to get to work, because we know it's only a matter of time before they pick up our trail between the convenience store, the cabin, and this morning's car wreck."

"Don't forget the two goons we left handcuffed at the storage unit," Olivia added.

"They've been brought in for questioning," Avery said, "but for someone supposedly needing to stay under the radar, you've really managed to get yourself in a lot of trouble."

Avery walked over to the white board they'd set up in the corner of the room and pointed to the photo plastered at the top left. "Starting with the convenience store robbery, we've got Simon Bunch. He's got a number of priors, including assault, robbery, auto theft, and drug dealing."

"Any connection to the cartel?" Michael asked, stepping up beside her.

"Oh, yeah. Right now we think it was simply a random robbery that put you in the wrong place at the wrong time, but we'll know more after Carlos finishes questioning him."

"What about the accident on the interstate?" Michael asked. "Can they trace it to us?"

"We don't know much, other than an eyewitness called 911 and it was classified as a hit and run. There's a BOLO out for the driver of the vehicle—that'd be yours—that left the scene first. The car that reportedly hit the guardrail was gone by the time the police got there."

How had he managed to incur both the wrath of the cartel and the US government in less than seventy-two hours?

"You're lucky so far," Avery said. "The car doesn't trace back to you—at least for now—and no leads have been called in yet."

"That's all very optimistic," Michael said, "but we both know that it's just a matter of time until they run fingerprints and check out the cabin where we stayed last night or check the video footage at the storage units. It's all going to come down very soon."

Michael stared at the board, where Avery had posted the photos of Tomas and Elias. "Are they talking yet?"

"Nope."

Avery pointed to the photos. "What can you tell me about these men?"

Olivia stared at the photos, wondering how she'd become involved as a witness against the cartel. "They work for my father. Obviously, they know my connection to Felipe."

A sick feeling hung in the pit of her stomach. The closest she'd ever come to facing death before this week had been when her mother died. Seeing the mug shots of the men who'd killed Felipe, then tried to kill her this morning, felt like an episode of some TV police drama.

But this wasn't television or some action movie. This was her life being ripped to shreds.

"Olivia?"

"If this is too much too soon—" Michael began.

"No, I'm fine." She nodded at Avery, then looked back up at the board. "Sorry. The one on the left, his name is Tomas. The other man is Elias. I'm sorry, I never heard their last names used. I always thought they were bodyguards, but clearly that's not all they do. Michael can attest to that."

"Anything else?"

Olivia shook her head. "What about Felipe's cabin?"

The shooting at the gas station and the near accident on the interstate had left her shaken, but the attack at Felipe's cabin had been personal.

"Details are still sketchy. Law enforcement is still going over the scene," Avery said, "but Carlos is doing what he can to keep us in the loop. The most surprising thing is that they found a safe under the floor, full of cash."

"Cash? I don't understand. Felipe lived a simple life. Why would he have a safe full of cash?"

"Maybe it belonged to the previous owners and was forgotten for some reason," Mason threw out.

"CSU will dust for prints inside the safe, and hopefully have an answer for us soon," Avery said.

Michael grasped Olivia's hand. "What about Felipe's body?"

Avery checked her notes. "According to the latest report . . . there were no fatalities found on the scene."

"And the two men I shot?" Michael asked.

"They must have escaped."

Olivia tried to respond, but she couldn't. Couldn't breathe. Couldn't move. Where was Felipe?

"I don't understand," she finally managed.

Michael squeezed her hand. "Look again, Avery, because that doesn't make sense. Felipe was shot and killed in that cabin."

"I'm just telling you what the report says."

"I shot two of the men," Michael said. "The other two shot and killed Felipe."

"They'll run the traces of blood that were found, but so far, there are a lot more questions than answers. More than likely, the men hightailed it out of there."

"And took Felipe's body with them? Why?" Olivia needed to breathe, needed to move. She stood and started pacing.

"I don't know."

"Were there any witnesses?" Olivia caught the panic in her voice as she spoke. "Someone has to know what happened to him."

"Uniforms are canvassing the area now to see if anyone saw anything. We should know more soon," Avery said. "I promise I'll let you know the moment I hear anything."

Guilt refused to lessen its hold. They never should have left him there. There had to have been a way to save themselves and Felipe.

"There is one other thing I need to tell you, Olivia." Avery pulled a file out of the stack on a table. "Felipe's name sounded familiar, so I started digging through my paperwork to find out where I'd seen his name before. Olivia, please understand, I know this is difficult, but did you know that your father and Felipe were brothers?"

"Brothers?" Olivia's voice caught. "No, that can't be true. Where did you get that information?"

"I dug up every mention I could find on the Cártel de Rey

in our files, going back four decades. According to one of the sources, Antonio and Felipe used to run the cartel together. Then about thirty years ago, something happened between them, and they split up, eventually causing rifts in their territories."

Olivia's head spun. Somehow, in some crazy illogical way, everything was beginning to make sense. The secrets hadn't stopped with her mother and Valez. Felipe had known the truth about Valez because he'd been a part of it all.

"There have been rumors circulating for months that La Sombra is dying and grooming a replacement."

Olivia sat back down on the couch and leaned forward, bracing her arms against her thighs. She'd noticed that Felipe had lost weight and seemed . . . different.

Avery continued on. "I know this is hard, Olivia, but what do you know about Felipe's relationship with your father?"

"Not very much." Olivia looked at Avery and tried to digest her question. She didn't want to deal with any of this. "Felipe and my father . . . I know they met at least once years ago, maybe twice. But I don't think they were friends, if that's what you mean."

Of course, all she had was the word of her mother and what she'd seen.

"Are you sure about that?"

"I never saw them together, and my father never mentioned him, but Felipe . . . When we were there at the cabin, Felipe told me he was in love with my mother . . . and that she was in love with him."

"Did Valez find out about their relationship?" Avery asked.

"Not as far as I know. Felipe told me my father would have killed him if he'd ever found out."

"Did Felipe ever talk about any involvement with the cartel?"

"Felipe?" Olivia narrowed her gaze, uncertain as to where

Avery was taking the conversation. "No. He never said anything about the cartel. Ever."

Avery's gaze shifted to Michael, then back to Olivia. "I know this might be difficult for you to hear, but we have evidence that Felipe was involved in the cartel also. That he disappeared for a while, but was still very much active."

Olivia felt her anger rise. This was nothing more than another crazy wild-goose chase in the wrong direction. And what did it matter anyway? Felipe was dead. "Felipe lived in a cabin in the woods with his dog. Kept to himself most of the time. Loved it when we visited, which was only a couple times of year. He was a hermit."

"What if he was there because he'd gone into hiding, Olivia?" Avery asked.

"No—"

"Avery's just looking for answers." Michael reached out and took her hand.

Tears welled in Olivia's eyes. "I know, it's just that you're looking in the wrong place."

She dug through the cluttered recesses of her mind, trying to unearth anything that connected Felipe to the cartel. He'd always been like a father to her and Ivan, much more even than her own father. Beyond his somewhat quirky behavior, she couldn't see him involved with the cartel.

Unless she'd simply ignored the truth like she'd done with her father. The thought made her sick. How easy it had been to see what she'd wanted to see and ignore what she didn't.

"Did he have any enemies?" Avery asked.

"I don't know." She reached up to rub her throbbing temple with her free hand. "Maybe. He did mention one time that he needed to keep a low profile for a while, but he didn't seem overly worried, and I never thought much about it."

"Did he ever have any visitors while you were there?"

She shook her head. "We didn't see him often, but when we did, he was always alone. I thought he preferred it that way." So many secrets had been kept. So many lies.

The room pressed in around her. Olivia struggled to breathe.

"I'm sorry." She pulled her hand away from Michael, unable to hold back the tears any longer, and ran toward the balcony.

CHAPTER
20

Olivia stepped out onto the chilly balcony overlooking the Atlanta skyline and drew in a ragged breath. A thin layer of snow covered the buildings framed by the green beltway in the backdrop. She tried to shake the feeling of being caged in, wondering by the time this was over how many more secrets would be uncovered.

When all of this *was* over, she was going to whisk Ivan away with her. They could move across the country. Disappear, somewhere safe, where her father could never find her. Except she wasn't sure there even was such a place.

Besides, maybe her father wouldn't come after her. Michael was the one he wanted. Michael was the one hiding from the police and searching for evidence that would take down Antonio Valez. Which meant that when all of this was over, there was the very real possibility that her father would spend the rest of his life in prison.

But Michael—the man she should resent was also one of the reasons she wanted to stay.

Emily stepped out onto the balcony, hair pulled back into a neat ponytail, with her double-breasted vintage coat and knee-high leather boots. She handed the wool jacket she carried to Olivia. "You're going to freeze out here."

Olivia took the coat and nodded her thanks as she slipped it on. She'd barely even noticed the cold.

"I wanted to make sure you're okay," Emily said.

"My nerves are a bit . . . strung out. I just needed some fresh air."

Emily rested her hand on Olivia's arm and caught her gaze. "If anyone can figure out what's going on right now, it's the team working inside. You can trust them."

Olivia nodded, wanting to believe her. "I want you to know I appreciate everything you've done for me. The clothes . . . the encouragement . . ."

For making her feel as if she weren't an outsider.

Emily smiled. "We'll have to go shopping together when this is all over. I have a few places where I can always find something unique."

"I'd like that." Almost as much as she liked the friendship Emily was handing her.

"Besides," Emily said, "our family owes you for saving Michael. I'm still trying to absorb the fact that he's alive. It seems like yesterday when we received the news that he'd been killed."

"I can't imagine what you've gone through."

"I think you can."

Fresh pain washed over Olivia, leaving her raw emotions feeling exposed. "Felipe was like a second father to Ivan and me. It's still hard to believe he's gone."

"You've been through a lot in the past couple days."

"How did you deal with the news of Michael's death?" Olivia asked.

Emily stared out across the city. "Michael's presumed death was hard on all of us, but I guess the fact that I knew he'd been doing what he knew was right helped in a small way. Unfortunately, even trying to make the world a better place doesn't always guarantee a happy ending."

"What about when you find out your family's running with the cartel?" Olivia asked. "How do you justify that?"

"I don't know, but I can tell you this. That fact doesn't influence Michael one bit. He asked me to put in a good word for him. He likes you. A lot."

Olivia brushed her hair back from her face and turned to Emily. "Which is exactly what scares me. I don't meet a lot of men my age—or shall I say, men I can see myself being with. They usually end up too busy with their career or on the other end of the spectrum, living with their mothers."

Emily laughed. "Believe me, I know the feeling. It took me a long time to find a man I can trust."

"Mason?"

A blush swept over Emily's cheeks. "Our whole relationship was completely unexpected. There was always a chemistry between us, I guess, but I was just the baby sister of his best friend. Everything that's happened over the past two weeks has reminded me what's important in life, along with the uncertainties life often throws at us."

"Michael told me a little bit about Charlie and how he ended up being a dirty cop."

Emily's gaze dropped. "I'm still trying to work through those emotions. Still trying to get the picture out of my head of what happened when he died. All I know for sure right now is that it'll take some time."

Olivia leaned against the railing, wondering how long it would take her to work through her own father's betrayal. "So how did you let go and trust? Especially after what happened with Charlie?"

"I'm finding it's not easy," Emily said. "But when you find the right person, in the end it's a decision you make to believe in that person. And the reality is that there are good men out there. Charlie betrayed me, but I know I can't generalize that all men are evil because of him."

"It still scares me. I'm suddenly faced with the realization that my father isn't the man I thought he was or—at the least—wanted him to be. It suddenly makes me question all of my relationships and why I didn't see the truth in front of me."

"I know I had to keep reminding myself that God didn't give me a spirit of fear and timidity," Emily said, "but of power, love, and self-discipline."

"Maybe it's time I grabbed on to that truth."

Mason and Michael walked out on the balcony, bringing with them a gust of hot air from the hotel room.

"Are we interrupting?" Mason slid his arms around Emily's waist.

"Yes." Emily smiled, then let him kiss her lightly on the lips. "Olivia and I have been talking . . . getting to know each other."

Michael stopped beside Olivia, making her long for him to gather her into his arms and kiss her too.

"Any more news?" Olivia asked.

"Not about Felipe," Michael said. "But I decided to try tracking down one of my informants from back when I was working undercover in Atlanta. We're waiting right now to hear back from his parole officer. Jinx has a talent for gathering information, which means if anyone has insight into what's going on within the local cartel right now, he will."

Olivia rested her hand briefly against his chest. "You walk outside this building, and they won't be able to protect you, Michael."

"I'll be okay. I promise."

She started toward the door with Mason and Emily, but Michael stopped her. "Olivia? Wait . . ." He grasped her fingertips. "Do you have a second?"

───────

As Mason and Emily stepped back into the hotel room, Michael let go of Olivia's hand, still trying to process the longing

she'd awakened inside him. There'd never been room for a serious relationship in his life. Never been someone he wanted
to make room for. He'd dated here and there, but finding that
person who changed the way he looked at life, who made him
want to find a place for her, was something altogether different.

"Is everything okay?" she asked.

"I wanted to ask you the same question. You've been through
a lot the past few days, and now this news about Felipe . . ."

"Part of me feels like jumping into a hole and hiding. The
other part of me wants to get up and fight. The bottom line is
that I'm still trying to sort through everything, but Emily helped
me put some perspective on a few things."

"I hope she didn't scare you off. I'm fully aware that our family can be a bit intimidating at first, and you haven't even met
my mother yet." Michael laughed. "She's the sweetest person
in the world, the best cook, and full of southern charm, but she
can also be a bit intense."

"I like your family, actually." Olivia felt some of the fear
start to fade. "Though, Emily did warn me about you and your
untamed ways."

"My untamed ways?" Michael glanced back at the partially
open curtains framing the sliding door. So much for his family
being on his side. "You can't be serious—"

"I'm kidding. She did tell me, though, that you'd asked her
to put in a good word for you. Do you think you need that?"

He swallowed hard, her smile making his heart pound. "Do I?"

"I'd say you're doing pretty good on your own."

He let out a slow sigh of relief. He wanted to tell her how he
felt, but it had been a long time since he'd let a woman in his life.
And that wasn't the only issue facing them. They were currently
standing in a lull in the midst of a storm, with no end in sight.

But for now, he was having a hard time looking past the moment. "I've made it a rule to never fall for someone I'm working

with, let alone someone I'm protecting, but sometimes—this time—my heart is refusing to listen."

Her smile broadened. "So this isn't some form of rescuer syndrome?"

"Far from it. All I see right now is a beautiful woman who challenges me with her strength and heart."

"So what are you going to do about it, Michael Hunt?"

He smiled and ran his thumb down her cheek. "I can think of a few things I'd like to do right now."

His heart raced, knowing the crazy reality was that he was falling for the daughter of the man he'd sworn to destroy. Her father wanted to kill him, while all he wanted to do was kiss her. He pushed Valez out of his mind, bent down, and did just that. Anticipation of their first kiss met every expectation as she melted into his arms and deepened the kiss.

The blast of heat from the hotel room rushed onto the balcony. Michael pulled away from Olivia, his arms still wrapped around her waist, and frowned at Mason's bad timing.

Mason shot them both a weak grin. "I'm sorry to interrupt, but we just heard from Jinx's parole officer. We've got an address."

CHAPTER
21

Michael turned onto the familiar street in one of the west Atlanta suburbs, hoping they'd made the right decision to track down Jinx. Time was running out, and chasing a false lead would waste what precious little they had of it left. But if Jinx was going to talk to anyone, it would be him, so at the moment it was a risk he was going to have to take.

He shook off any lingering doubts and focused on the run-down neighborhood with its vacant lots, gutted storefronts, and shoddy duplexes that sat waiting for a string of developers to step in and revitalize the once-thriving neighborhood.

It had always bothered him that television painted a portrait of most drug dealers as men like Valez, who could afford fast cars and loose women. The truth was that most of the dealers he'd had contact with over the years had a hard time simply keeping a roof over their heads. Their days were spent trying to get enough cash to avoid being evicted while feeding their addiction. It was a horrid life that far too many found impossible to escape.

Mason grabbed a piece of gum from the console between them and peeled off the wrapper. "Are you sure this guy can help?"

"If anyone will have information on what's about to go down,

Jinx will have it. It's been awhile since I've seen him, but he owes me a favor or two." Michael glanced at his former partner and saw the frown on his face. "What's wrong?"

"Still trying to absorb everything that's happened since your text." Mason scrunched up the wrapper and dropped it in the litter bag hanging on the gearshift. "In some ways, it's easy to forget that you've been 'dead' the past eight months, until something's said that brings it all back."

Michael nodded. Mason was right.

"Driving together feels like old times, yet at the same time, everything has changed."

"I'm still trying to take it all in myself."

He slowed down as they passed a row of apartment buildings. There was a marked police car a quarter of a mile ahead. He turned left, opting for the back way into the neighborhood. With every police officer in the city looking for him, he couldn't take any chances he didn't have to.

"Funny how you can step out of the picture for so long, yet still expect everything to be the same when you return," he said. "Except clearly it isn't. Everything feels familiar, but there's still that feeling that something's off."

"I guess it's true that life goes on with or without us."

"Like you and Emily?" He posed the question, needing the distraction from the current situation. Like his former partner, love—or at least attraction—seemed to have taken him by surprise. He was still trying to decipher the unexpected rush of emotions that came over him when Olivia looked at him. Unexpected. Unpredictable. He knew he shouldn't have kissed her, but kissing Olivia had only managed to cement those feelings he knew now he wanted to explore. When all of this was over, he planned to ask her out on a proper date and see what came of it.

Mason looked at him incredulously. "You still don't approve?"

"Actually I do approve, but that doesn't mean that it isn't going to take a bit of time for me to get used to all the changes. I think part of me expected life to stand still while I was gone, and that . . . that certainly didn't happen." Michael turned onto Jinx's street. "Besides, when it comes to Emily, I'm just doing my job."

"Your job?"

"As a big brother. It's my responsibility to protect my little sister from the likes of scoundrels like you."

"A scoundrel? Really?"

Michael laughed, helping to break some of the tension of the morning. "You know I couldn't choose a better brother-in-law, if it comes to that one day."

"Well, I'm glad to hear that, though I can't say I was planning to ask for your approval."

"You always did have a stubborn streak."

"Tell me more about Jinx," Mason said, bringing them both back to the present.

"Last I heard, he's been toeing the line pretty well, but I'm pretty sure he's kept his ties with the cartel. At least he should have some information for us." Michael pulled up against the curb, then turned off the engine. "We're still half a block away, but we'll check out the neighborhood a little. The address his parole officer gave you is the same place he lived the last time I saw him."

Michael pulled the keys from the ignition and exited the car, hoping they'd get lucky and find Jinx on their first stop.

The neighborhood was filled primarily with duplexes and other lower-end houses. At least a third of them looked empty, with plywood over the windows and overgrown grass in the yards. A group of kids played basketball in a vacant lot down the street.

"This reminds me of where I grew up," Mason said.

Michael nodded at Jinx's house. "There it is. And I recognize the car in the driveway. Jinx never could get rid of anything."

An old junker sat in the carport. Jinx was reaching for the car door when Michael saw him.

Michael started up the driveway. "Jinx . . . it's been a long time."

Jinx hesitated, then started running toward the back of the house.

"Jinx!"

Mason threw Michael an apologetic glance. "You up for this, partner?"

"Not sure I have a choice. I'll take the back. You cut him off around the front."

Michael felt the sharp jerk in his rib cage, and instantly regretted the movement. Pushing through the pain, he ran under the carport, ducking beneath a ladder hanging from the ceiling.

Jinx slipped into a narrow alleyway behind the house, then headed south.

"I just want to talk with you, Jinx," Michael shouted.

Jinx turned again onto a small side street, allowing Mason to cut off his only escape route and giving Michael the chance to wrestle him to the ground.

Michael paused to catch his breath and make a mental note to take some more pain relievers once they were back in the car while Mason slapped a pair of handcuffs on the fugitive.

Jinx squirmed into a sitting position. "I heard you was dead."

"As you can see, I'm alive and kicking. And I said I just wanted to talk."

"Sorry. I got a couple goons after me for a few . . . unpaid debts. Didn't know it was you, considering I thought you was dead."

"Fortunately, that rumor wasn't true." Michael kept his tone

casual. "So, my partner had a talk with your parole officer earlier today."

Jinx held Michael's gaze. "I ain't done nothin' wrong."

"I'm happy to hear you've been staying out of trouble." Michael grabbed Jinx's arm and pulled him to his feet. "But personally, I'm getting too old for this. A bit of cooperation would
have gone a long way in softening me up. Because now, not only
do I need something from you, but I'm in pain."

"That's not my problem."

"Really?" Michael asked. "I'm sure if I did a bit of digging,
I'd find something I could take you in for."

Michael caught the fear in the man's eyes. Jinx might have a
habit of playing on the wrong side of the law, but he wasn't stupid.
He'd learned long ago how to play the system to his advantage.

"So how have you been?" Michael asked.

"I've been workin' long hours. Got a job not too far from
here."

"Good for you. At the moment, we need some information,
and as I remember, you were pretty good at knowing what was
happening on both sides of the fence."

"My days of being an informant are over."

"Think of it as a get-out-of-jail-free card. There are rumors
of a list. Dirty cops working for the cartel. What do you know
about it?"

"That I'm smart enough not to get involved in somethin'
stupid like that."

"Good answer, but we need information. We know you've
been in contact with Bernie, which, as you know, is a violation
of your parole."

"He gave me a lead on a job. Nothin' more, I swear."

"And I'm supposed to believe that." Michael turned to Mason.
"I say we haul him down to the station and book him for fleeing
a police officer."

"I told you, I'm clean. I'm not goin' back there."

"Then tell us what you know, and we'll put in a good word to your parole officer."

Jinx stared down the street. "Fine, but first take off the handcuffs and come inside. I don't need no one seein' me talkin' to cops."

Michael smiled. "You've got a deal."

Inside the duplex Jinx dumped a load of laundry onto the floor, nodding to the leather couch across from him. He lit up a cigarette and sent a puff of smoke into the already stale air.

Michael let out a low whistle as he looked around the place. Jinx had learned how to live under the radar, but clearly that didn't mean he was willing to give up certain luxuries, starting with a sixty-inch flat-screen TV with surround sound and a three-piece leather furniture set. A soccer game played on the screen, sound muted. Pizza boxes sat on the kitchen table beside a two-liter bottle of Coke.

"You've done well for yourself," Michael said.

"I get by okay."

Mason crossed the carpet and cracked the blinds on the front window. Other than the wind blowing through the line of trees out front, the street was quiet.

"I seen you on the news last night. Did you kill those guys?"

Michael sat down across from Jinx. "Just like the rumors of my death, don't believe everything you hear on the news."

"So what's all this about? I need to be at work in forty-five minutes."

"Tell us what you know about that list."

"Who says I know anything?" Irritation flickered in Jinx's eyes. "I'm clean now, remember?"

"And smart enough to keep tabs on what's going on, in order to make sure you benefit from that knowledge."

"A man's gotta protect himself. Knowing what's going on has

always worked good for me." Jinx let out a sharp huff while Michael waited for him to answer. "They call it the Canary List. It's a list of dirty cops and government guys paid off by the cartel."

"What else do you know?" Michael asked.

"There's a turf war gettin' fueled up. Some say La Sombra's involved."

"Do you know who La Sombra is?"

Jinx stilled, and glanced to the right and left. He ignored the question and said instead, "I've heard rumors someone is trying to take over."

"Who?"

"I'd start lookin' into a man by the name of Julio Salazar," Jinx said. "He hasn't made much noise yet, but they're sayin' he's quickly makin' his way up the ladder."

"So Salazar's planning to take over?" Michael said.

"There're rumors of a hit," Jinx said.

"Any idea how this is going to play out?"

"No, but from what I've heard, Salazar's plannin' somethin' big."

"Like what? A bomb?"

"You know of anything bigger?" Jinx said with a sneer.

Michael ignored the jab. "Is Salazar the one who tried to take out Valez earlier this year?"

"Maybe. This time, though, he wants to make sure everybody knows who the new boss is. Make a statement to stop any future uprisings," Jinx said.

Michael felt a chill race through him. That wasn't how the cartel normally worked. At least not on this side of the border.

"Where?" Mason asked.

"I don't know, but it'll be soon."

"How do we stop it?"

Jinx shook his head. "Stop it? You don't cross these people

and live to tell about it. They have resources even the police don't have."

"Do you know anything else?" Michael asked.

"I know you ain't the only one wantin' that list o'names."

"Who else is looking for it?" Michael asked.

Jinx looked up and caught his gaze. "Salazar."

"Because whoever gets ahold of that list," Mason said, "will be one step closer to controlling the entire territory."

"My, my, ain't you the smart one." Jinx stubbed his cigarette out. "You better hope those smarts can keep you alive, if you go after Salazar."

Michael walked to the front window and looked out again. "Sorry to interrupt the reunion, but we've got company."

"Who is it?"

"An unmarked car with what looks like a couple of detectives."

Jinx frowned. "You went and got me in trouble? Even after I told you all that stuff?"

"I don't think they're after you, Jinx. Mason, we got about thirty seconds to get out of here before they find us."

"You told them where I am—"

"No one knows we're here, except your parole officer."

Jinx hesitated. "Where'd you park?"

Michael pointed. "A few doors down."

Jinx started toward the back of the house. "We gotta go over the back fence. Follow me!"

Michael hesitated briefly. *Over the back fence? Right.*

They were banging on the door. "Jinx Cawley? Police! We have a warrant for your arrest."

Michael was the last one out the back door. He slammed it shut behind him.

CHAPTER
22

Michael scaled the fence at the back of Jinx's property, biting back the pain that shot through his rib cage. He landed on his feet in a puddle of mud in the neighbor's backyard. Like it or not, he was definitely getting too old for this. Of course, Tomas and his hit squad hadn't helped either.

He ran behind Mason and Jinx toward the neighbor's side gate, noting the wooden doghouse in the corner of the yard. *Great.* The last thing they needed right now was yet another complication to their escape.

The three men slipped through the gate into the front yard and slammed it shut, just as a German shepherd rounded the corner of the house. Michael stopped to catch his breath, bracing his hands against his knees, his lungs burning.

"You okay, man?" Mason asked.

"Yeah, but as soon as this is over, I'm applying for a job as a greeter at my local hardware store."

"Funny."

Jinx looked back at them like they were crazy. "Come on, man!"

They made their way through the yard of a vacant house toward their parked car. Michael hit the button on his key fob, and all three men jumped into the car. Michael took the wheel, zigzagging through the narrow streets for a good ten minutes, until he finally pulled into the back of a deserted parking lot.

"You going to be okay?" Michael said, as Jinx opened the car door.

"Yes, but just don't forget one thing," Jinx said before getting out.

"What's that?"

"After this," Jinx said, "we're even." He took off running and disappeared.

Michael stepped out of the car onto the pavement, anger from the encounter still seeping through him. "If the arrest warrant was just a ruse, how did they know we were there?"

"I don't know." Mason walked around the car, then leaned against the front. "I was sure we weren't followed."

"Me too."

He'd driven using every trick in the book to lose any tails. Either he'd lost his touch, or they'd found another way to track them.

"They used a tracking device on Gizmo's collar to find us the first time," Michael said.

"You think they're tracking my car?"

"If they were tracking your car, they wouldn't have bothered going to Jinx's house. They'd have been waiting for us when we got back to the car."

"What about Jinx's parole officer?" Mason asked. "It wouldn't be the first time when one had been bought to look the other way. Maybe if we found that list, his name would be on it."

"Or maybe the visit was legit."

But from the look on Mason's face, neither of them believed this was simply a coincidence.

"I'll call Tory," Mason said, as he took his phone from his pocket. "She'll be able to find out if there's a warrant out for Cawley."

A minute later, Mason hung up the call. "She can't find any official record of anyone being called to that address, but she's going to keep looking into it."

"So they were either dirty cops or men posing as cops, which means they had to have found out where we were going from a dirty cop."

"These guys are smart, Michael. We thought the leak had been plugged with the death of Charlie, but this goes much deeper."

Michael scuffed his shoe against the pavement, knowing exactly what his partner was thinking. Somehow they'd managed to land smack-dab in the middle of a turf war.

"We need to get ahold of that list," Michael said. "Because people are going to die if we don't stop this."

"I know."

"What about the hotel room?" Michael watched a line of starlings congregating on the power line. The worry in his gut was growing. They needed that list. "Do you think they're safe?"

The intensity of his emotions surprised him. Especially surprising was how Olivia was included in the same, intense concern he felt for his family. Working undercover might have taught him to control his emotions, but Olivia had managed to cross his boundaries, something no other woman had ever done before. Taking risks with his own life was one thing. He wasn't willing to risk hers. Not even if it meant losing Valez.

Mason shoved his hands into his pockets. "We could change locations, but we run the risk of being found no matter where we are."

"I know."

"Which is why I think the hotel is probably the safest place right now. Tory's made sure all of our electronics are clean, and she's swept for bugs and tracking devices. I don't know what else to do."

Michael would have preferred to keep the team limited to just his family and Mason, but he trusted Avery, her judgment, and her team's expertise. And he wasn't sure they had a choice. He couldn't keep them all safe on his own.

"What now?" Michael asked.

Mason shoved his phone into his pocket. "For now, let's get going. You shouldn't be out here."

Michael tugged on the edge of his cap. "I can't stay holed up in that hotel room, either. I promised Olivia I'd take care of her and her brother. Because of me, their lives are in danger."

Mason turned to get into the car, then stopped. "What about Olivia?"

Michael's defenses rose. "What about her?"

"You know I have to ask the question before we go any further. Do you believe she's telling you the complete truth?"

"What?" Michael frowned. "You think she's in on all of this with Valez? You think she let him know we were coming to see Jinx?"

"Honestly, I don't know, but neither do I think we can overlook the possibility. She is his daughter."

"Who saved my life, risking both hers and her brother's in the process. She didn't have to do that. And now you want to start pointing fingers at her?"

"All I know is that someone knew we were coming. We're out here risking our lives to find out the truth, and if she is involved in this—"

"You're wrong."

Mason held up his hands and moved around to the front of the car to where Michael stood, his voice rising. "Before you start blaming me, don't tell me you haven't at least considered the idea. Or are you so caught up in her irresistible charm that you've simply accepted everything she's told you at face value?"

Michael clenched his fists. "This has nothing to do with how I feel about her."

"It has everything to do with how you feel about her. You're attracted to her. I get that. But you can't let those feelings get in the way of the truth. You of all people know that."

"She saved my life—"

"I don't care if she saved the president of the United States' life. She's the daughter of a cartel leader, yet you're telling me she knew nothing about his involvement. So forgive me if I'm not on board a hundred percent, but I'm starting to have a few doubts about your girlfriend. How does someone that close to Valez not know the truth?"

Michael took a step back, fighting the urge to slug his friend. "How many cases have you dealt with where friends and family were the last to know? How many women are shocked when their husbands walk out on them? Shocked that they've been having an affair or gambling away their savings? The truth is that we see what we want to see."

"Exactly." Mason looked up and caught his gaze. "I need to make sure that you're not seeing what you want to see instead of the truth."

Michael bit back a sharp response as his defenses began to fall. As much as he wanted to deny it, Mason had a valid argument. It was telling that neither man was worried about Ivan's trustworthiness. They both knew that Olivia was the weak spot in Michael's professional armor.

"We have to look at everyone," Mason continued. "And if you're wrong about her, you're putting us all at risk."

Michael stared across the empty lot where weeds had popped up through the broken pavement, between shattered glass and empty bottles. The problem was, Mason *was* right about some things. This had gone far enough. It was time to put an end to it.

"Maybe it's time I turn myself in."

"I'm not asking you to do that," Mason said. "You know I'd do anything for you. I'd do anything for your family, but we're all putting our lives and our jobs on the line here. We have to be able to trust each other. And just like I have to trust you, I have to be able to trust her as well."

Michael slumped against the car, his emotions drained. "I know that she risked her life to save mine. She could have walked off the island without me. She could have dumped me off somewhere that first night, but she didn't."

Mason caught Michael's gaze. "Do you trust her completely?"

Michael nodded. "Yes. Completely. Have Tory look into her background and check her out for yourself—"

"She already did."

"Did anything come back?"

"Except for a speeding ticket fourteen months ago, no. She doesn't seem to be close to her father beyond a visit once or twice a year and the support money he sends her that seems to go primarily to her brother's schooling."

"I trust her, Mason. And it's not because she's somehow managed to make her way into my heart." Admitting it out loud made it seem real. "Am I crazy?"

Mason shot Michael a smirk as he headed for the car. "Love has a tendency to make you feel like you're crazy. I know. Emily's managed to turn my world upside down, but I wouldn't have it any other way. I just wanted . . . needed to make sure."

"In the meantime," Michael said, "we need to find that list."

———

Olivia dumped the last swirl of coffee down the sink and started a fresh pot. At the rate they were going, they'd run out of coffee before the afternoon was over. But a potential coffee shortage was the least of her worries. Michael still wasn't back. Avery and her team might not fully trust her, but she needed to do something to keep from worrying about him.

She marched into the living room and stopped in front of

Avery, who was writing on the white board. It was time to prove she was trustworthy.

"I want to be a part of this investigation," she began. "I can't sit around making coffee and reading the hotel directory while the rest of you work. In case you've forgotten, I'm a reporter. I know how to search for information, follow leads, and investigate. I might not be a detective like the rest of you, but I can dig up information with the best of them."

Avery nodded. "Okay."

Olivia paused. "Okay?"

"I do have something you can do, actually." Avery grabbed a laptop from the desk where Ivan was still working with Michael's father and handed it to her. "I've got a name for you. I need to know everything we can find out about Julio Salazar. Mason told Tory that according to Michael's informant, the man apparently has his sights on taking over Cártel de Rey. We need to know exactly what we're up against."

Olivia breathed out a sigh of relief. She didn't care if they were only placating her, she needed the distraction. Needed the chance to focus on anything besides the fact that Michael was out there, risking his life, and that Felipe's body was missing. Doing something productive was the only way she was going to make it through the next twenty-four hours.

"I'm on it."

She found an empty armchair in the corner of the room and went to work.

Tory picked up her phone across from her, read the text message, and frowned.

"Something wrong?" Olivia asked.

"It's nothing." Tory swept back a strand of dark hair behind her ear. "I just had to cancel my dinner plans for the third time this week."

"I'm sorry."

"We're both used to it, so there are no expectations other than my mother's for grandbabies. She doesn't understand how it can take me weeks just to get that first date."

Olivia chuckled as she clicked on the first link with Salazar's name. At least she wasn't the only one with relationship issues.

The information on Salazar was limited, but there was enough for her to put together a basic background that alluded to a connection to the cartel. She grabbed a pad of hotel stationery along with a pen someone had left on the table beside her. This might be the twenty-first century, but sometimes a pen and paper worked best.

Olivia started jotting down notes, trying not to worry about Michael. Trying not to think about his kiss. She'd spent so much of her life being the protector to both her mother after she got sick, and then to Ivan. Michael had made *her* feel protected, and she liked that feeling. But when this was over, things between them would change. And besides that, she had a pretty strong feeling that his southern-born mama wouldn't exactly welcome the daughter of a cartel kingpin into her family with open arms.

Still, as crazy as it seemed, part of her wanted to hold on to the dream fantasy, even if it was nothing more than a grand illusion that would vanish at the stroke of midnight like Cinderella's carriage turning back into a pumpkin.

Fifteen minutes later, she signaled to Avery that she'd found something.

"What have you got?" Avery asked.

Olivia started to answer when the hotel door opened and Michael and Mason walked in.

The men hung their coats on the coatrack, then walked into the room. Michael tossed his cap onto the table, fatigue masking his expression.

"You're limping," Olivia said.

"I'm fine." He shot her a smile. "Just the normal chasing

down a suspect and scaling security fences. Though I admit, it made me wish I was Ivan's age again."

Avery laughed. "Well, while you were out gallivanting, Olivia's been researching the name you sent us and was just about to tell me what she found."

"That's great." Michael turned to Olivia. "Did you find anything?"

"I did."

"Good," Mason said. "Because according to Jinx, Salazar is moving up the ranks and has plans to take over."

"Salazar's father had known ties to the cartel," Olivia said, "though most reports say that Julio never wanted anything to do with the drug empire. He's smart, well educated, and has somehow managed to stay so low profile that even his digital footprint is light. He has a squeaky clean bio."

"Too clean if you ask me," Michael said.

"You might be right, because I did find one interesting fact." Olivia glanced down at her notes. "According to one source, six years ago, Salazar's father was brutally murdered by La Sombra, and at the time, Salazar promised revenge."

"So Salazar killing La Sombra becomes a win/win situation," Michael said. "Not only does he avenge his father's death, but he gains new territory."

"Exactly." Avery grabbed her coat off the rack. "I'm leaving you all on your own for a bit. I'm going to talk to Jackson about looking through Michael's file at the medical examiner's office. In the meantime, Mason, see if you can track down Longhurst, the ME who signed off on Michael's death. I want to talk to him again as well. If he was paid off, like I've always suspected, it could help us connect the dots."

"You got it, boss."

Avery rubbed her hands together. She'd chosen to meet Jackson in the town center—still decked out with Christmas decorations and lights—and now wasn't at all certain the ambiance was worth having to face the dropping temperatures. She needed to talk to him on a professional level, as a medical examiner. But she also needed to talk personally with the man she'd fallen in love with.

A minute later, Jackson approached the bench where she waited, carrying two cups of coffee.

"Hey." She took one of the paper cups, smiling as he brushed his lips across hers, lingering just long enough to set her heart racing.

"We might have to do this more often," he said, smiling back.

"I agree, plus you're a lifesaver. I needed this." She took a long drink of the coffee, letting its heat spread through her chilled body, thankful for the distraction. And even more thankful for Jackson.

"When you told me where you wanted to meet," he said, "I thought you might be able to use warming up with a bit of pumpkin spice."

"It's perfect." She nodded toward the empty sidewalk lining

the shops and businesses. "I thought we could walk while we talk."

"Sure."

He matched her stride as they started down the sidewalk. Most of the stores, with their brick-face buildings, were decorated in holiday garlands and lights, but with the cold weather, the number of shoppers was minimal, making the setting quiet for now.

She offered him another smile, hoping he didn't notice the fear in her eyes. "Thanks for coming."

"You're welcome, though as a born-and-bred Texan, I have to admit, it's a bit too cold for me out in these lower-than-normal temperatures." He slipped his free hand into hers and laced their fingers together. "Why do I have a feeling you're about to cancel our dinner date?"

She shot him a weak smile. "I promise to make it up to you."

"Yes, you will, with one request attached."

"Anything."

"Hmmm . . . I was thinking of dinner, just you and me, and with no talks of mother-in-laws or wedding plans."

"Are you saying you don't like my mother?" she teased, throwing out the question more as procrastination than anything. The inevitable storm had already hit, but she knew if she didn't find the answers soon, the swells would eventually take her under.

"I love your mother almost as much as I love her fried chicken," Jackson said. "But I miss you. Since moving up the wedding—and all the work that's entailed—I don't think I've seen you alone for more than ten minutes."

She smiled back at him. "In about six weeks that will all change."

She'd much rather focus on the two of them and put aside everything else, but that wasn't possible—not with all that was happening.

"Married to the most beautiful woman in the world with seven days in the Caribbean." Jackson took another sip of his coffee. "Just you and me and a cruise ship . . . I'm already counting the hours."

Avery's mind longed to follow Jackson there, but instead, Michael's face kept flashing in front of her. Memories from the crime scene after the explosion. His funeral. And now . . . seeing him again. The distraction wasn't working.

"As soon as I wrap up the case I'm working on, I'm all yours. I promise. With no talk about cake flavors, flowers, or appetizers."

"Just so you don't forget I was right. Eloping is sounding better every day."

They slowed down in front of an open bakery, the scent of fresh-baked bread and pastries reminding her she'd skipped breakfast again.

Jackson reached up to stroke her cheek. "But we both know you didn't call to talk about wedding plans. What's wrong?"

Avery hesitated, wishing there was a way to delay the inevitable conversation. Talking about Michael's death was only going to make what had happened today feel all the more real.

"What is it?" he asked.

Avery took another sip of coffee. She'd gone back and forth in her mind on the drive over, unable to decide if she should tell Jackson that Michael was alive. Because once he knew the truth, he'd be honor bound to turn him in. Putting Jackson and his career at risk wasn't something she was prepared to do.

But on a personal level, neither did she want to start keeping things from the man she was about to marry.

"Avery . . ." He stopped and caught her gaze. "When I asked you to marry me, it meant I was ready to go through everything in life with you. The good, the bad, and the ugly. We're in this together."

"Then I don't know how else to tell you but to just come out and say it." Her voice caught. "Michael's alive, Jackson."

"He's alive?" She clearly had his full attention now. "I don't understand. How is that possible? The ME signed his death certificate, there was DNA evidence . . ."

"Trust me, I'm still struggling to figure everything out myself."

"Tell me what you know."

"I told you about the video of the gas station robbery and the rumors that he'd been spotted there."

"Yes."

"They aren't just rumors. I met with him this morning."

"You met with Michael?" Jackson asked. "What did he tell you?"

Avery started walking again, thankful it was too cold for most shoppers and dog walkers to be out in this weather. "It's a long story, and I don't have a lot of time to tell you everything now, but I do need your help. His life is in danger."

"You know I'll do anything I can, but I'm not sure how I can help. You know I wasn't working for the ME here when Michael . . . died."

"I know." She nodded. "But now, not only does the cartel have a hit out on him, there are people in the department who are convinced that if he really is alive, that he's guilty of murder and more. If he lets the chief know he's alive, he'll be arrested."

"What can I do?"

"You did the recent autopsy on Russell Coates, and as you know, we suspect that his death was an inside job, handled by someone who didn't want the information he had to get out, and if Michael's arrested . . ."

"They could just as easily do the same thing to him."

She nodded. "I can't lose my brother again, Jackson, but the police now believe he's responsible for the death of an FBI agent and for the convenience store shooting."

"And you believe he's telling the truth?"

"I know you've never met Michael, but trust me. He's not guilty. I've known men who'd betray their own mother if it was to their advantage, but nothing—not even the evidence stacked up against him—will convince me of Michael's guilt. Michael would die for his country before betraying it. And we've also got Ivan's eyewitness account of Agent Kendall's murder."

"Who else knows about all of this?"

She tossed her empty cup into a trash container as they walked past. "Mason. Emily. Tory, Levi, Carlos, and my father. We're holed up in a hotel, trying to figure out how to clear his name."

"You haven't brought the captain in on this?" he asked.

"I'm supposed to be working the case to track Michael down, but until we know what's going on and who's behind this, I'm afraid to trust anyone."

"You could lose your job over this, Avery."

"I know. And so could you, if you do what I ask." She studied Jackson's face as he struggled to take in what she'd just told him. "Which is why you can walk away from this right now, and I'll never bring it up again."

"What do you need me to do?"

She let out a sigh of relief at his response. "Donald Longhurst, the medical examiner who signed off on Michael's death, has already been interviewed, but I need to know what you know about the man."

"Longhurst . . ." Jackson slowed his steps. "He was a member of the committee that hired me, but I can't say I know much about him. He was a bit reserved, but not unfriendly. Very knowledgeable. He left a month . . . maybe six weeks after I was hired."

"What do you know about him personally?"

"Not much. He wasn't very social. Never saw him hang out with colleagues. I remember his mother was sick. Not sure what was wrong with her, but I know he took care of her. Don't think she was supposed to live much longer, but after he retired I never saw him again. I believe he has a daughter in the Atlanta area. He had a photo of her on his desk. I think her name was Sally . . . or Molly. I don't remember."

"Did you notice anything strange about him around the time of his retirement?"

Jackson shrugged. "Like I said, I didn't really know him enough to recognize any changes in his behavior."

"How hard would it be to alter DNA evidence, falsify a death certificate, and not get caught?"

"You'd have to breach the chain of evidence, but I suppose it wouldn't be impossible. Foolish and even risky, but not impossible."

"Enough money can make all kinds of things happen."

"So you think Longhurst was paid to change the results on the death certificate?"

"Yes."

"That's quite an accusation."

Avery hesitated, praying she wasn't running in the wrong direction. "I know, which is why we have to move carefully. But on the other hand, we don't have a lot of time."

"You know I'll do anything I can to help, Avery."

"I know, but before you agree too quickly, let me tell you exactly what I'm asking you to do. The captain knows that I'm looking into the possibility that Michael faked his death. What he doesn't know is that I've found him," she said. "I've been given permission by the captain to open up Michael's case. I need you to go back through the autopsy reports and see if you can find anything that stands out. If necessary, we'll exhume the remains of the body that's in the casket."

Avery's phone rang. "Mason?"

"We found Longhurst and the information you wanted from the files. He's living at his daughter's house."

"I'm on my way." Avery reached up and kissed Jackson's cheek. "We might have just caught another break. I'll call you as soon as I know something."

———

Thirty minutes later, Avery knocked on Molly Parker's door. A pretty woman with bright blue eyes opened the door, letting the scent of pine and baking cookies escape from inside the house.

"Can I help you?" she asked.

Avery held up her badge and introduced herself and Mason. "We're looking for Donald Longhurst."

"Just a minute." Ms. Parker stepped back into the house. "Dad, someone's here to see you."

A moment later, the former associate medical examiner, Donald Longhurst, a skinny man with a matching thin face and crooked nose, stepped into the doorway. "Is there a problem?"

"Dr. Longhurst," Avery began, "we're currently investigating the death of a Michael James Hunt, and we need to speak with you. You were in charge of his autopsy eight months ago and signed off on his death certificate?"

"You'll have to forgive me if I can't remember that case in particular . . ." Longhurst slipped his hands into his front pockets. "You must realize that I handled hundreds of cases a year. But I'm retired now and am no longer with the medical examiner's office."

"How long did you work as a medical examiner?" Avery interrupted.

"Thirty-five years, but—"

"I understand you had aspirations to be the chief medical examiner."

"I don't see how that has anything to do with this."

"Just answer my questions, please, Dr. Longhurst."

"I once had that career goal, but working as an associate was very satisfying."

"Satisfying, maybe, but not nearly as lucrative. I understand you have a bit of a gambling habit you struggle to support."

Dr. Longhurst pinched the bridge of his nose. "You know, that's none of your business."

"But you would agree that your finances are in a bit of a mess?" Avery asked.

Dr. Longhurst shut the door behind him and stepped out onto the long veranda. Definitely nervous. Definitely hiding something. "What does my financial situation have anything to do with any of the hundreds of autopsies I performed over the years?"

Avery pulled out a photo of her brother from the file she held. "This man was declared dead after a bomb explosion in a warehouse eight months ago, but we now have information that he is actually very much alive. Does that ring any bells?"

"I . . . yes . . . remember that case. While there was little left of the bodies, we found the DNA of Mr. Hunt at the crime scene."

"While I don't doubt that Mr. Hunt was at that warehouse that day, I do, however, question the fact that he died there, which brings me back to you. I want to know why you falsified Michael Hunt's death certificate."

"I don't know anything about falsifying—"

"I find that hard to believe, because according to your record, the case involving Mr. Hunt wasn't the first time something like this happened. Your tenure, Dr. Longhurst, was, in fact, marked by questions about accuracy several times, isn't that correct?" Avery said, not waiting for a response before she continued. "And if anything else were to show up, formal disciplinary action would have been taken against you."

"I told you, I don't know—"

Avery held up a piece of paper. "We have evidence that eight months ago, there was a payment deposited into your bank account in the amount of seventy-five thousand dollars."

Longhurst patted his front pocket and pulled out his reading glasses. "I've already spoken to the police about this case, and I explained that the money was from my mother's estate. She died this past year."

"This is not a statement from your local bank here in Atlanta, Dr. Longhurst. This is a deposit of seventy-five thousand dollars in an off-shore account we were able to link to you."

"No." Dr. Longhurst reached for the paper. "The only money I received was from my mother's estate."

"*Those* funds were deposited by the insurance company into your personal banking account."

"Then there must be some mistake."

"Like the mistake of falsifying autopsy papers?"

"No, I would never—"

Dr. Longhurst flipped over the paper as if looking for something to exonerate him, but it was too late.

Mason spoke up. "Game's over, Longhurst. We have further evidence of another large deposit into that same account eighteen months ago, and even more incriminating, we have records that prove who put it into your account."

Longhurst's face paled. "If you know who it is, then you'll know I'm going to need protection. They'll kill me if they know I've been talking to you."

"First tell us exactly what you were told to do."

"He told me I would find DNA at the scene from Mr. Hunt, and that I needed to ensure that he was listed as one of the fatalities in the explosion. But I never thought anyone would get hurt. You have to believe that."

"How very noble of you, Dr. Longhurst," Mason said. "But is that what you really thought? What about Mr. Hunt's family, who watched their son and brother buried, never knowing that he was alive out there somewhere, maybe even needing their help?"

Dr. Longhurst rubbed his fingers against his temples. "I figured if I was doing a favor for the cartel, he deserved whatever he got just for being mixed up with them."

"And did you know if that man was, indeed, 'mixed up with them' as you put it?"

"No, but—"

"But you decided to play God."

"I didn't have a choice. He threatened to hurt my daughter if I didn't comply."

"I know how hard that had to have been, trust me. A week ago, I almost lost my daughter," Avery said, pulling out her handcuffs. "But you could have gone to someone instead of taking a payoff that hurt other innocent people."

Dr. Longhurst's expression darkened. "So is Mr. Hunt alive?"

"You know how the cartel treats its victims. There's a good chance that they tortured him and you helped them cover it up."

"I never meant to hurt anyone."

"Dr. Longhurst," Avery said, "you're under arrest for falsifying autopsy reports and—"

"Wait, I need protection, and if you cut me a deal—"

"You lost out on making a deal the moment you signed on with the devil."

CHAPTER 24

Olivia stood up and paced the beige carpet of the hotel room as Michael debated with Avery—who'd just returned with Mason—on whether or not it was time to bring in the captain. She glanced at her watch for the umpteenth time, realizing that this decision wasn't the only thing bothering her. Ivan had been gone twenty-six minutes with Gizmo. And the fact that they'd sent an officer with him did little to ease her worry. She kept giving them more minutes. Believing that any second they'd come in the door, reminding her once again that she was overprotective when it came to him. Reminding her that there was nothing to worry about.

But after all that had happened over the past few days, not worrying was getting harder and harder. She wished she knew how to get rid of the constant knot in her stomach that had settled there over the past twenty-four hours. The only thing keeping her going was the reality that she didn't have to go through this alone. Michael, his father, his sisters, and the rest of them had swept in and set up the place until it looked like a war room. And they'd promised her they wouldn't stop until this was over.

"Olivia?" Emily called to her from the small kitchen. "Would you like some hot chocolate? I for one am tired of coffee."

Olivia joined her in the kitchen, thankful for the distraction. "That would be great. Thanks."

Emily dumped two packets of powder into empty mugs, then filled them with hot water. "Are you hanging in there?"

Olivia hesitated, wondering if she should stay quiet. Michael had been right. Ivan wasn't a child anymore, and she did tend to overreact.

"I guess I'm doing just that . . . hanging in there."

"I know this is hard on you." Emily's gaze softened. "I have a feeling we're a lot alike." She leaned against the counter. "I don't even want to be in that other room right now, because I think too much, and definitely worry too much."

Olivia grabbed a spoon and started stirring the lumps of powder, thankful she wasn't the only one who overprocessed everything.

"I've been thinking what you said about fear . . . and Michael." Olivia felt a heat cross her face at the thought of Michael. "My main concern is—and has always been—making sure Ivan is okay. Michael's entrance into my life has been—well, like you said—completely unexpected."

"I'm the perfect case in point. Sometimes love comes unexpectedly. So the question becomes, what does your heart say?"

Olivia didn't even have to try to imagine those blue eyes smiling down at her. Or what those eyes did to her heart.

"There's a chemistry between us I can't ignore," she said. "In some ways I feel as if I've known him forever, but the reality is, I haven't, and that's where my heart starts warning me to back off."

"That's fear speaking again."

Olivia nodded. "But Michael and I . . . we live in two different worlds. I'm not sure I could handle waiting for him to come home every night, not knowing if something might have happened to him. Even now, I find my stomach in knots, worried that something's going to go wrong. That in the end my father and whoever else is involved will win, and I'll lose him before I ever know what might have been between the two of us."

"Don't borrow trouble, as my father always used to say. This situation won't last forever. And when it's over, I'd say both of you will have earned some time off to explore whatever feelings have come to the surface."

Excitement mixed with sweet anticipation spread through Olivia. So much had changed over the past few days, both good and bad. Only time would tell which was going to outweigh the other.

"I have no idea what the future holds," Emily said, "but Michael needs someone in his life like you. I can see it in his eyes. You make him happy."

"The question is, can I be with someone who lives on adrenaline? You thought you lost him once, and the chances of him finding himself in another situation like that are very, very real."

"You're right." Emily nodded. "Michael's a cop, and nothing's going to change that. Not even falling in love."

"So how do you live with the fear that he might not come back? Or that Mason won't come back? My life is predictable. Michael's life is more like a constant firecracker in a hornet's nest. I'll be honest, the thought terrifies me."

"I might come from a family of cops, but you can bet it scares me too. I'm a teacher with a pretty predictable life. I might spend my days teaching about revolutionaries and wars, but my own day-to-day life is routine. I eat oatmeal and blueberries for breakfast, drive the same route to school every day. I buy Chinese takeout on Tuesdays and eat dinner with my family on Wednesday nights. Falling in love with an undercover cop who also thrives on adrenaline wasn't exactly on my to-do list."

"Maybe a bit of unpredictability isn't such a bad thing for

the two of us after all." Olivia's smile faded as she glanced toward the door.

"So what else is bothering you?" Emily asked.

"Ivan . . . he's been gone too long."

Michael stepped into the kitchen with an empty coffee cup in his hand and grabbed the half-full pot off the counter. "I'm sure he's fine. This hotel was chosen because of the security."

Olivia frowned, hoping he hadn't heard the first part of their conversation. But no matter what Michael thought about the safety of the hotel, they shouldn't have let Ivan take Gizmo out. These weren't ordinary circumstances. Whoever was after them was involved with the cartel, which meant these weren't run-of-the-mill thugs involved in petty crime. If they found Ivan . . . if they knew he'd witnessed a murder . . . knew he was the son of Antonio Valez . . .

She drew in a deep breath, trying to get rid of the doubts. She knew Michael was right. But letting go of the fear wasn't easy.

Michael put a spoonful of sugar into his coffee, then set his mug on the counter. "You know, I could use a few minutes to stretch my legs."

"Did you and Avery come to an agreement?"

Michael nodded. "Before things progress further, we decided we have to let the captain know what's going on."

"Can you trust him?"

"I have no reason not to at this point. In the meantime, let's go for a walk."

She nodded, then grabbed the coat Emily had loaned her before heading out the door with him.

In the hallway, Olivia pressed the Down button, then watched the elevator's numbers count as it made its way slowly to their floor.

"Thank you," she said.

"I know what it's like to worry about family."

"How does it feel to be back with yours again?" she asked.

"Surreal. I've thought about being together again so many times over the past few months. And then more recently, I wondered if I ever would see them again."

"It's clear how much they love you."

"Which I'm very thankful for." Michael chuckled as the elevator finally dinged and its doors slid open. "Even though my sisters are always trying to mother me, and Mama tends to be more of a mother hen now that we're grown and have been out of the house for a decade. Nothing happens without her either knowing about it, or finding out soon afterward. But she does make up for her inquisitive nature with invites to a home-cooked meal a couple nights a week. You can't get much better than her chicken fried steak and banana pudding, unless it's her Christmas dinner. I'll have to bring you to one of our family dinners."

She caught his gaze in the mirror as they stepped into the empty elevator, wondering if he'd still want to invite her to a family dinner when all of this was over. Because she'd say yes. She loved the sense of family he brought with him. The stability that came with his family, despite the hazards of the career he'd chosen to follow.

"I don't think I'd mind putting up with a bit of overbearing mothering if it included meals like that." She laughed as the elevator approached the lobby. "Ivan's had to put up with my cooking for the past ten or so years unless we go to a church potluck or the occasional invite to someone's house. He usually gets something from a box or from the freezer, though I am known for my death-by-chocolate brownies."

"Oh, now that's definitely not a bad rep to have."

"Ivan's actually a better cook than I am. I watch cooking shows, then pull out the handy frozen lasagna."

He laughed as they stepped out of the elevator into the lobby and headed toward the grassy area in the back. Olivia drew in a deep breath, still trying to settle her nerves. Worrying had been a foolish waste of energy. Of course Ivan was fine. She knew him. He tended to get distracted and lose track of time. How many times had she found him sitting in front of his computer at two in the morning, wrestling with some problem he'd been trying to solve? Today was no different.

But even those reassurances did little to ease her worry. Everyone she saw was a possible enemy working for her father. The man in a dark suit talking on his cell phone, clearly angry about something. The couple sitting beside a stack of luggage. Even the manager behind the counter looked suspicious.

Michael opened the door and Olivia walked past a stack of chairs. There was a thin layer of snow on the ground, though the sky had cleared up, with promises of warmer weather by midafternoon.

She glanced across the lawn, looking for her brother.

"He's not here, Michael."

Michael took her hand. "Don't worry. I'm sure they're just around the corner."

"Gizmo?" She called the dog, trying to mask the desperation in her voice. "Come here, boy!"

The familiar surge of panic raced through her. She was eighteen again. She'd taken Ivan to the carnival, knowing he was determined to ride the roller coaster even though he was barely tall enough. They'd let him through, though she'd been convinced he'd been standing on his tiptoes.

She'd waited for him at the exit, minutes clicking by in slow motion. And then the ride had ended, and he never got off.

She found him fifteen minutes later. He'd chickened out and slipped out of the line but had been too embarrassed to tell her. The threat might have been minimal, but she'd never forgotten those moments of panic. Just like she'd never forgotten her mama's dying wish that she make sure Ivan stayed safe.

Olivia stood in the middle of the green space, cold and scared. There was no sign of her brother.

"Michael . . ." She turned around to face him, her heart pounding. "They're gone."

The fenced-in area was quiet except for a young woman, bundled up in a hat and scarf, with a miniature poodle.

Olivia walked up to her, forcing a smile. "Did you see a young man, nineteen years old, and a dog? They would have been here a few minutes ago."

"Sorry . . . no. I just got here."

Olivia turned back to Michael. "We should check the parking lot."

Five minutes later, they stood on the edge of the parking lot, with no sign of Ivan or the dog.

Something caught her eye near the fence. A man lay motionless on the asphalt. "Michael . . ."

"It's the guard we sent with Ivan," Michael said, rushing toward the body.

Panic slowly seeped through her as Michael knelt down beside him and checked for a pulse.

"He's dead. Shot in the head."

"They took Ivan, Michael."

"I'll send someone out here, but I want you back inside immediately." He pulled out his phone as he hurried her in the direction of the hotel. "We can search the security cameras, as well as traffic cameras in the area. Wherever Ivan is, we're going to find him."

Olivia struggled to keep up with Michael as he shouted out instructions to his sister. He stopped outside the back entrance of the hotel, pulled out his keycard, and whisked her inside the building.

Something that had been nagging at her clicked as they stepped into the elevator. "What if someone took Ivan for leverage against my father? What if, in this war involving Salazar, La Sombra, and my father, we somehow both become prime targets?"

Michael's brow furrowed as the doors shut. "It's possible."

Olivia's throat constricted as she tried to speak. "Whoever it is, they won't think twice about killing him."

He gathered her into his arms. "Don't go there."

She rested her head against his shoulder, feeling the weight of the world against her as the elevator started moving.

"Avery's putting out an APB," he said, "and my father is on his way to hotel security to start checking all the videos. We'll find him."

She pulled back, her eyes wide with question. "Michael, what do you do when something horrible happens, when fear takes hold so deep you can hardly breathe?"

He pulled her against his chest, feeling the warmth of her closeness as the tears she'd bottled up over the past few days began to flow. "All I know to do is to dig deeper until you remember that God knows exactly what's happening at this very moment. He cares, and no matter what happens, He will never leave you or Ivan."

"You make it sound easy. Like if I wish hard enough, there'll be a silver lining when this is all over."

Her statement made him pause. It was easy to spout out words of advice. What was difficult was actually putting them into practice. Memories of sitting in that cottage, waiting for Tomas to pull the trigger, waiting to die, flashed in front of him. He'd made peace with God, but even that didn't take away the terror of facing death. They'd bound him and beat him, forcing him to dig deeper than he ever had.

He'd repeated every verse he could remember. *Even though*

I walk through the valley of the shadow of death, I will fear no evil . . .

I will fear no evil . . .

Surrounded by that evil's very presence had forced him to look at not just why there was evil, but to look to the One who would triumph over that evil.

"Michael?"

Her eyes pleaded with him to give her the answer. "It isn't easy. But I know He's there. Every moment. He's given me strength to face some of the darkest situations. And things haven't always turned out the way I've wanted them to. My brother-in-law was killed almost four years ago. Sometimes bad things happen to good people.

"So no, I can't promise you that everything is going to be okay, but I can promise you that we won't stop until we find Ivan. Until we put those who are responsible for this behind bars. But I've learned something else. Sometimes, you never get the answers to all the questions you ask. But sometimes, maybe that's okay."

"What do you mean?"

"Over the past few days and weeks, I've found everything that I ever believed in questioned and at times stripped away. I've been forced to look at God in a different light. Sometimes there simply aren't answers. At least not the answers we're looking for. Walking through the fire forces us to face God. To strip our souls of all of the charades we play, until we see only Him. And in the end, we know Him better."

Because God was good. God was truth. Even when he couldn't see the truth or get the answers he wanted.

Michael wanted to tell her how sorry he was for everything, wanted to find a way to fix everything . . . and tell her how he was falling in love with her.

He tried to shove the last thought back where it had come from, as the elevator doors slid open, but there was no going back. No matter how hard he tried to fight it, no matter what happened at the end of the day, his feelings for the woman walking beside him had blossomed into something he hadn't even known he wanted. They'd already moved passed the typical superficial chitchat most relationships started with. Playing the dating game wasn't what he wanted. He wanted a woman who could love him for who he was. Who encouraged him emotionally and spiritually, and yes, who made his heart race like he was that high school geek on a date with the prom queen.

He laced his fingers between hers as he checked the hallway, then hurried toward the room. There were so many things he wanted to tell her when this was over. So many questions he wanted to ask her. He wanted to spend the next six months and beyond getting to know her dreams and aspirations. For now, though, he needed to deal with the whole tenuous situation. There would be time to focus on their relationship later.

"What do we do now?" she asked.

"We find Ivan. Find out who's behind this. Find that list of dirty cops."

She squeezed his hand. "I don't know how you do this, trying to save the world every day."

"I learned a long time ago that I'll never save the world. There will always be one more person who needs me. But I can help one person at a time, and today that person is Ivan."

"Good, because I'm so scared right now, I need to know I'm not in this alone."

He hesitated in front of the hotel door and held her against him until he could feel her breath on his face. "We both know that this might not end up all nice and packaged in a neat bow, but you're not in this alone. My family has a way of sticking together—and sometimes driving you crazy in the meantime— but it also means that we're in this together until it's over. That I can promise."

He hated that he couldn't guarantee a happy ending. That he couldn't simply make everything okay for her. They needed to find Ivan. Needed to find that list. And needed to ensure that more innocent lives weren't taken because they were protecting him.

CHAPTER
25

Ivan watched the van door slam shut and felt the vehicle swallow him and Gizmo. He felt for the dog's leash and gripped it tight between his fingers, then struggled to sit up. They'd tied his hands behind him and gagged him, but at least they hadn't blindfolded him. Losing his sight terrified him.

He leaned down and nuzzled his head against Gizmo, wishing he could believe everything was going to be okay. But while he might not know names, he knew who he was dealing with. Every time he closed his eyes, he could still see Kendall lying on the ground. See the blood trickle down the dead man's skull. They'd murdered him in cold blood. Just like they'd murdered Felipe.

Now they had him, and he didn't even know why, unless it was because they preferred their murder witnesses at the bottom of the ocean.

He lifted his head, forcing himself to stay composed. He'd given his captors nicknames based on their physical features, like he did with most people. The Scarecrow was thin and pale, and clearly not the brains of the operation. The Tin Man was cold . . . and heartless.

He checked the time on the dashboard as they made another right turn. Three minutes later they were on the highway heading north.

They were talking, laughing about something. He scooted to the right until he could see the Tin Man's face in the rearview mirror, hoping he could catch something they were saying.

But the bottom line was, if they'd kidnapped him because he was Valez's son, and thought that would give them an advantage, they didn't know his father very well. His father might not blink at paying the bills, and he might have even loved their mother, but there'd never been much of a connection beyond the shallow relationship he had with his son. A reality Ivan had accepted years ago.

While his friends' fathers showed up for Little League games, Olivia had been the one standing along the bleachers cheering him on. There had never been father-son outings or trips to the beach. Antonio Valez had always been too busy to see that all Ivan had ever wanted was a father.

Now he understood why.

And maybe he'd been lucky, not knowing what his father had really been doing. But somehow, despite the distance between them, he still felt as if the sins of the father had piled on him as well.

The van pulled off onto a gravel road. Five minutes later, the Tin Man parked under a tree and shut off the engine. The van door slid open and the Scarecrow flashed him a cold smile before pulling his weapon from his holster and motioning for Ivan to get out. Ivan obeyed and started praying, because the only thing that could save him now was a miracle.

CHAPTER 26

Michael sat on the couch in the center of the hotel room, his fingers drumming on the armrest as they waited for the captain to stop pacing. The man had been furious when Avery had made the initial phone call asking him to meet with them. Livid when he'd arrived and discovered that Michael had been found and Avery's entire team had been working behind his back the past six hours. Irate when he was introduced to Antonio Valez's daughter.

Now the captain stood in front of them, arms crossed, and a deep frown marking his ebony features, making Michael feel as if the consequences for every choice he'd ever made were about to all come due at the same time. More than likely, he was about to be tried and convicted in one breath, because Captain Peterson had the demeanor of a firing squad. Michael had no desire to be on the receiving end.

But it was already a bit too late for that.

Captain Peterson glared at Avery. "I'll be honest, I'm not even sure where to begin. I trusted you with this investigation, Detective North, even though it was against my better judgment for you to take on this case. But because you know more about it than anyone else on the force, it seemed the right thing to do. And now what do I find out? I find out that your brother has been here for hours, while I thought I made it extremely clear that if you heard from him, I would be the first to know."

"You did, sir."

"And yet somehow"—the captain continued his pacing—"I'm the last one in this room to know what's going on.

"And you, Detective Hunt . . ."

The captain shifted his attention toward Michael, who winced, feeling as if he were five again, in trouble with the school principal.

"From what I've heard, you were involved in quite a bit of havoc over the past seventy-two hours, starting with a shooting at a convenience store, a stolen car, leaving the scene of an accident . . . and most recently, video surveillance shows that those two thugs our uniforms picked up this morning handcuffed to a pole were your work."

Michael nodded. "Yes sir."

"They are currently being held for questioning, but even that doesn't begin to explain the past eight months, your faked death, or Agent Kendall's death."

Michael struggled with his answer. "I was following orders, sir."

"And your plan . . . did it work?" the captain asked.

"No sir, it did not. Not completely."

Avery looked up at the captain, her gaze steady. "Sir, there were a number of unexpected details that have come into play in this situation since we spoke last."

"Details that I should have been made aware of."

"We needed time to guarantee that Michael would be safe once he came forward."

"And you didn't think you were able to trust me with that decision?" The captain continued speaking, not giving Avery a chance to respond. "You've led this team with integrity in the past, which is why I trusted you, but after today . . ."

"Yes sir."

"And as much as I might sympathize with your position, I'm not sure at this point how this is going to end for you."

"I'm willing to take full responsibility for my actions and those of my team, but we believe, sir, that Russell Coates was murdered by someone on the inside. We believe there are a number of officers being paid off by the cartel for information, and that this information puts my brother's life at risk."

"You will all be dealt with later for not keeping me in the loop—"

"There's also the matter of a possible bomb, sir," Michael said.

"A bomb?" The captain's frown deepened.

"We believe that someone—possibly a man by the name of Julio Salazar—has his eyes on Valez's territory and is planning to take it over with a bomb attack."

"Where?"

"We're still working on that, sir."

"Well, now that I'm a part of this—unofficial—party, would you mind clueing me in on your plan to find out where that bomb is going to go off?"

Olivia cleared her throat beside him. "I might have something."

"Go ahead," the captain said.

"While we were staying at Felipe's, we watched the news report about Sam Kendall's death and Michael being a person of interest. I'd like to go speak to the reporter who broke the news. Her name is Rebecca Pearce, and I believe we might be able to get some answers from her, in exchange for a few exclusive leads."

"She's already been interviewed by the police, and didn't tell them anything," the captain said. "Why should I send you to talk with her?"

"Because we go back a long way. If we could get the name of her source, it could help."

"You think she'll give her source up?"

"I don't know, but I've already contacted her."

"You've talked with her?" Michael asked.

Olivia nodded. "She's agreed to meet with me."

"When?"

"Right away."

"It's not safe for you to go out, Olivia—"

"Michael, my brother's missing. I'm not going to sit around here doing nothing, and I might be able to get her to talk."

"It's not a bad idea," the captain said. "Someone wanted that information leaked, and we need to know why. But in the meantime, let me advise you to heed this warning." The captain's frown deepened the creases on his forehead. "If anyone in this group here so much as needs to sneeze, you'd better get permission from me first."

Olivia shivered, despite the warmth radiating from the car's heater, as Michael pulled into the paved circular driveway at the front of the cemetery. She pulled her coat tighter, wishing for something heavier. Pressing her fingers into the edge of the seat, she wondered why Rebecca had wanted to meet here. She'd always hated cemeteries and the memories they dredged up of her mother's death. The scent of roses, the color black. And the icy feel of an engraved marble headstone.

She'd been twenty-two when her mother had died, two months after her college graduation. Ivan was just about to enter his teen years, and his mother's death left him feeling angry and deserted. It had been at her mother's graveside, watching the priest toss dirt onto her coffin, that Olivia had realized for the first time that she now had a brother to raise.

Somehow, she'd managed to hold on to her faith, but in the

dark places of her mind, and in times when God seemed far away, she couldn't help but ask the question, why?

She felt Michael's hand brush against her shoulder and turned to him, wondering how it was possible for her to come to trust someone so deeply whom she'd known for such a short time.

"Olivia?"

She caught the concern along with a hint of understanding in his eyes. "I'm sorry. My mind's wandering."

"They're doing everything they can to find your brother."

"I know."

She wasn't even sure how to explain. She trusted Michael. Trusted his instincts and wisdom in the situation, but it was more than that.

"Are you having second thoughts about meeting with Rebecca?"

She blew her nose. "No. It's just that being here reminds me of when my mother died."

"How old were you?"

"It was right after I graduated from college. I'd just landed my first job but had no idea what I was doing. I wanted to take care of Ivan. And I was independent enough to believe I could do everything on my own."

"Where did you live?"

"With one of my mother's younger sisters for a while, but she had four kids of her own. She worked long hours and saw me as a free babysitter, cook, and chauffer. As much as I wanted to help, it didn't work."

"What about your father? How often did you see him?"

"Not very often. He traveled a lot and didn't have time to be tied down with the two of us. He arranged financial help, and I got legal custody of Ivan. I was able to rent an apartment, and somehow we made it."

"You've done a good job. Especially for someone who was given so much on her plate at such a young age."

"Ivan's a good kid." She laughed. "I know he'd cringe if he heard me calling him a kid, but sometimes I still see him as that young, vulnerable boy. He'd hate hearing me say that, because the truth is, he isn't that little boy anymore. He has more courage than most people I know."

Including herself.

He'd been the one who'd encouraged her to stand up and do what was right, even if it cost her something. Without Ivan, Michael would be dead.

"What about Rebecca? What do you know about her?"

"Rebecca has an ear for a good story, but I'm worried she's gotten involved with the wrong kind of people to get what she wants."

"Why would you say that?"

"We went to college together. She has a tendency to be a bit ruthless. She goes after what she wants, not caring much about how it affects the people around her. We were friends for a while, but it didn't last long. She stepped on a lot of people on her way up the ladder. I eventually decided that that kind of competitiveness wasn't for me. I just wanted to report a good story."

He wrapped his hands around her fingers that were cold from the dropping temperatures. "Just promise me you'll be careful."

For a moment, she allowed herself to imagine him pulling her into his arms and kissing her again. To let him promise her that everything was going to be okay.

Instead, she pressed her fingers against the door handle, trying to gather the courage to face the truth she'd been wrestling with for three days. Her father wasn't the man he claimed to be. And her life and Michael and Ivan's lives were still at risk.

"She's coming." Olivia saw Rebecca walking toward their car from the east entrance of the cemetery.

Michael switched off the motor. The hot air began to dissipate in the chilly afternoon. "Are you sure we can trust her?"

"I'm not sure we can trust anyone, but if someone told her that you killed Sam Kendall, then she has to know who's behind this. She wanted me to come alone, so let me go first. I'll tug on my left ear when I'm ready for her to talk to you."

Michael laughed. "You're sounding like a true spy."

"Very funny."

He caught her hand before she got out of the car. "I'll be right here. If you need anything."

"I know."

"And if anything seems off—anything at all—walk away."

She nodded, wishing she could simply walk away. But she had to find a way out of this and ensure Ivan's safety. Running wasn't the answer.

A moment later, Olivia was walking along the sidewalk, surrounded by tall evergreens, letting the wind whip through her coat. Nerves twisted reality, making every shadow look like a monster. A man waited beside an older woman who laid a bouquet of flowers on a tombstone. So much sorrow. So much loss.

You will know the truth and the truth will set you free.

She grabbed onto the verse, refusing to give in to the fear. For the past few days, she'd been afraid of knowing the truth, but she'd been wrong. She needed to know the truth. Needed to find that freedom.

Olivia walked on, watching as Rebecca passed the older couple, headed in her direction, dressed in one of her typical outfits. Expensive Armani jacket, a pencil skirt, and a pair of ankle-strap pumps. Olivia's budget would never allow for the thousand-dollar price tag Rebecca doled out for her outfits.

"Rebecca?" Olivia brushed a loose strand of hair away from her face. "I wasn't sure you were going to show up."

"Your phone call intrigued me, and you know I've never been able to pass up a good story."

"You chose an interesting place to meet."

Rebecca laughed, but there was a hint of caution behind her smile. "I've always loved cemeteries. Just think of all the stories that were never told. Family secrets. Lies. Affairs . . . Perfect fodder for a reporter."

Or some seedy reality show host.

"I promised you a story," Olivia said. When they'd spoken on the phone, the promise of a story had been all the bait she'd needed. "But I need some answers from you first."

Rebecca's brow rose, marked with a hint of doubt. "I've been thinking about what you said on the phone. I think you're digging for your own story."

"This isn't about competitiveness or even our professions. It's about someone's life."

"Someone's life?" Rebecca frowned. "You've always been a bit overly dramatic, which is why I'm poised to move into television and you're still working for some podunk local paper."

"Did you ever think I might like my job and the people I work with?" Olivia tried to ignore the jab as she tugged on her ear. There was no use delaying the inevitable. "I didn't come here to argue with you. I want you to meet someone."

Michael stepped onto the walk behind them.

"He's a friend, and we're here together. He has some questions to ask you."

"Wait a minute. You're the man I reported on the other night. Michael Hunt." Rebecca took a step forward, the smile back on her face. "Maybe you were right when you told me you were bringing me a story."

"He didn't murder that agent."

"And you know that how?"

"I can't tell you everything—yet. You're going to have to trust me."

"Trust you? Listen, I have no idea how you got involved in this, but you don't realize what you're mixed up in."

"Unfortunately, I do." Olivia shook her head, wondering who was playing who. "Which is why we need to know your source."

"My source? Are you kidding me? He'd kill me if he knew I was talking to you. I came as a favor, nothing more."

"We need to know your source," Michael said.

"No way."

Olivia tried a different angle. "Listen, you came because you were expecting a story. I promise that I'll give you the exclusive when this is over—and trust me, it's going to be worth it, but I need answers. We know you leaked the story, and that the information you had didn't come from the police. Who told you Michael murdered Sam Kendall?"

"I'm not giving away my source. You of all people should understand that."

"Please, Rebecca."

"I'm in too deep, Olivia." This time there was a hint of fear in her voice.

"Michael can help you. He has connections. He's a police officer."

Rebecca scowled at them. "Listen, I already spoke to a couple of officers about what I know, and I don't intend to tell you anything more than what I told them. My sources are confidential. Period."

Michael stepped forward. "If you come in with me and answer our questions, I'll make sure you're protected from whoever you're afraid of."

"I'm not afraid."

"Rebecca?"

"Listen, even if I did think my life was in danger, then what?

You put me in some witness protection program and send me off to some isolated cabin in the middle of Alaska in hopes no one finds out? I'm a television reporter, with my eye on prime-time news. I don't plan to spend the rest of my life hovering in the wings."

"Is that worth your life?"

"There's nothing to tell. I was contacted by one of my sources. I don't even know the guy's real name. He told me that Michael Hunt murdered Agent Sam Kendall. He sent me the photo of Michael that we aired. I dug around a bit and discovered that Michael Hunt—that you—were an undercover cop. And that you were supposed to be dead."

"Why did someone want that story on the air?" Olivia asked.

"I have no idea, but it certainly didn't hurt our ratings."

"But there's more at stake here than just a story, Rebecca." Michael took another step forward. "We believe someone is planning to set off a bomb in a public place, and whoever gave you this information is more than likely involved in it."

Rebecca pulled her purse strap across her shoulder. "I've already given you more than I should have. I need to go."

"You have my number." Olivia felt the frustrating tug of failure. Not every contact provided the information needed, but this time the stakes were too high to make a mistake. "Promise me you'll call me if you change your mind."

"Forget it, Olivia. You go out there and get your own story."

Olivia watched her walk away. "I'm worried about her, Michael."

"Not every lead pays off." Michael gathered her up in his arms. "We'll find out who's behind this."

"When? After more people are caught in the crossfire, or that bomb goes off and innocent lives are lost? Or Ivan—"

"We're going to find Ivan."

Michael's phone rang as they headed back to the car. He grabbed it out of his pocket and answered it.

"That was Avery," he said, hanging up. The furrow in his brow deepened.

Olivia's heart stopped. "They found Ivan?"

"No. They found Felipe. He . . . he's alive."

CHAPTER
27

W hat do you mean, Felipe's alive?" Olivia took a step backward, stumbled, then caught her footing before Michael had time to grab her. "That's not possible."

She'd seen the bullet hole in his forehead. Touched the blood running down the side of his face. Checked for a pulse. There had been no pulse. She'd been certain of that. But clearly, in the smoke and gunfire, she'd made a horrible mistake.

She looked back up at Michael. "How is it possible that he's alive?"

"Avery said that the hospital just made a positive ID of a John Doe brought in last night."

"Felipe."

Michael nodded. "The people who found him were driving to their own cabin a couple miles up the road when they saw that the cabin was on fire. They called 911, then stopped to see if anyone needed help. According to the police report, Felipe was sitting outside the house, completely disoriented."

Olivia ran through the scenario in her mind, while a sick feeling settled in her stomach. There were clearly things Felipe had lied about. Things he'd purposely kept from her. But in the end, she'd failed him.

"This is all my fault." Her chest heaved. The chilling reality of what they'd done swept through her. They'd left Felipe to die in that fire. "He was alive, Michael, and I just left him."

"Olivia, stop." He braced his hands against her shoulders. "This wasn't your fault."

"It wasn't my fault? You can't be serious." She pulled away from him and started for the car. She needed to see Felipe. To find out if he was all right. "He was alive, and we left him there."

He grabbed her arm and turned her around. "Stop. I know this is a huge shock, but at least he's alive. You and I both know that we did everything we could. They were shooting at us, the place was on fire and filling up with smoke. We were out of options, Olivia."

"Then we should have come up with another option."

Feelings of anger resurfaced. She shouldn't be snapping at Michael, but she wasn't just angry at herself for what had happened back in that cabin. She was angry at Felipe for lying to her. For pretending to be someone he wasn't. She was tired of the games and the secrets.

And now she'd just been given the chance to hear the truth from him herself.

She slipped into the passenger seat while Michael started the engine. Warm air began slowly circulating again but did nothing to melt away the fear surrounding her heart.

"Do you think Felipe is La Sombra?" She looked at him, knowing he didn't have any more answers to that than she did.

"I think it's possible, but that's a question you'll have to ask him."

"I need to see him."

"I know." He nodded. "I'll drive you there now."

Michael pulled out of the circular drive and headed toward the hospital, their security detail trailing behind them.

Thirty minutes later, Olivia stood outside Felipe's hospital room, trying to find the courage to step inside and face him.

Michael stood behind her, attempting to rub the kinks out of her shoulders. "No matter what he's done, no matter what he might regret or not regret about his life, one thing was clear to me when we were with him at the cabin. He loves you, Olivia. And nothing's going to change that."

Nodding, she stepped inside. Felipe lay against the pillow, his skin sallow against the white sheets. There was a bandage on his forehead, and his arm was hooked up to an IV.

"Olivia."

She crossed the speckled tile, breathing in the scent of disinfectants and hospital food, while trying to settle her nerves. "I thought you were dead. I saw them shoot you . . . I saw you lying on the floor—"

"This wasn't your fault, Olivia."

Tears streamed down her cheeks. "I couldn't find a pulse—"

"You're not the only one." He shot her a weak smile. "It took the doctor awhile to find my pulse this morning. Apparently there's a problem with my arteries not pumping enough blood. And this"—he touched the bandage on his forehead—"turned out to be a shrapnel fragment from the shooting that required a bit of stitching, but not near as deadly as a bullet would have been."

He looked past her, toward the doorway where Michael stood, giving them some privacy. "Where's Ivan?"

"They . . ." Her voice broke. "They took him."

"During the attack at the cabin?"

"No, this afternoon. They tracked us to Atlanta, following the GPS device on Gizmo's collar, then somehow tracked us to the hotel."

"Who?"

"My father's men? Or maybe men working for you? I don't know." She wiped away the tears on her cheeks, trying to erase the resentment from her voice, but knew from his expression that he'd heard it. "I was hoping you might be able to tell me."

"Then that attack . . ." Felipe struggled to sit up, but Olivia stopped him. "They were after me, and I led them straight to you, because of a decision to protect that crazy dog of mine? But why take Ivan if they were after me?"

"Leverage, maybe? Trying to draw out my father? I don't know. We're still trying to put the pieces together."

"Did you receive a ransom message?"

"Nothing yet. There's a team out there doing everything they can to find him."

"I'm sorry, Olivia. I never meant for my sins to affect you and Ivan."

"It's a little too late for that." Sorrow mixed with the anger brewing inside her. But she didn't want any more apologies, or excuses, or lies. She wanted answers. "There have been far too many lies, Felipe. My mother and father weren't the only ones hiding the truth. I know that you and my father are brothers. I know about the money you had hidden at the cabin."

Felipe's fingers pressed against one of the strips of tape securing his IV. "I should have disappeared a long time ago. Retired to some island in the South Pacific."

"Why didn't you?"

"I think I lost the desire to start over." Felipe lay back against the pillows. "Maybe if your mother hadn't died, things would have been different."

"Why didn't you just tell me the truth?"

"She thought it would be better for the two of you if you never knew the truth." He looked away, as if not able to handle her pain. "She thought she could shelter you—protect you—from the life she lived. From the lives all of us lived."

"So she really did know everything?"

"Your mother had the bad fortune of falling in love with the wrong people. She loved your father, and while I know he loved her, he didn't love her as much as the business, so eventually she turned to me."

"And my father . . . what was his role in all of this?"

"Your father was never interested in leading the cartel. Instead, he became successful running his real estate company and used it to help launder the cartel's money. He managed to avoid getting caught . . . until now."

"Why didn't you just continue to lie to me? Why are you telling me the truth now?"

"Because I believe that his role of laundering money isn't enough for him anymore. I believe he's planning to take over." Felipe shook his head. "There have been a number of my men killed over the past few months, all in an attempt to take over my territory."

"Why did you go into hiding?"

"I'm not afraid of your father, if that's what you're implying." This time he didn't avoid her gaze. "I went into hiding because I'm dying, Olivia."

"Dying?"

"I always figured I had more lives than a stray cat, but this time I've pushed fate one too many times."

"You could have told me."

"I wanted to . . . at the cabin, but the timing never seemed right. Cancer's spread through my body. The doctor's given me a couple months at the most," he said. "It's humorous in a way. I always assumed I'd either die with a bullet in my head or in prison. Never this. But I knew when those I worked with found out I was sick, I'd lose the control."

Olivia frowned. "Are you La Sombra?"

"You want the truth?"

"Yes."

"La Sombra was our father." Felipe grasped her hand. "I took over as the head of the cartel when he died, but it was best for others to believe he still lived. I can live with the consequences of the life I chose, but I didn't want that for you. Which is why I tried to warn you about your father."

"So the emails?" Pieces of the puzzle clicked into place. "You're the one who sent them to me."

"I was worried about you, Olivia. I can't protect you from what is happening."

"Do you know who took Ivan?"

"I swear I don't know."

"If it's my father, trying to get to you, how do we stop him?"

"I don't know."

"People are going to die if we don't, Felipe. You can't tell me you're not in a position to fight back and put a stop to this."

"Do you think I haven't already tried to stop this?"

Michael stepped into the room. "What if your father isn't behind this?"

Felipe looked up at Michael. "Then who?"

"Julio Salazar."

"I killed his father." Felipe shook his head. "With my death, the entire territory will be up for grabs."

"And the cartel isn't the only one with lots to lose." Michael stopped beside the bed. "What do you know about the 'Canary List' that supposedly has names of dirty cops? Does Valez have that list?"

Felipe hesitated, as if weighing the impact of his answer. "Valez doesn't have that list. I do."

"You do?"

Felipe unclasped a thin chain necklace from around his neck, then slipped a small silver key from it.

"What is that?" she asked.

"My insurance policy. I almost gave it to you at the cabin," he said to Michael, "but I wasn't sure you wouldn't use it against Olivia and Ivan. But now . . . now something tells me you need it more than I do."

"What kind of insurance policy?" Michael asked.

"It's a key to a bank safe-deposit box." He looked at Olivia. "Your name's already on the permission card, Olivia."

"What's inside it?"

"It's the list you need. The list that will allow you to come in, Michael. Every person who's associated with Cártel de Rey, from Atlanta to the Mexican border. Dirty cops, government agents. Even a local senator."

"The story Rebecca's after," Olivia said.

Felipe pressed the key into the palm of her hand and closed her fingers around it. "If I can't win this war, I might as well take them all down with me."

————

Michael walked out of the room beside Olivia, the key tucked away in his pocket. He should be relieved they had it, but instead of relief, alarm still hovered over him. This wasn't over. They needed to find Ivan. Needed to stop that bomb. And he had no idea how to do either.

Carlos and Levi met them in the hallway where they'd been waiting. "Everything okay?"

"He was able to clarify a few questions we had." Michael weighed his options. If everything Felipe said was true, then the man's life was in danger. And it was only going to be a matter of time before he was tracked down.

"I want the two of you to stand guard here until Avery can set something up," Michael said.

"Avery told us to stay with you—"

"I know what Avery said, but Felipe is a key witness in

bringing down the cartel, and his life has already been threatened at least once." Michael slipped his hand into his pants pocket and grabbed the key. "We'll go straight back to the hotel room. I promise. But he's going to need round-the-clock protection until we can get to the bottom of this. I also want a formal confession taken as soon as it can be arranged."

"You got it."

Michael took Olivia's hand as they started down the hall toward the elevator, taking in everything around him. A man talked with one of the nurses at the nurse's station, wearing jeans with a turtleneck and jacket, holding a gray cable-knit hat. An elderly couple sat next to each other in a small waiting room. The woman cried quietly beside her husband. Michael's mother's image flashed before him, how she must have cried the day she'd been told her son was dead.

As they stepped out of the elevator into the parking garage a minute later, a chill swept over him. He shook it off. Their footsteps echoed across the concrete. Past rows of cars and concrete columns.

Michael looked behind him, unable to shake the feeling they were being followed.

"What's wrong, Michael?" If someone knew they had the key . . .

"I don't think we're the only ones here to visit Felipe."

Michael grabbed Olivia's hand and pulled her behind a cement pillar, then pressed his finger to his lips. He was tired of all the games. Tired of constantly feeling one step behind.

Michael reacted the second the man in the gray cap walked by. He grabbed for the man's gun, spun him around, and pinned him against the pillar.

CHAPTER
28

Michael held the gun against the man's chest. "Don't move."

"Whoa!" The man held up his hands, obviously terrified. "I'm not going anywhere."

"Why are you following us?"

"Following you . . . why would I do that?" His voice cracked. "I'm here to see my grandmother. She was admitted last night for heart problems, and—"

"Enough," Michael said. While he didn't believe his story, the guy seemed far too green to be cartel. "I don't have time to play games, and since you were clearly not on the cardiac wing to see Grandma, I'm going to assume I'm right. So I'll ask you for an answer nicely one more time, and after that I'll consider using this." He pressed the barrel of the gun firmly against the man's chest. "Why are you following us?"

"I wasn't—"

"What did I just tell you?"

The man's jaw tensed. "Fine. I'm a PI. But I have a license and a permit to carry."

Michael glanced at Olivia. "I don't know about you, but I always carry heat while visiting my grandmother."

"There are no gun restrictions in a hospital—"

"Who hired you?"

"I'm not at liberty to say."

"He's not at liberty to say." Michael looked at Olivia again and rolled his eyes, before turning back to Atlanta's own Barney Fife. "You need to understand something. I've had a very, very bad beginning to my day, and so far, it has yet to get any better. I've been shot at and side-swiped, and if that isn't enough, there's a hit out on me by the cartel and the cops want to arrest me, so if you think I'm playing games—"

"No, please. If I'd have known you were involved with the cartel . . . What do you want? I'll give you money. There's an ATM around the corner. I've got a couple hundred dollars in my account, which I know isn't much, but it's all yours."

"I don't want your money," Michael said. "I want to know who hired you."

It took all of five seconds for the man to cave. "Rebecca Pearce."

"Now that wasn't so hard, was it?" Michael asked, smiling for the first time. "Now tell me why she hired you."

"She wanted me to follow you."

"So you're not involved in the cartel?"

"Me? Involved with the cartel? Are you crazy?" He pointed to his jacket pocket. "I'm just an investigator. If you'll just let me show you, I've got my license. I wasn't lying."

Michael took a step back. What in the world was a green detective doing involved in a cartel investigation?

Fumbling, the man pulled the card out of his wallet and held it up. "See. My name's David Coleman."

"Coleman Investigations," Michael read.

"That's my father, actually." He pulled out another card. "Here's my driver's license. It's all legal. And my—"

"I believe you. Put those away. How long have you been working as a PI?"

"I've had my license for three months."

Michael held up the man's handgun. "Have you ever fired this before?"

"Yes . . . well . . . at the firing range."

"Have you ever had to aim it at a person?"

"No . . . I . . ." He shoved his glasses up the bridge of his nose. "I spend most of my time locating records or . . . or divorce filings. Stuff like that."

"Locating records and divorce filings . . . sounds like fun." Michael aimed the gun at the ground, ejected the clip, then turned on the safety. He dropped the clip into his jacket pocket and handed the man back his weapon. "Let's go back to the original question. Why are you following us?"

"Rebecca's a friend of mine from high school. I've done a few jobs on the side for her, though normally she has me digging through someone's trash . . . or doing various kinds of research."

"Where is Rebecca now?"

"I'm not sure, exactly. She told me she'd talk to me later after I found out where you were going."

"I think it's time we gave Rebecca another call. Where's your cell phone?"

Mr. Coleman pulled it out of his jacket pocket.

"Perfect. Now, call her and have her meet you here immediately. Tell her it's important."

"I don't usually tell her where to meet me—"

"Just call her."

A minute later, he hung up the call, the message passed on. "Can I leave now?"

"Are you kidding, Mr. Coleman? The fun's just beginning."

"For you, maybe. If she finds out I blew my cover—"

"Relax. Trust me. Rebecca's the least of your worries."

Ten minutes later, Olivia watched Rebecca pull into the parking garage and stop her vehicle where they waited, blocking a row of parked cars in the process.

"Your little charade is up, Ms. Pearce," Michael said as she exited the car.

Her glare shot arrows right through him, but she wasn't the only one ticked.

"Why did you have Mr. Coleman here follow us?" he asked when she didn't respond.

Rebecca let out a sharp huff. "I figured Olivia might be on to something. And if I had you followed, I might be able to find out what it was."

"What, exactly, did you think she was on to?" Michael asked.

"For starters, I know that you're the son of the former police captain, and you've been presumed dead. And now you've shown up after spending eight months working for the cartel. But you already know that." Her smile widened as she turned to Olivia. "For you, it took a bit more digging into your background, but I came up with something I'd somehow missed all these years."

"That my father is Antonio Valez, leader of the Cártel de Rey?" Olivia asked.

"Exactly." Rebecca didn't try to mask the suspicion in her eyes. "Kind of makes one wonder which side you both are working on."

"A question that should be cleared up soon," Michael shot back. "What exactly are you looking for, Rebecca?"

"Proof to back up the story I've been working on."

"What story might that be?"

"Forget it," Rebecca said. "That's where this conversation stops—"

"I don't think so." Olivia moved across the pavement in front of Rebecca. "Not this time. I'm guessing that you stumbled across something far bigger than you can actually handle. And considering the direction our day has gone, I have pretty good reason to believe you're about to find yourself in a lot of trouble."

"Especially if it has anything to do with government officials and a story involving the Canary List," Michael added.

"The Canary List?" Rebecca's face paled. "How do you know about that?"

"I'm guessing your source keeps you supplied with small tidbits of information that work to his advantage, while you wait for the promise of a big payoff. But somehow you found out about that list," Michael said. "And that list is the story you want. Am I on the right track? A list that has the potential to switch the balance of power between cartel leaders?"

"You're correct." Mr. Coleman pushed his glasses up the bridge of his nose. "Atlanta is a key territory for the northeast as well as in parts of Europe, so whoever holds this territory stands to gain tremendously in profits. And that list will ensure whoever has it continues to dominate the drug market in this area."

"David—"

"Sorry, Rebecca." Apparently, Mr. Coleman was tired of feeling unappreciated. "But I've been doing my own research."

Rebecca headed back to her car. "I have nothing more to say."

"Please, Rebecca, stop!" Olivia ran toward her, not willing to give up. The woman knew something. Maybe it was time to appeal to whatever sliver of humanity she had left. "They've taken my brother, Rebecca. Ivan has nothing to do with the cartel, or the Canary List, or any of this. Whoever took him thinks they can use him as a pawn because of who his father is."

"Don't even try a guilt trip on me." Rebecca walked back toward Olivia. "That stopped working a long time ago."

"I'm not trying to make you feel guilty, I'm trying to show

you that there are lives at stake. They're planning to set off a bomb. People are going to die."

"Rebecca!" Olivia turned to see Michael staring at the entrance as a car came into the parking garage. He yelled her name again. "Rebecca, were you followed? If your informant knows you're talking to us . . ."

"I don't think so. I—"

Olivia jumped at the sharp crack of a gun going off.

"Everybody get down." Michael grabbed Olivia's hand and jerked her behind Rebecca's car.

Olivia pulled Rebecca down with her as the driver slammed into the side of Rebecca's car.

Michael eased out from behind the trunk of the vehicle and fired back. The car continued up the ramp past them.

"They're going to circle back." He ran around to the driver's side. "Give me the keys to your car."

Rebecca stared at the keys, her hands shaking.

"The keys, Rebecca."

Olivia grabbed the keys out of Rebecca's hand and tossed them to Michael.

Michael opened the back door and shoved Rebecca into the car. He yelled at the others as he jumped into the driver's seat. "Get in the car and get down."

Tires squealed as the other car started back toward them.

The windshield shattered as Olivia crawled into the backseat after Rebecca and David.

"Go . . . go . . . go . . ."

Michael stomped the accelerator and headed toward the exit of the parking garage, while the occupant of the other car continued firing shots at them. The tires screeched as Michael broke through the arm gate and onto the street.

"They shot me." David leaned back against the seat, looking as if he were about to pass out.

Olivia pulled off the man's coat, struggling to keep her balance, while Michael tried to lose the shooters.

"How bad is it?" Michael took another sharp left turn.

She ripped off David's sleeve at the shoulder and found a half-inch shard of glass sticking out of his arm.

"Am I going to die?" he asked.

"It's not a bullet, it's a piece of glass, and it's barely a scratch. You're going to live."

"Are you sure?" He held up the coat and showed her the patch of blood from the injury. "I've lost a lot of blood."

"It's a piece of glass, David," Rebecca said. "I'm pretty sure you're not going to bleed to death."

"Hold on," Michael said, making another sharp turn.

"You were followed," Olivia said.

Rebecca gripped the handle above her. "I'm sorry."

"Who's your source, Rebecca?" Michael asked.

"I can't tell you."

"This isn't just a story you're chasing," he continued. "People's lives are at stake."

"I think I sort of figured that out. They were shooting at us," she yelled back.

"Who is it?"

Rebecca blew out a sharp blast of air. "His name is Javier. He's a member of the Cártel de Rey."

"Can you get ahold of him?"

"Probably."

"Was that so hard?" Michael asked. "I'll have my sister try to pick him up, but in the meantime, I'll make sure I've lost these jokers, then head back to the hospital and drop you both off at the emergency room, where Coleman can have his arm patched up."

"No way," David said. "I'm not getting out of this car until we've put as much distance as possible between us and those shooters."

"He has a point," Olivia said.

"Fine, I'll even make sure you're both protected until this is over, but in the meantime, I think it's time to find out who's on the Canary List."

CHAPTER
29

Ivan stared at the bomb, an organized jumble of cylinders, wires, and a timer in the open silver case, counting down its destruction.

Three hours. Forty-five minutes. Thirteen seconds.

Twelve.

Eleven.

Ten.

Ivan forced himself to look away from the table where the bomb sat next to the floral drapes hanging over the closed window of the hotel room. His sister was out there somewhere looking for him. Worried about him like she always was. And this time, she had every reason to worry. Because that bomb marked the inevitable countdown to his death.

Unless he could find a way out.

Fear had brought with it a steady trickle of adrenaline dripping through his veins, urging him to run. But with his hands tied behind him, a gag in his mouth, and a DO NOT DISTURB sign posted on the outside of the hotel door, his captors had guaranteed there was no way to escape and nowhere to run.

The only good thing was that Scarecrow and the Tin Man had continued to talk in front of him, blissfully unaware that he was following their conversation. If Michael and Avery could locate him in time, they would need information. Anything he could discover might be the clue they needed to put an end to this.

He kept his head down as the men finished up room service. Hoping they'd continue to believe the falsehood that he wasn't interested in their conversation. Their discussion switched from the room service menu to the upcoming NFL playoffs, like sitting in a hotel room with a bomb and a hostage was just another ordinary day.

Scarecrow swung his legs down from the desk, grabbed his empty coffee cup, and slam-dunked it into the metal trash can. "Have you heard from the boss?"

Ivan leaned forward, intent on not missing any of the conversation. He waited for Tin Man's response, but the man was turned away from him.

Ivan felt his lungs tighten as he held his breath. *Turn around . . . turn around . . .*

Tin Man turned back to the bomb and carefully closed the lid. "Everything's on schedule. We leave the bomb downstairs. And the boy, we'll leave alive . . . for now."

Scarecrow's grin broadened. "As soon as we get our hands on that list, every dirty cop across the city will be forced to change loyalties."

Ivan focused on the Tin Man's lips, careful to keep any hint of interest off his face. No interest at all in the game playing out in front of him.

Tin Man turned to Ivan as they headed toward the door. "I hope you'll be . . . comfortable while we're gone."

Ivan watched as the hotel door slammed behind them. He needed a plan. Because when the bomb went off, everyone in the vicinity of the blast would die.

CHAPTER
30

Olivia reread the email from her father on the laptop Avery had loaned her. Antonio Valez, money launderer and cartel leader wannabe, wanted to see her. She heard a soft knock on the bedroom door. She called out, "Come in," and looked up as Michael entered the room. "Hey."

"Hey yourself. I thought you were supposed to be sleeping."

"I tried." Sleep had become elusive as her jumbled thoughts tried to put the pieces together. Trying to find resolution from her past.

"Emily said she had some sleeping pills you could take."

"I'm fine for now. I'm not sure I want to sleep. Any updates on Ivan?"

"Nothing yet, but this is far from over."

"I know. What's happening out there?" She'd come back exhausted from the bank where they'd retrieved Felipe's list. Now she was hoping that something they found would lead them to Ivan.

"Tory's arranged to move you to a safe house. We'll be ready to leave in the next fifteen to twenty minutes."

"What about Felipe?"

"He was telling the truth about the list. They're working on getting arrest warrants. The fallout is going to be significant."

"What happens to him now?"

"Turning over the list won't save him from prison, Olivia."

"I know. And my father?"

"Avery's team was able to track down Rebecca's contact. He hasn't said much yet, but we believe Salazar was using him to pass on information to her to manipulate the situation as he moves in to take over the territory. He also confirmed that Salazar is planning to kill your father, who, it appears, has gone into hiding." He sat down on the edge of the bed beside her, where she clutched her phone. "What is it?"

She hesitated, unsure of how much she wanted to tell him. "I checked my email. There was a message from my father."

"Your father?" Michael frowned as he glanced at the computer.

"Said he needs to meet with me." She looked up at Michael. "I need to call him and arrange to see him."

Michael grasped her hand. "It's too risky. You need to be somewhere safe."

"I need to talk with him. What if he knows where Ivan is?"

"What if it's a trap?" he countered.

Olivia pulled away from his touch, her mind spinning with the possible implications. "Even after all that's happened, even after knowing the truth about who he is, I still don't believe he would hurt either of us. And I don't believe he's the one who took Ivan. I think his life is in danger."

"You might be right about every single bit of that, but even if he didn't take Ivan, that doesn't mean you can trust him."

Olivia's gaze dropped. "After I meet with him, you can bring him in."

Michael nodded. "I'll give you a phone to use. We'll be able to make it look as if the call is coming from your phone, and we'll trace his cell."

Two minutes later, Avery gave her the go-ahead from the

middle of the hotel room, and Olivia dialed her father's number. He answered on the fourth ring.

"Olivia?"

"Yeah. It's me."

He paused. "I . . . I wasn't sure you'd call. I'm worried about you. I got to the island, and they said you'd left. I know I missed Christmas, but—"

"It's okay. I'm sorry we missed you." She licked her lips, wondering how long he was going to keep lying to her. When the deception was going to end.

"We need to talk," her father continued.

Olivia tapped the speakerphone function and glanced at Michael. She wasn't sure what to say. Wasn't sure what she wanted. She didn't want to believe he'd hurt her or Ivan, but how could she trust him?

"I'm listening." Olivia pushed through the pain of knowing this man on the phone wasn't the person she'd always believed him to be.

"I heard about Ivan."

"How?"

"I received a phone call about thirty minutes ago."

"A ransom demand?"

"There were no demands. At least no financial demands."

"What do they want?"

"I'll tell you everything, but we need to meet. In person."

Michael shook his head. She hesitated, knowing he was probably right. But she also knew that she wanted—needed—to give her father a chance to explain. A part of her was still holding on to the possibility that maybe . . . just maybe . . . things weren't as they appeared. But even more than that, she needed to find Ivan.

"Olivia?"

Her legs were suddenly weak, and she sat down on the edge of the couch, praying, weighing her options.

"What did you have in mind?" she asked.

"I'm on my way to Atlanta now."

"I don't know—"

"Please, Olivia. There are things I need to tell you."

"About your involvement with the cartel? Isn't that what this is all about?"

"This isn't a conversation I can have over the phone."

"Apparently, it's not a conversation you're able to have, period."

For a moment she was ten years old again. Trying to gain her father's approval. Standing at the boat dock, waiting for him to arrive. Opening up another monthly check with the hope he might have included a personal note.

But how was he supposed to have told her? *Would you mind passing the mashed potatoes, and by the way, in case you were wondering, the real-estate business is just a sideshow. I'm actually laundering money for the local cartel.*

"I don't see what's complicated," she continued. "You've lied to me all these years and now, because of those lies, Ivan's life is in danger." She caught her breath. "Do you know who has him?"

"Not yet, but I can't talk about it over the phone." There was a long pause on the line. "Are you with Michael?"

Olivia looked at Michael. "Yes."

"Ivan's life is at stake here, Olivia, but I need your help. No cops, or they'll kill him. You have to come alone."

Tears formed pools in her eyes. This couldn't be happening. "What time will you get here?"

"I'll call you in an hour with further details."

It was crazy how badly one part of her wanted to see him while the rest of her wanted only to run. There was no way she could know if it was safe.

"I'll wait for your call," she said.

"Olivia." Michael spoke as soon as she hung up the call. "You're not—"

"Don't." She set the phone down on the table. "I have to see him."

"No, you don't." Michael turned to his sister. "Avery, back me up here."

"This is my decision," Olivia said.

"She's right, Michael." She turned to Olivia. "We can do everything we can to protect you, but—"

"You heard what he said." She wasn't doing anything that could jeopardize Ivan's life. "No cops. I won't risk it. Do whatever you want, but not until after we talk, and I find out what he knows about Ivan."

Michael sat down on the couch beside her and took her hand. "What if it's a trap?"

"I'll have to take that risk, but I don't think he's planning to kill me. I'm sure he's got an assassin or two on the payroll that could take care of a little issue like a daughter who's in the way. That wasn't why he called."

"He's lied to you his entire life, Olivia. Manipulating everyone around him. I know. I worked with him and saw firsthand what he's capable of doing."

"You don't get it, do you?" Olivia pulled her hand from his and pressed her fingers against her temples. "Everything important to me has turned out to be nothing more than a bunch of lies. I need some kind of explanation that only he can give me."

"I'm sorry, Olivia . . . I really am. I can't imagine how difficult this must be for you."

"Why?" She pointed to his sisters and father across the room watching the scene play out. "Because you have the perfect family?"

"Don't make me out to be the bad guy."

Anger bubbled inside her. Maybe it wasn't his fault the Hunts were the model for the perfect southern family. "Just stating facts, like you are."

Michael let out a sharp huff, echoing her own frustration. "You can ask my mother about perfection. I'm sure she'd be happy to give you a long list of my flaws."

———

Like my short fuse, for one.

Michael closed his mouth, feeling his defenses drop. He could see the determination in Olivia's eyes, but more than that, he could see the hurt. He'd pushed too hard in trying to protect her.

He fumbled for what to say. "I'm sorry. I just don't want to see you hurt."

She got up and strode to the door leading to the hallway and flung it open. "I've got to get some air."

"Olivia . . ."

He started toward the door.

"Let her go for now, Michael."

He turned back to his sister. "But—"

"She won't go far." Avery nodded at Mason to follow Olivia and keep an eye on her. "I know you're worried about her, but you can't fix everything. She's lost a lot these past few days. She's going to need time and space to work through this."

"And if Valez's intentions aren't on the up-and-up?"

"I just wouldn't be so quick to dismiss her going ahead with this." Avery nodded toward the kitchen. "Come on. I could use a cup of coffee, and I have a feeling you could too."

Michael hesitated, then followed his sister into the kitchen, still torn between his desire to run after Olivia and try to make everything right or Avery's advice to back off. This was why he never let his heart get involved in a case. Why he needed to step away emotionally before he got pulled in any further.

Avery filled the coffeemaker with water and flipped it on. "She's stronger than you think."

"Maybe, but that's not the issue."

"Then what is the issue?"

"I just believe . . . it's too dangerous for her to be out there. I've worked with Valez for months. I know the kind of man he is. My job was to collect enough evidence to put him and as many as I could in prison—"

"I understand that, but there's more here. Your heart's involved."

Michael grabbed two mugs from the shelf. "I'm an undercover cop, Avery. I know how to work a case without getting my emotions involved."

"Really?"

"And even if there is . . . something . . . between us, I'm not letting it cloud my judgment."

Avery folded her arms across her chest, clearly not buying his excuses.

"I don't even know if what is there has a chance of going anywhere." He fumbled with his excuses. "I haven't even known her for a week."

"Does it matter? We all have concerns when it comes to relationships. For me, it was the fear of what a relationship would require of me. I wasn't sure I was able to give Jackson a chance."

"So you're saying what . . . that I'm scared?"

"Of a girl?" Avery laughed. "Yeah. Pretty much. Admit you like her and it'll make your life a heck of a lot easier." She turned around and leaned against the counter, facing him. "But you also need to admit that she can handle this. She's strong. Stop trying to protect her from every possible complication that might arise, and give her some credit."

Michael grabbed a couple of spoons and stuck them in the mugs. "I still don't think it's a good idea for her to meet with her father. This is your chance to go in there with your team and arrest him."

"What if he knows where Ivan is? Or has information regarding his captors?"

Michael leaned back against the counter, feeling as if all of his options were going to get someone else hurt.

"You know, little brother, you've spent most of your career working the tough cases. Undercover, risking your life . . . Have you ever thought about quitting and putting yourself first for a change?"

He shook his head, not following her train of thought. "And switch to what? A desk job?"

"Hardly. There are lots of other choices out there that would work better with getting married, starting a family."

"Whoa." He held up his hands. "I'd say you're jumping the gun a bit."

"Maybe, but I think you understand what I'm saying. Don't use your job as an excuse to run away. Your career doesn't make you who you are. Listen to your heart for once, Michael." She reached up and hugged him. "And now that Olivia's had a few minutes to calm down, go talk to her. She needs your support right now, as much as you need hers. Just don't be afraid to let her do what she needs to do. She needs a friend right now more than a bodyguard. Be that for her."

Michael stepped out into the hallway and nodded for Mason to leave him and Olivia alone. She sat on the floor at the end of the hallway beside a floor-to-ceiling window overlooking the city. Snow fell in the background, covering rooftops in a blanket of white. If this had been any other moment, any other circumstance, he'd follow his heart, sweep her into his arms, and kiss her like she'd never been kissed before.

"Olivia?" He slid down the wall beside her. "My sister thinks I was out of line in there. And she was right."

She looked up at him, her eyes red from crying. "You know what's funny?"

"No."

"The fact that I've been doing the exact thing to Ivan that you've been doing to me. I've protected him because I thought I was keeping a promise I made to my mother."

"It's easy to do, isn't it?" He ran his fingers down her arm, then laced their fingers together. "I was just so scared, thinking of what might happen if you went to see your father. But it has nothing to do with not trusting you. It's my not being sure I can keep you safe."

"Would that matter to you?"

He matched her smile. Liking the way she looked at him. Liking the way she flirted with him. "I wouldn't want anything to happen to you or your brother, you know that."

"So this is just about our safety?"

"Hardly. It's about these crazy feelings I have for you."

A part of him feared he was going to regret giving in to his heart, but maybe Avery was right. Maybe it was time he stopped running. Living two lives had become unbearable.

"This is personal," he continued. "Very personal. In the short time we've known each other, I've seen so many sides of you. The way you care for your brother. The way you seek out truth no matter what the cost. I don't want to lose you, Olivia, because . . ."

"Because what?"

She was close enough that he could read the question in her eyes.

"Because I can see the two of us together when all of this is over."

She reached up and played with the lapel of his bomber jacket, then looked up at him with those wide, brown, questioning eyes. "We've been through a lot together these past few days. I know how easily emotions can spiral out of control and make you feel things you wouldn't necessarily feel if there wasn't a crisis happening. But when you kissed me on that hotel balcony . . . was that as real to you as it was to me?"

"Are you asking me how I feel about you?"

She nodded.

"I wasn't expecting someone like you to walk into my life. So yes, when this is over, I'd like to spend a lot of time with you and find out."

She smiled up at him, causing his heart to trip again. "I was hoping you'd say that. But first, I need to do this. I need to know the truth. I need to have this part of my life closed, and that will never happen unless I confront my father."

"Then we do this right. You go and see your father, while Mason, Avery, and I provide security."

She shook her head. "You can't be there. My father knows you. Besides, I can't do anything that might risk Ivan's life."

The elevator dinged. Michael looked down the hall as the doors opened. Two men, dressed in black, stepped into the hallway carrying rifles. Michael felt his adrenaline surge.

They'd found them.

CHAPTER
31

Olivia saw the two men the moment Michael hauled her up beside him onto her feet. Her mind struggled to decipher what was happening. Tattooed necks . . . heavy boots . . . assault rifles . . .

How in the world had they slipped past the added security Avery had insisted on?

The panic that had been simmering in her gut all day exploded. She glanced down the adjoining hallway. There were only two ways off this floor. The elevator, and the stairwell twenty feet ahead of them. With two armed men standing in the middle of the hallway, the elevator wasn't an option.

Michael pulled her toward the stairwell as the first bullet hit the wall behind them. She ran beside him down the narrow hallway, past a blur of room numbers and a maid's cart. Michael shoved the cart behind them down the hallway as the men rounded the corner. He fired two rounds from his weapon, then threw open the heavy metal door that led to the stairs.

He grabbed his phone from his pocket and thrust it into her hand, then pulled her in front of him toward the stairs. "Call Avery. Tell her we need backup. Now."

Olivia fumbled with the phone as Michael followed her down the stairs to the next floor, his gun aimed at the top of the stairs.

"Michael?" Avery answered on the first ring.

"It's Olivia. They're on our floor and they're after us." She fought to catch her breath as she continued down the staircase beside Michael. "Two armed men."

"We're already in the hallway. Where are you?"

The stairwell door opened above them. Footsteps pounded on the landing.

"In the east stairwell headed downstairs."

The phone slipped out of her hand, tumbling to the floor as she turned to head down another flight of stairs.

She started to grab for it. "Michael—"

"Leave it!"

Steps reverberated in the stairwell above them as the men gained on them. Another shot fired, hitting the stair rail.

Michael tugged at her hand. "Keep moving."

Olivia rounded the next flight of stairs, her lungs burning for oxygen. The door above them slammed open again, followed by Avery's voice. "Police."

Someone else was shouting. Footsteps pounded above them. More shots fired—

Michael moved her against the wall, pressing against her like a shield.

The stairwell fell quiet.

"Michael?" Avery's voice called down the stairwell. "We're clear."

Still holding Olivia's hand, Michael steadied her for a minute. Then he tilted up her chin and caught her gaze. "It's over."

Her eyes filled with tears. "It's never going to be over."

Her shoulders dropped as he led her back up the stairs, the terror settling like the aftermath of a fire. Avery and Mason were handcuffing the men.

"Do you recognize either of them?" he asked after they'd hauled them up the stairs.

Olivia shook her head.

"I don't either."

Olivia started back up the stairs, her heart still hammering. "It's time for me to go see my father and try to put an end to this."

———————

Michael felt his blood pressure rise as Olivia stepped out of the hotel bedroom. She looked beautiful bundled up in the jeans and heavy coat Emily had loaned her, but he knew this wasn't about his growing feelings toward her, or even his fears of losing her. This was about confronting her father, and putting an end to everything that had happened over the past couple of days. Which was why he'd thrown out every objection he could think of to deter her from meeting him, but he knew she wouldn't listen. She was determined to go through with this.

She stepped in front of him, her eyes full of questions. "You okay?"

"Just wishing I was the one taking you out somewhere tonight." He bit back the word of warning poised on the tip of his tongue, swapping it for a compliment. "You look beautiful."

"Thank you, but I know that's not all you're thinking. I can't back out of this for the same reason that you couldn't stop working for my father."

"I know."

"I'm not walking into this blindly, Michael, but I need to do what's right—whatever the cost."

He smiled down at her. "You're a brave woman, Olivia Hamilton."

"Not really." She took his hand in both of hers and squeezed it tightly. "I'm terrified, but you keep reminding me of what's important and what's really at stake here. I just wish it didn't include having to consult with the enemy."

Which was exactly what had him scared.

"When this is over," he said, wrapping his other hand around hers, "how about doing something boring together, like an afternoon at some stodgy museum, or maybe a really dull poetry reading."

She laughed. "I'd like that. Spending a normal, boring day with you."

Avery walked into the room, reminding him that there would be no normal, boring days ahead for the two of them if they didn't end this tonight.

"You two about ready?"

Olivia nodded.

"As soon as you're done talking with your father, we're moving you to that safe house," Avery said.

"What about Felipe's list?"

"We're closing in on the uniforms involved. Four arrests have already been made tonight, and the captain is expecting at least a dozen more to follow."

"I'm glad, but the evidence . . ." She turned to Avery. "Will it stick?"

"I think the DA should be able to make a strong case against them."

"I hope so."

Michael studied his sister's somber expression. He might not have been around the past few months, but he still knew her well enough to tell when something was wrong.

"Avery?"

"I have good news and bad news."

Michael glanced at Olivia. "Okay."

"The good news is we were able to confirm from the hotel video footage that the two men who grabbed Ivan were the same guys we just arrested in the stairwell."

"And the bad news?"

"We know how they got in. Two of the security guards were found dead."

Olivia's grip tightened on his hand. "Are they talking?"

"So far all we know is they work for Salazar, and that they were ordered to find you and Ivan." Michael's frown deepened.

"So we are being used as leverage. What else?"

"I'm sorry, Michael, but they found Jinx. They murdered him too."

"No . . ." Michael's voice caught as a wave of nausea pooled in his gut. This was the kind of guilt he'd never be able to shake.

"They apparently found out from his parole officer that you were going to talk to him. They were waiting for him when he eventually returned to his house."

"He paid the price for my decisions."

"You can't blame yourself," Avery said.

"I can and I do. They killed him because I went to him for information." Michael's jaw tensed. "The bottom line is that these people don't play games, Olivia. And now you and Ivan are being used to draw your father out—"

"That's why we have to stop this before more people are killed."

He took her hand and laced their fingers together. All he knew to do was keep praying that they could get through the next few hours without anyone else getting hurt. "You know the plan for tonight?"

"Yeah."

Her father's directions had been simple. He'd chosen the busy food court of a nearby mall, and given her specific instructions. Come alone. No cops. She was to sit down at a table and he'd find her. They'd worked on a plan with the captain to get around the no-cops condition by using handpicked, plainclothes officers to secure the area, but the mall would be crowded, with multiple exits, something Valez was no doubt counting on. Michael could only pray their plan was enough to keep Olivia safe.

"Avery will meet you there when you're done talking with him and escort you out of the mall. We'll be able to hear everything you say."

"And then they'll arrest him." She reached for the button on the front of her coat jacket that would catch both audio and video. "Is it wrong for me to still want to believe that my father's somehow innocent in all of this?"

"No. I'd say it's completely normal."

She moved away from him until she was standing in front of the window overlooking the lit-up city. "I've always seen life as black and white, with a few areas of gray, but part of me wants to try and justify everything that my father did. I want to tell the DA that it's not my father's fault that there are drugs in the world. He never forced anyone to use them, he was simply doing business like any other businessman would have done . . . meeting the demand."

She turned away from the window to face him. "I want to blame what's happened on the millions who demand what he sells. Is that crazy?"

He waited for her to continue.

"The other thing I want to tell him is that you can arrest my father, Salazar, Felipe, every lieutenant, hitman, and local drug dealer under them, along with every single person on the Canary List, and there will be others who will rise up to take their places. Maybe the problem will move down the street or into another neighborhood, but it's not over. It's never going to be over. Not as long as people keep demanding the drugs."

"Maybe, but in the end, your father is responsible for his actions, just like every other dealer and user out there," Michael said. "And what we do today will make a difference."

Avery walked into the room, adjusting her earpiece. "Are you ready?"

Olivia drew in a deep breath. "Yeah, let's go."

———

Forty-five minutes later, Olivia crossed the crowded food court, with its loud music playing in the background, praying that after tonight all of this would be over. Praying that Avery and her team would find Ivan. And that maybe . . . just maybe . . . she'd get a chance to get to know Michael without the threat of someone trying to kill them.

People lined up in front of the dozens of food venders still decorated for the holidays, buying everything from pizza, to burgers, to Chinese fare. Families with young children, teens, and couples filled the tables and chairs across the open space. She couldn't see them, but she knew that the team Avery had put together was out there as well, ensuring her safety. But even that wasn't enough to settle her nerves.

The calmness she'd tried to emulate on the drive over had been nothing more than a false front, because inside, she was still terrified. She'd take sitting in front of her computer, miles away from any real conflict, to chasing down the bad guys like an adrenaline junkie any day.

But she could—she would—do this for Ivan.

She found one of the few empty tables with two chairs and sat down as she'd been instructed, sipping the milkshake she'd bought while trying to look as if she were simply taking a break from shopping. A moment later, she saw him walk toward her, carrying a shopping bag. He looked older than she remembered. His hair was grayer than it had been a year ago, his hairline had receded, and there were creases across his face from the hard life he'd led. He didn't look anything like a drug lord or money launderer. He looked like someone's husband—or someone's father—birthday shopping after a day's work at the office.

He slid in across from her and set his shopping bag on the floor beside his chair.

The smile he gave her was tempered with an edge of caution. "I wasn't sure you'd show up."

"You told me this had to do with Ivan. What choice did I have?"

"There are so many things you don't know. But as much as you probably hate me right now, I want you to know that I never regretted loving your mother. Never regretted you and Ivan."

Olivia's jaw tensed. It was too late to start over. Too late to erase the damage from the past. And she was tired of his excuses.

"What I know," she said, "is that I've spent my entire life living a lie. Surrounded by secrets that no one would tell me. Maybe you and my mother were only trying to protect me, but Ivan could lose his life because of those secrets. It has to end. Now."

"Can I assume that Michael filled you in on some of those secrets, *mi princesa?*"

Olivia flinched at the pet name. "Does it matter? And maybe we should skip the pleasantries and just focus on where Ivan is."

"Salazar has him."

"Why?" she asked.

"For the past few years he's been setting up a place to operate out of northern Mexico, supplying heroin, cocaine, marijuana, and meth that he plans to flood the region with. He's in the process of centralizing the shipping, warehousing, and distribution of the drugs, then the collection and transport of the money back to Mexico. He's setting himself up to take over Cártel de Rey."

The pieces were beginning to snap into place. She knew some of the answers, but wanted to hear them from him. "How do Ivan and I fit into all of this?"

"He's using you to get to me."

"What are they asking for?"

Her father tapped his fingers against the table, clearly taking in everything that was going on around him while he spoke. "There's a list of names some call the Canary List. It's a record of cartel informants within the government and police department. He needs that list in order to ensure loyalties."

Olivia felt her stomach clench. "That's what they're asking for?"

"If they don't get that list, they've said they'll kill your brother." Her father reached out and grasped her hands. "No matter what kind of father you think I've been, I don't want to be responsible for my son's death. But I swear, I don't have the list."

The panic was back. Did her father have any idea that with the Canary List in the hands of the police, it had become worthless to Salazar? Olivia felt her head pound, not knowing how much to tell him, or how much she could trust him. But the bottom line was that their leverage to save Ivan's life had just vanished.

"How much time do we have?"

"I don't know yet." Her father glanced at his watch. "I'm waiting for Salazar to call me back and tell me where to meet him, but there are rumors that Felipe gave you the list. Is that true?"

Olivia ignored his question. "And without the list? How do we save him?"

Her father's gaze darkened. "Why? What do you know, Olivia?"

"I know it's too late." Olivia felt the darkness of the room close in on her. They'd torture and kill him. "The police already have that list."

"Making the list completely worthless to Salazar." Her father raked his hands through his hair.

"What do we do?"

"I don't know, but what I do know, *mi princesa*, is that all those years I kept my distance from you, it was never because I didn't care. It was because I was afraid of this very thing happening."

"Then what do we do now? There has to be a way to get Ivan back alive." The panic was rising again. The noise from the crowd and the music pressed in around her, making her want to bolt. "They've already made a number of arrests. It won't be long before Salazar knows that list is worthless, if he doesn't already know."

Her father reached into his coat pocket and pulled out his phone to check his messages.

Olivia leaned forward. "What is it?"

"I have to go."

"Wait. It's Salazar, isn't it?" She reached out and grabbed his arm as he stood up to leave. "Tell me what he says."

"He's given me a meeting place. He's expecting that list."

"Where?"

"I don't want you involved in this. Salazar doesn't just want that list. He wants me. And he'll use you to get to me, just like he's using Ivan."

"Tell me where." She grabbed his hand holding the phone and pulled it toward her.

The Addison Hotel.

"Stay out of this, Olivia," he said.

She stumbled away from the table and tried to follow him through the crowded food court. He dodged the woman cleaning a table, sidestepping her cart by slipping through a bunch of rowdy teenagers.

"Excuse me." Olivia pushed her way through the group. If they lost him now . . .

She caught sight of him again briefly, heading down the crowded corridor of the mall. He was pulling out a jacket and a ball cap from his shopping bag and slipped them both on as he disappeared into a sea of shoppers. Her stomach cinched. He'd planned for everything, and now they were going to lose him . . .

A moment later she was finally at the edge of the congested food court. And her father was gone.

She spoke into the mike. "He put on a jacket and cap . . ." Her words trailed away. She hadn't been close enough to be able to describe them. And she had no idea where he'd gone.

Avery met her at the edge of the food court and swept her down an empty hallway, toward the back exit.

Olivia forced down the rising despair. "We lost him."

"Maybe," Avery said. "We've still got men on all the exits."

"They won't find him." He'd spent his life staying one step ahead of the cops. "But he received a text message right before he left. He's meeting Salazar at the Addison Hotel."

Avery passed on the information to the rest of the team on her radio, then turned back to Olivia. "We can have backup there in the next ten minutes, and we'll pick up Salazar and Valez."

"Ivan could be there too."

"I'll have security start searching the video footage from the time he was taken until now." Avery rested her hand on Olivia's arm. "If your brother's there, we will find him. For now, Carlos is waiting to pick us up outside."

Olivia wanted to cry, wanted to scream, but all she could do was follow Avery down the hallway, letting the shock of her father's words consume her. "We've just lost all our leverage to save my brother. They want the list. Ivan's life for that stupid list, and if they don't get it they're going to kill him."

How could she save Ivan when there was no way to give them what they were demanding?

CHAPTER
32

Olivia struggled to keep up with Avery as she escorted her out of the mall and into the cold Atlanta night. "Where's Carlos going to take us?"

Avery buttoned the top of her coat. "The captain secured a safe house where you can stay out of the line of fire until it's over."

They paused in front of an unmarked car at the edge of the parking lot, making Olivia feel as if she were trying to escape the paparazzi.

She slid into the seat ahead of Avery. "I want to go to the Addison Hotel with you. If my brother's there, I can help find him."

"I need you to trust me. It's not safe, Olivia."

As soon as Avery shut the door, Carlos drove off. "Where's Michael?"

"He'll meet us at the safe house."

Olivia leaned back against the seat as they pulled out of the mall parking lot and tried to relax, but all she could think about was her brother. They would kill him without the Canary List, and the list was worthless. How had doing the right thing turned into this?

Five minutes later, Carlos pulled onto the freeway, passing neighborhoods still lit up for the festive holiday season. For most people it was another ordinary Friday night watching television and eating pizza. For her, nothing was ordinary about today.

God, the past few days have felt like one nightmare after another. And this time . . . this time I can't see a way out. We don't have what they want. Can't get what they want.

Her fingers gripped the armrest. Ivan could be at the hotel, but the reality was they could have taken him anywhere.

Olivia looked at Avery, who'd just answered her cell, trying to gauge by her expression what was going on.

"What is it?" she asked as soon as Avery had hung up.

"They found something."

"Please. Tell me what's going on."

Avery hesitated as if deciding whether or not she should tell her. "Security at the Addison Hotel started going through the footage for us, and they think they found your brother."

"So he's there? Where my father is going to meet Salazar." Olivia gripped Avery's arm, the first seed of hope she'd felt all day springing to life. "Where is he?"

Avery shrugged. "That's the problem. They don't know. Not yet, anyway. Ivan was caught on the security footage as he got into one of the elevators with two men, but the problem is that there are over a thousand rooms, 150,000 square feet of indoor meeting spaces, laundry, pools, underground parking . . ."

There had to be a way to find him. "So you're saying he's at the hotel, but you have no idea where."

"I'm sorry, Olivia, but at least we have his whereabouts narrowed down."

"They're going through the rest of the footage to see if he left."

A chill ran up Olivia's spine. "I want to see the footage."

"The captain doesn't want you involved in this."

Olivia shook her head. "Please. Ivan is smart. He might have found a way to communicate."

"They said there's nothing there—"

"Please. Just let me see it."

Avery made another call, then spoke to Carlos.

"You're in luck," she told Olivia. "The captain agrees you should look at the footage, but then I want you out of there."

Olivia nodded. "Thank you."

Avery's expression softened in the light of the passing cars. "Listen . . . I know this has all been hard, but you did what was right. And I promise we'll do everything we can to find your brother."

Then why did doing what was right make her feel as if she'd just betrayed someone? "Do you think my father was telling the truth? That he really is concerned about Ivan's life, or do you think he just wanted the list for himself?"

"I wish I could answer that question for you, but I don't know. All we can do right now is focus on finding Ivan."

Carlos took the next exit, heading for the hotel. Avery was right, but Olivia still couldn't help but wonder what her father was thinking. Wonder what his real motives were for asking her to come and help. Was it because he cared about Ivan, or because he needed the list for himself?

Something told her it was the latter. He'd spent his entire life building his empire, oblivious to what was going on in her and Ivan's lives. They had been an inconvenience to deal with and nothing more. It was easy to have an accountant write a check every month. How could she ever have expected anything more?

At the hotel they entered through a back entrance, and Olivia was ushered into a nice-sized office behind the front desk, where Tory was working with one of the employees at a computer.

"Tory, I need you to show Olivia the footage of her brother," Avery said.

"Give me just a second," Tory said. "The resolution isn't

great, but it's clearly Ivan. This is Brett Fuller," she continued, making quick introductions. "He's with the hotel security."

Olivia nodded at the balding, uniformed officer, then turned her eyes to the computer screen, her heart pumping fast in anticipation. If Ivan *was* here, with or without the list, they needed to find him.

With a few clicks of the mouse, the footage appeared on the screen. "This is what they found of Ivan getting ready to get on the elevator."

Olivia braced her hands against the desk, studying the footage. Ivan walked between two men. He looked up at the camera as they passed by right before getting into the elevator.

Five seconds later, Tory froze the footage.

"Where did they get off?" Olivia asked.

"That's the problem. We don't know. It looks like two of the cameras aren't working, since we never see him get off the elevator. We're still trying to find out why."

Which meant this was all they had to go on.

"Can I see it again?" she asked.

"Sure." Tory rewound the grainy footage, then played it again.

Olivia watched Ivan look at the camera again. His hands were behind his back. He looked away . . . "Stop. Rewind the footage ten seconds, then zoom in on my brother's hands."

"Okay."

"There. Slow down the speed."

Olivia held her breath as she watched the footage replay in slow motion. Ivan glanced up . . .

"Stop . . . Right there."

"What's he doing?" the guard asked.

Olivia smiled. "Signing. My brother's deaf. He can read lips, and he must have caught something important that he's trying to tell us."

"What is he saying?"

"Run it back one more time."

Olivia watched for the fourth time. There was no mistake. "Three hundred twenty-two. It must be a room number."

"Are you sure?"

"Positive."

———

Michael slipped into the hotel lobby behind Mason and clicked on his radio. "Avery, we're here. What have you got?"

"Olivia found something in the surveillance video. Looks like Ivan might be in room number 322."

"I'm on it."

"Can you meet us there with a key?" Mason asked.

Michael passed a row of elevators, opting instead for the stairs at the end of the short hallway, praying as he went. Praying for Olivia and Ivan . . . and for a way to end all of this without anyone else getting hurt.

He paused to catch his breath at the third floor before opening the metal fire door.

I need to find him, Lord . . .

Avery met them at the room, where he shoved the key card into the lock and waited for the green light to come on, then burst into the room.

"Ivan!"

They swept the room and bathroom, but there was no sign of Ivan.

Michael turned to Mason, frustrated. Another dead end meant they were back to square one. "He's not here."

"Do you think Olivia made a mistake with the numbers?" Mason asked.

"I don't think so." Michael picked something up off the floor and walked across the room to where Mason and Avery were opening drawers, looking under the chairs, anything to find a clue.

"What's that?"

"Part of a detonator." Michael's heart pounded. "There's a good chance that bomb is somewhere here in this building."

"What about the bomb squad?" Michael asked Avery.

"I've already got them here on standby, just in case."

Michael turned back to Mason. "If Salazar wanted to make a statement, where would he set it off?"

"Wait a minute." Avery had pulled back one of the chairs from the table and looked underneath it. "I think Ivan left us a message."

Michael knelt down beside his sister and read the message scratched into the underside of the table.

Balrom.

"Balrom?" Mason asked.

"Ballroom." Michael checked his watch. "I glanced at the schedule earlier. There's some kind of event going on here tonight in the ballroom, and the master of ceremonies is scheduled to speak right about now."

Michael turned to Avery. "Have the bomb squad meet us on the first floor with the bomb dogs to make a sweep . . . and start evacuating the hotel."

"I'm on it."

Michael radioed Tory as they started for the stairwell and gave her a quick update. "Have you found Valez?"

"Not yet."

"And Olivia?"

"She's here with me."

"Make sure she goes somewhere safe. Please."

"I will."

"And pray we find that bomb before it goes off."

Three minutes later, Michael ran through the lobby, his pulse racing. The fire alarm screamed in the background. Staff members were trying to keep order with walkie-talkies while guests hurried toward the exits.

One of the K9 handlers called Michael and led him down a hallway behind the ballroom. "I think we might have something. It's a storage room, but it's locked."

"Can we get a key?" Mason asked.

"We don't have time for a key." Michael kicked open the door of the storage closet with his heel and flipped on the light. Ivan and Valez sat tied up and gagged in the shadows beside the bomb.

Michael pulled out their gags.

"Don't bother with me—get him out of here," Valez said. "We're out of time."

Michael radioed the captain. "We've found the bomb. It's in the storage closet behind the main ballroom."

"How much time?"

Michael glanced at the timer. "Five minutes, twenty-nine seconds."

Ivan was trembling. "You should go."

Michael shook his head. "Are you kidding? I'm not leaving without you, Ivan. You did good, leaving the message under the table."

The bomb squad moved in and got to work defusing the bomb. Michael worked on the duct tape wrapped around Ivan's wrists that secured him to a metal pole behind him, while Mason worked to free Valez.

"Listen, there's nothing for you to worry about. The bomb squad knows what they're doing." Michael freed Ivan's second arm with his pocketknife. "Besides, there's someone waiting for you outside. I'm pretty sure she wouldn't forgive me if I let something happen to you."

He started on freeing Ivan's legs.

He glanced at the bomb as he struggled to unloose Ivan. The fire alarm screamed in the background.

Three minutes, fifty-two seconds.

"Come on . . . come on . . ."

With three minutes left on the timer, Mason finished freeing Valez, who refused to budge until Ivan was also free.

All four men ran toward the hotel exit.

They found Olivia standing behind the yellow police line with Carlos, who was talking on his radio.

"The bomb squad just gave the all clear," Carlos said. "It's over."

Ivan flew into his sister's embrace, then stepped away, nodding at Michael.

Adrenaline still raced through him. But that wasn't the only reason his heart was pounding. He took a step forward, cupped her face between his hands, and paused a moment to breathe in her sweetness. "I was so afraid I might lose you."

She smiled up at him, and he kissed her softly before pulling her into his arms. "You didn't lose me, Michael. You didn't lose me."

CHAPTER
33

Michael sat in his car outside his parents' home, feeling the weight of how his choices hadn't just affected himself. He turned to his father sitting in the passenger seat, thankful for his strength and presence. "How has she handled the news that I'm alive?"

"It's been a shock. I'm not sure she'll truly believe it until you've been home for a while. For months, she's believed her only son was dead. Someone once told me that you can lose a spouse or a parent and move on, but losing a child is different. It's something that isn't supposed to happen. And I saw on a day-to-day basis how that's affected your mother."

Michael whispered, "Do you think she'll ever forgive me?"

"She already has." His father laid his hand on Michael's shoulder. "But that doesn't take away the consequences of that decision. Your mother—both of us—love you. Losing you was like losing a part of ourselves. It doesn't matter if you're five or fifty-five, we still see the little boy and all the hopes and dreams we have for you."

Michael pressed his fingers against the armrest, replaying in his mind what the outcome would have been if he'd done things differently. If he'd gone to his father from the beginning instead of trying to play the game on his own. He'd believed he was protecting his family. In the end, it felt as if he'd hurt so many people.

"The bottom line, son, is that the choice has already been made. And while your decision brought about a lot of pain, it also brought about a lot of good. I can't say that your mother will ever agree 100 percent, but I'm proud of you for taking the difficult road. For standing up for justice and what you believed to be right, even knowing that the cost would be great."

Michael shook his head. "I'm no hero. I feel as if I still need to apologize. To you and to Mom . . . to the whole family. What I did affected everyone, and while I don't regret what I did, part of me—a big part—wishes I'd never had to make that choice. Wish I'd walked away from it all before I ever got in as deep as I did."

"You'd never have met Olivia. What happens now that all of this is over?"

It was the question Michael had asked himself over and over the past few hours. "Part of me feels as if I haven't known her long enough to make that decision, but another part of me knows I don't want to let her go."

"I've seen the two of you together. She's good for you."

"You sound like Avery and Emily. So you think it's time for me to settle down too?"

"I know your mother would appreciate another grandchild or two."

"Whoa . . . let's not jump ahead there yet. I'm looking forward to spending some time getting to know Olivia outside a situation where we're constantly running for our lives. And then in time, who knows? You might get that extra grandchild."

Michael couldn't help but smile at the thought. It had been a long time since a woman made him want to settle down and find a hint of normalcy in his life. They might still need time to explore their feelings together, but as far as he was concerned, she'd already stolen his heart.

He set his empty coffee mug down between them and cleared his throat. "There is one other thing I need to tell you before I go inside."

"What's that?"

He hesitated, unsure what his father would think about his latest decision. "I've asked for a transfer out of undercover work."

His father's brows rose. "Did Olivia have anything to do with this decision?"

"In part, though I haven't even told her yet. All I know is, if our relationship is to have any chance at all, I can't be spending my time living another life. She needs to get to know me. *I* need to get to know me."

He'd almost lost himself the last few months. It was time to take a different road. Finding someone to take that journey with him had been unexpected. But his father was right. There was something about Olivia that was very, very good for him. "I think you're a wise man. When the right woman comes along, you have to hold on to her."

"I believe she's worth it," his father said.

He looked at the house where he'd grown up. He'd bring Olivia here sometime, but for now, there was another woman he needed to see.

"Go on in and see your mother. She knows you're coming, but it's still going to be a shock for her to see you. She struggled for eight months to resign herself to the fact that you weren't coming back. I'll wait out here a few minutes before coming inside."

Michael walked slowly up the driveway toward the front door of his parents' house. Memories flooded through him. Water balloon fights in the summer, running through the sprinkler, camping in the backyard and roasting marshmallows. He'd grown up here in this house, listening to his father's wise advice, eating his mother's southern cooking.

Before he'd even reached for the handle of the front door, his mother was suddenly standing in front of him.

"Michael."

"Mama . . . I'm sorry . . . so . . . so sorry for everything."

She gathered him into her arms. It was the second chance none of them had expected. "Welcome home, son. Welcome home."

CHAPTER
34

Olivia sank into the comfy couch she'd picked up at an estate sale last year, grabbed the TV remote, then stopped, dropping it onto the seat beside her. She needed a distraction, but reruns or infomercials weren't what she was looking for. She'd spent the past hour praying, trying to settle her mind as it sorted through everything that had happened the past few days.

Ivan walked into the room with Gizmo—who'd been found wandering the hotel parking lot—right behind him and flipped on the lamp on the end table. "Can't sleep?"

"No," she signed, squinting against the light.

"Me either." He motioned for the dog to lie down, then sat down beside her on the couch. "They told me it would be normal to have trouble eating and sleeping."

"Nothing that happened this past week was normal." Emotion teetering on the edge of her heart welled up. "I thought I lost you."

"But you didn't."

She nodded, realizing that the memories of the past few days would eventually fade, but for now, they were still all too present.

"There is one other thing we need to talk about."

Olivia fought against the initial panic. "What's wrong?"

"Nothing's wrong. It's just something I've put off telling you, because . . . because I didn't know how to tell you."

He pressed his palms together in front of him, his eyes bright. "Ivan . . ."

"A few months ago"—he began signing again—"I applied to another school."

"Why?" she clipped back.

"I want a change. More of a challenge."

After high school Ivan had offers to universities in several other states, but had eventually decided to stick with their local community college for the first two years. She hadn't argued. She liked having him home.

"Two weeks ago, they sent me an acceptance letter."

"Wow. That's fantastic. What school?"

Ivan's gaze shifted. "MIT in Cambridge."

"Cambridge?" She hadn't expected this. "I thought you meant a school here in Atlanta."

"It's only a day's drive—"

"A very long day's drive."

Options ran through her mind. She could always get another job with a newspaper in Boston. The only thing she wasn't sure about was leaving Michael.

She pushed aside the thought. "I've got a friend in Boston who could help us find a place to live and—"

Ivan shook his head. "You don't understand. You're not coming with me. I need to do this by myself."

Olivia let his words sink in.

"Please," he continued. "Please don't think I'm not grateful for everything you've done for me. You gave up everything to take care of me, and I don't take any of that for granted."

"Of course not." She blinked back the tears. "We're family. Families stick together."

"And just because I'm in Cambridge and you're still here doesn't mean any of that changes, but this is something I need to do. Last week proved to me that I want to focus on computer forensics. Plus, Tory said she would try to fix me up with someone she knows for a possible internship."

"That's wonderful, but—"

"Please, let me finish. While I was in the hotel room with those men, and then in that storage room, I thought I was going to die. All I could do was pray that you or Michael or one of the officers would find me. But I also realized that I rely on you too much. I need to prove I can get out in this world and make it on my own."

"You don't have to prove anything. Because you're right."

"I'm right?"

She pulled the throw pillow to her chest and fiddled with one of the tassels. It was a conversation they should have had a long time ago. "I've spent my entire adult life trying to protect you, but what I didn't do was let you set off on your own. It's time I let you fly, because I have no doubt that you can."

"So you're not mad?"

"Mad? Are you kidding me?" She pulled him into a hug, then drew back and caught his gaze. "My genius brother's going to MIT."

"I think you gained something as well this past week. Or shall I say, someone." Ivan's smile widened. "I like Michael, and his family. I think you need to hang on to him. He's good for you."

She brushed back a tear and laughed. "Yeah, he is good for me."

"Is he going to drive you to the prison this morning?"

She nodded, some of the anxiety returning. Her father had asked her to visit, and she'd agreed, despite strong feelings of uncertainty. "You still don't want to come?"

"Maybe one day, but not now."

She gave his hand a squeeze. "That's completely up to you."

Olivia stopped in front of the prison lobby, the nerves in her stomach feeling more like a host to a large flock of starlings than a few butterflies.

She looked up at Michael, thankful for the calming effect he had on her. "Do you think I made the right decision in seeing him?"

"I can't make that call for you, but I do think you need answers to your questions, and this isn't something I can do for you." He ran his thumb down her cheek. "I just want you to be safe."

The answers she had so far had left her more unsettled than at peace. Tomas had confessed to betraying her father and working for Salazar, the man he believed would soon rise to power. Kidnapping Ivan had been an attempt to draw out their father, but it hadn't been enough. Felipe had vanished from the hospital, presumed to have overpowered the guard whose only crime had been to protect him. Two nights later, Salazar and four of his men had been gunned down in a brutal attack outside of Atlanta, their bodies left on the side of the road, tortured and beheaded. No one knew for sure who'd ordered the attack, but rumors were running rampant that La Sombra killed them before fleeing the country.

Olivia grasped Michael's hand. He was right. This was something she had to do on her own. "I always believed that the truth would set me free. Maybe this is the final step in finding that freedom."

Olivia showed the officer her driver's license, then signed the visitors' log. She walked past the security guard into the visitors' waiting room, mouth dry, palms sweaty.

Antonio Valez sat on the other side of the room, looking lost, no longer able to hide behind his expensive suits.

"I appreciate your coming to see me," he said as she walked up to him.

Olivia nodded, then let her gaze sweep his orange jumpsuit,

wondering how to respond to the man who'd spent his life deceiving others. A man who more than likely would spend the rest of his life in prison. It had taken her a week to come to the point where she could walk into this room. Now she was wondering how much could be said in fifteen minutes.

She sat down across from him with the knowledge that nothing was ever going to be the same again. All the memories of the summers she'd spent visiting the island had now been shoved into the past where she wanted them to stay.

Her father broke the uneasy silence between them. "How's Ivan?"

"He's doing well. He's been accepted to MIT, and wants to work in computer forensics."

"Wow. That's fantastic."

"Yeah, it's going to be strange not having him around, but it's the perfect situation for him."

"Sounds as if he's doing what he's always wanted to do."

"He is."

Olivia folded her hands together and rested them on the table between them. Part of her wanted to bolt. The other wanted to find a chance for their relationship to work. She'd never seen him so humble and unassuming. So engaged with what she had to say.

"And you? I'm assuming you're going to stay here?"

"Yes." She leaned back and started to play with the zipper of her coat. "I did a story for the paper and ended up getting a promotion, actually."

"Congratulations."

"Thanks."

The decision to stay had come easier than she thought. Realizing that Ivan could take care of himself without her had stung at first, but then came with it the knowledge that the boy she'd raised really was grown up.

"Does your staying have anything to do with anyone in particular?"

She felt a blush cross her cheeks. "There is someone. He's . . . someone I met recently."

How did she tell him she was in love with the cop who'd taken him down?

"It's Michael Hunt," he said.

Olivia frowned. "How did you know?"

"I've gotten used to checking up on you over the years, to make sure you're okay." He sat back in his chair and folded his arms across his chest. "I still find it hard to believe that I spent a year and a half working with him, never knowing who he was. Never imagined he might betray me . . . or one day, perhaps, become my son-in-law."

"Just like I never imagined my father was connected with the cartel." She looked up at him, wondering what she was looking for. Proof that he had a conscience? That the men he'd ordered killed had somehow deserved it?

He leaned forward and caught her gaze. "We live in two different worlds, Olivia. We always have and we always will. But there are some things we have in common."

"Like?" she asked.

"Michael completes the missing pieces in your life . . . just like your mother completed me. And you and Ivan . . . I meant what I said before. I'll never regret having you."

She drew her finger slowly across the table, not ready to go there. "I read that they denied your bail."

"I might not be the big fish they were after, but the list of crimes against me—even with my cooperation with the state—is enough to keep me here for a very long time."

"Can I ask you something?"

"Anything."

"Why wasn't a family and a growing business enough for you?"

"You mean why weren't you enough?"

His words punctured straight through her. Hadn't that always been the question?

He shook his head. "If you were hoping for a bunch of profound answers, I don't have them. I got involved with the cartel when I was twelve years old, because my father was involved with the cartel. Still, I thought I could play both sides of the fence, live life the way I wanted while helping Felipe launder money. In the end I couldn't get out."

"What about my mother? Did she ever ask you to walk away?"

He chuckled. "She knew I never would. The world I was in was as seductive as your mother. I thought I could do anything, and there was power in being in control."

"How did my mother fit into this?"

"Maybe she was the only thing real about my life. But she also believed what she wanted to believe about me. For some reason she loved me for who I could have been, not for who I really was."

Olivia flinched at his words. "Did you love her?"

"From the first day we met." There was no hesitation in his answer. "No matter what you think about me, that is the one thing I need you to believe. I really did love her. I loved all of you in my own way. I know none of this makes sense to you, but I guess I spent my life trying to live in two worlds. The world where I had a family, your mother, you, Ivan . . . and a life where I had power to control what was going on around me."

Emotions tangled inside her, as she realized she'd never really known the complicated man sitting across from her.

"I don't know what else to say," he continued. "But the truth is that I can't pretend to be someone I'm not. I don't expect you to accept that, but this is who I am."

The man who hired hitmen to kill his enemies.

The man who'd loved her mother.

The man who'd tried to save her brother's life.

She pressed her lips together as the guard walked toward them. "I need to go."

"Maybe I'll see you again?"

She stood up, her heart still conflicted as she nodded. "Maybe."

"Olivia?"

She turned back around to look at him.

"When you leave here, there will be a box on your car. Take it. Please. It's a gift from me."

———

She found the box outside the prison on the hood of her car, while the morning's gray skies loomed above them. She looked around at the lot filled with other vehicles, but no people. She set her bag down, then carefully slid the contents out of the package.

"What is it?" Michael asked.

"My mother's music box." Olivia's breath caught as she opened the lid, letting the music from her childhood spill into the cold morning air like a salve across her fractured heart. "I'd always wondered what happened to this."

For a moment, she was a child again, dancing with her mother and brother in the middle of the living room while the music box played in the background. She pulled out the picture that had been pressed into the lid and held it up to show Michael.

"She was beautiful," Michael said. "Just like her daughter."

"My father thought so. He took her to Switzerland one winter. She'd never traveled overseas, and he once told me that watching her reaction made it seem like he was seeing it all again for the first time."

Olivia ran her fingers across the inlaid wood, then closed the lid before sliding it back into the box.

"A lot has happened over the past few days," he said.

"Some days I still feel as if I can't catch my breath." She looked up at him. "In some ways, I feel as if I've lost everything. My father's going to prison, Felipe's vanished, Ivan's moving away . . . But then I remember what I've been given."

She looked up at him with tears in her eyes, a feeling of gratefulness and hope beginning to nudge out the hurt and loss.

"Speaking of what we've been given, I think the initial shock of having her son show up on her doorstep is beginning to wear off, because I just got a text from my mother. She's planning a huge family meal for all of us tonight." He grasped her hands and pulled them against his chest. "I thought I might invite someone to join me."

"Really." She smiled up at him. "Who did you have in mind?"

"There's this woman I met. She's intriguing, fun, and beautiful."

"Should I be jealous?"

He laughed. "Say you'll come."

"Your family won't mind?"

"My mother actually insisted that both you and Ivan come."

"I'd love to come."

"Good, because while you've already received quite a crash course on the Hunt family these past few days, you still haven't met my mother."

She leaned into him. "Stop trying to scare me away, because I already like her. Your sisters . . . your father . . . They remind me that there are still good people in the world who are actually making a difference."

The family she'd never had.

"They like you. And even more important than that—because while I love my family, some decisions are personal—I like you, Olivia Hamilton. I like you a lot."

Anticipation of what lay ahead for them and their relationship fluttered inside her. He was the kind of man she wanted to spend the rest of her life with, and while she didn't know if that was where things would end, she was ready to find out.

"There is one other thing. I've been praying about a slight change in my career direction."

"Like what? I can't exactly imagine you at a desk job."

"Even after all that's happened, I'm not exactly ready to give up life as a cop altogether."

"What do you have in mind?"

"I've been asked to head up a special task force with drug enforcement, but I won't be working undercover anymore."

"With your skills I'm not surprised at all. Sounds as if you're perfect for the job."

"As excited as I am about the possibilities, there is one other thing on my mind right now."

"And what would that be?" she asked.

"You and me."

She felt his arm slide around her waist as he pulled her against him. The wind blew against her face, but all she could see at the moment was the one man who'd managed to capture her heart.

"Do you always fall for the women you rescue?"

"If I recall, you're the one who rescued me."

"I did, didn't I?" She laughed. "Which turns out to be very fortunate for you, because after all that has happened the past few days, I'm ready to go back to *reporting* the news instead of *being* the news."

He leaned down and kissed her in the middle of the parking lot until everything else around her was completely forgotten.

At seven o'clock, Olivia sat down beside Michael at the lavishly decorated Hunt dining room table, with its gold-trimmed place settings, red roses and white tallow berry centerpiece, and flickering candles. She bowed her head while Thomas Hunt prayed over the food and the family, asking for safety and health for those gathered at the table, making her realize that while lies had been exposed and so much had been taken, much more had been given in exchange.

Michael squeezed her hand at the amen as everyone began passing his mother's roast turkey, giblet gravy, and cornbread dressing. She paused in the middle of the laughter and talk filling the room, absorbing the feeling of family she'd always craved. Already, she'd somehow been pulled into helping plan Avery and Jackson's wedding, amidst rumors of another impending engagement between Emily and Mason. They'd asked for her suggestions and input like she'd always been one of the family.

Claire Hunt, elegantly dressed in a red, sparkly holiday dress, tapped her fork against her glass.

Thomas Hunt set down the bowl of green beans he'd been about to pass around the table. "I think my wife has something to say."

The room fell quiet as everyone's attention shifted to Michael's mother. "Before y'all get too engrossed in the meal, you might have noticed that tonight's meal isn't our typical New Year's Eve fare. But nothing about tonight is typical."

Michael reached down and grasped Olivia's hand as his mother continued.

"I never once dreamed over the past months of loss that my son would once again be sitting here at the table with us. Or that he'd bring with him a stunning young woman and her brother— two people that I will forever be grateful to for saving his life."

A couple of amens filled the room.

Michael cleared his throat. "May I say something as well?"

"Just so it's not too long." Avery shot him a grin. "My dinner's liable to be cold by the time you finish talking."

"Very funny, sis." Michael laughed. "I just want to say, as I look around this table, I realize that the past few months have been full of both victories and defeats, love and heart-wrenching loss. I've missed being a part of that more than you will ever know. But as I sit here tonight with my family, listening to the talk of New Year's resolutions, Avery and Jackson's upcoming wedding, and Ivan's acceptance into MIT, I'm struck with the profound truth that God is good. He never promised us that life would be easy, but He has promised to walk with us. Which is what He's done. Which is why I can't begin to thank Him enough for a second chance at life, for getting my family back"—Michael pulled Olivia's hand against his chest—"and for the woman sitting here beside me."

Cheers and hoots went up around the table, but all Olivia saw was the man sitting beside her who leaned over and brushed his lips across hers, reminding her that this wasn't a fleeting moment, but the beginning of a relationship they both would ensure lasted. Because while the truth had brought pain, that pain had also brought with it so much more. Michael, his family, their new relationship were all based on truth, a truth setting her free.

ACKNOWLEDGMENTS

I absolutely enjoyed every moment of writing this series and getting to know the Hunt family. But as with every book or series, it's never a one-man job. I'm so thankful to those who have helped me along this writing journey. For this book in particular, to Andrea, Ellen, and Barb for your amazing editing skills. To Beth, Lynne, and Kellie for your support and inspiration. And for my wonderful family, who has always stood with me and encouraged me each step of the way. I am blessed.

Lisa Harris is a bestselling author, a Christy Award finalist for *Blood Ransom*, Christy Award winner for *Dangerous Passage*, and the winner of the Best Inspirational Suspense Novel for 2011 from *Romantic Times*. She has sold over thirty novels and novella collections. Along with her husband, she and her three children have spent over ten years living as missionaries in Africa where she homeschools, leads a women's group, and runs a nonprofit organization that works alongside their church-planting ministry. The ECHO Project works in southern Africa promoting Education, Compassion, Health, and Opportunity and is a way for her to *"speak up for those who cannot speak for themselves . . . the poor and helpless, and see that they get justice"* (Proverbs 31:8–9).

When she's not working, she loves hanging out with her family, cooking different ethnic dishes, photography, and heading into the African bush on safari. For more information about her books and life in Africa, visit her website at www.lisaharris writes.com or her blog at http://myblogintheheartofafrica.blog spot.com. For more information about The ECHO Project, please visit www.theECHOproject.org.

meet
LISA HARRIS

lisaharriswrites.com

AuthorLisaHarris

@heartofafrica

Don't Miss the Thrilling Start
to the *SOUTHERN CRIMES* Series

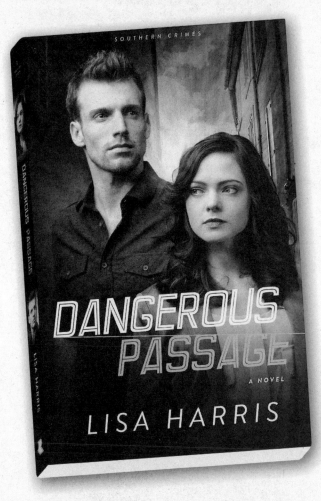

"Readers looking for a strong female protagonist and a unique murder mystery will find much to admire in Harris's work."

—*Publishers Weekly*

Desperate times create desperate people.
And desperate people are dangerous . . .

Introducing MEN OF VALOR,
a New Series from Bestselling Author
IRENE HANNON

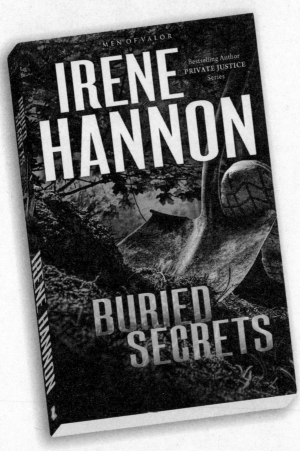

Police chief Lisa Grant and detective Mac McGregor
join forces to investigate an unmarked grave, only to discover
that someone will stop at nothing to make certain a
life-shattering secret stays buried.

"Keep your eye on Patricia Bradley.
With her stellar writing and edge-of-the-seat suspense, there is no telling what she has in store for readers next."

—*Sandra Robbins, award-winning author*

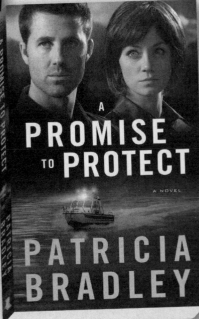